Joseph's Coat

Joseph's Coat

AN ANTHOLOGY OF MULTICULTURAL WRITING

edited by
Peter Skrzynecki

Hale & Iremonger

This collection © 1985 by Peter Skrzynecki
This book is copyright. Apart from any fair
dealing for the purposes of study, research,
criticism, review, or as otherwise permitted
under the Copyright Act, no part may be reproduced
by any process without written permission.
Inquiries should be made to the publisher.

Typeset, printed & bound by
Southwood Press Pty Limited
80-92 Chapel Street, Marrickville, NSW

For the publisher
Hale & Iremonger Pty Limited
GPO Box 2552, Sydney, NSW

National Library of Australia Catalogue Card no. and
ISBN 0 86806 185 9 (casebound)
ISBN 0 86806 186 7 (paperbound)

for Al Zolynas and Andy Milcz

Coming, going, the waterfowl
Leaves not a trace,
Nor does it need a guide.
       DOGEN

Contents

Introduction *13*

Walter Adamson
 Five Minutes *15*
 Laughter and Tears *16*
 Pietro *17*

Alma Aldrette
 The Black Skirt *18*

Gary Catalano
 from *Remembering the Rural Life*
  Four poems *23*

Mariano Coreno
 You Can Go Men *27*
 The War Stopped at Cassino *27*
 For a Spanish Girl *28*

Jack Davis
 Urban Aboriginal *29*
 The Girl in the Park *29*
 Bombay *30*

Margaret Diesendorf
 The Escape *31*
 Reading Akhmatova *34*
 Woman Alone *34*
 From Exile *35*

John J. Encarnação
 Coming of Age in Australia *36*
 Football Like She is Played *40*

Silvana Gardner
 Fox Fur *42*
 The Burial Dress *43*
 Villa Gardone *44*

Gün Gencer
    Mekong   *45*
    Killer Prayers   *45*

Kevin Gilbert
    Baccadul   *47*
    Soft Sam   *48*

Loló Houbein
    Fighting for Peace   *49*

Jurgis Janavicius
    Morning Frosts in Dungog   *55*
    from *Family in Exile*
        Land of Mark   *55*
        Silver Plains   *56*

Manfred Jurgensen
    object-lesson   *57*
    bonegilla 1961   *58*
    ethnic food   *58*

Vasso Kalamaras
    Mademoiselle   *59*
    A Christmas Gift   *68*

Antigone Kefala
    from *European Notebook*
        Parish Church   *77*
        The Old Palace   *77*
        Family   *78*

Stephen Kelen
    The Intruders   *79*

Rudi Krausmann
    The Art Critic   *85*
    The Poem   *88*

Yota Krili-Kevans
    On the Other Side   *90*
    To the Adopted Mother   *91*
    Migratory Birds   *93*

Maria Lewitt
    Refugee 1944   *95*

Serge Liberman
    Envy's Fire   *99*

Uyen Loewald
    Nightmare   *107*

Angelo Loukakis
    Being Here Now   *116*

David Martin
    Letter to a Friend in Israel   *123*
    Gordon Childe   *124*
    The Turkish Girl   *124*

Franco Paisio
    The Enemy   *132*
    Under the Sun   *133*
    Autobiography   *133*

Liliana Rydzynski
    The Husband   *134*
    The Polish Sculptor   *134*
    The Father   *135*
    Greece in Winter   *136*

Barbara Schenkel
    The Anniversary   *140*
    from *Israel — Impressions of a Journey*
        Judea   *149*
        On the Site of Jericho   *150*
        Olive Trees   *150*

Peter Skrzynecki
    Migrant Centre Site   *151*
    Hunting Rabbits   *152*
    Going to the Pictures   *153*

Tad Sobolewski
    Free As a Bird   *160*

Tutama Tjapangarti
    Getting a Wife   *175*
    The Payback   *177*

Dimitris Tsaloumas
    Prodigal   *179*
    The Return   *179*
    The Pale Knight   *180*
    Televised Message of Comfort   *180*

Vicki Viidikas
    Darjeeling   *181*
    To My Father, Viidikas   *181*
    The Relationship   *182*

Cornelis Vleeskens
    Street Talk . . . Two Sonnets on a Theme   *185*
    At Every Step   *186*

Kath Walker
    Namatjira   *192*
    Acacia Ridge   *192*
    Bwalla the Hunter   *193*
    The Curlew Cried   *194*

Ania Walwicz
    europe   *195*
    stories my mother told me   *196*

Judah Waten
    A Writer's Youth   *198*

B. Wongar
 Bralgu   *207*
 The Drought   *207*
 The Legend   *207*
 U$_3$O$_8$ *208*
 The Defectors   *210*

Spiro Zavos
 Elvis Is Dead   *212*

Nihat Ziyalan
 Pigeon Flight   *217*
 Poem of Missing Home   *218*

Acknowledgments   *219*

Biographical Notes   *221*

Introduction

In Australia today, whole new areas of social awareness and educational curricula have developed out of multicultural studies; these interests are reflected in schools, community centres, the visual arts, crafts, drama and literature. *Joseph's Coat* reflects and enforces these changes. It is not a collection prompted by academic needs, nor does it espouse an intellectual cause. It is a compassionate and humane collection of poetry and prose that is indicatve of the changing nature of our society.

Needless to say there will be criticism aimed at demonstrating how the collection 'discriminates' against one group of writers: how it isolates the so-called 'ethnics' and doesn't include writers from Anglo-Saxon backgrounds. Critics and reviewers may resuscitate literary cliches, invoke nationalistic pride and political debate to argue that we are all Australians. Yes, we are, no one disputes that; but, at the same time, we are not. It is a paradox, like the answer to a Zen koan; and if there is a solution, perhaps it is in harmonious co-existence. But that will only happen when we lose our prejudices, when we destroy our fears, when we look beyond the self.

Whether they are Aboriginal, whether they are first or second generation immigrants, all the writers here have or had a basic language other than English. If there has been discrimination, it has been against people such as these because they were 'different' — because they spoke a foreign language and were unwilling to sever the roots from which they grew.

Often they were tolerated, politely and formally, but this was nothing more than condescension; and yet, many of them succeeded in communicating their art despite the absence of language and the barriers encountered in day-to-day living. Those who have not experienced this kind of discrimination may smile in disbelief and choose to remain sceptical. That's all right. There are plenty of others who know differently.

Still, one can't help sensing that a change of attitude is on the way — a change associated with social structures and the influx of new immigrants in the 70s and 80s. Many of the writers in *Joseph's Coat* came to Australia as a result of the upheavals in Europe during World War II. The newest arrivals, such as the Vietnamese and those escaping from wars in the Middle East, have yet to make their presence felt in our literature. But they will. Their lives, and the lives of their children, will influence our cultural history even more diversely in the decades to follow.

Change has already occurred and more is on the way. One hopes that further acceptance will follow. One can only stand by one's beliefs — and if *Joseph's Coat* incurs the displeasure of the bigots, then that's their misfortune: they are still living in an irretrievable past, while Australia has already become a part of the twenty-first century.

* * * *

Thank you to all the contributors who submitted work. My one regret is that more writers could not have been included.
Limitations of space and money exist; they have to be adhered to. Initially, the *Ethnic Arts Directory* was used as a basic source of contact. Circulars were sent out and people were invited to submit work. Replies were received from all States except Tasmania. Some writers failed to reply; others wrote and submitted work after hearing of the anthology in progress from other authors. I haven't always agreed with points of view or reviews that some of these authors have published; but I have been an admirer of their own poetry and prose and have no hesitation about promoting it. For several of them, also, this is the first opportunity of having their work included in an anthology. Welcome! I hope it's the start to many more.

Peter Skrzynecki

WALTER ADAMSON

Five Minutes

The sister in charge said: five minutes, no more, are you friends, relatives, neighbours? Five minutes... She vanished before we could assure her that five minutes was a long time for the dying. There were about a dozen beds and twice, perhaps three times as many people. It was visiting time. Most of the patients were propped up against pillows like dolls in the window of a toyshop. At the very end of the room a screen. We made a beeline towards it, knowing instinctively that it was ours, already separated from the rest.

He looked as if he were asleep. His eyes shut, his breathing inaudible, only a slight heave beneath the blanket. We stood there for at least a minute. He opened his eyes. A question mark.

Have we met before? Let's pretend we have. It must be a comfort for the dying not to be alone or with strangers. We are from the same country. That was a long time ago, his eyes replied. We nodded. Why pretend it was yesterday? Life is shorter than its last five minutes.

He didn't try to fool us. He was in pain. But no longer in physical pain. The hospital saw to it that he was spared the indignities of the body. Flesh and bone had ceased to exist. He was past his physical death. But the dying of the mind had yet to be done. Coped with. Got over with.

We've come because it might please you. Inadequate, but what else could we say? Besides, it was true. To please him. The ball was now in his court. To be pleased.

He kept us waiting. He seemed to have all the time in the world. We only had five minutes. We couldn't see his hands. He kept them under the blanket. It occurred to me that I had never seen his body. Perhaps he had none. Only a head. But it was his head to be reckoned with at this moment. It projected his entire life and all he had ever done, been, thought, was concentrated in that head behind those eyes, behind that forehead. Strange, I thought. Is it really necessary to have a body to be alive?

Yes, it is, I decided, but not in order to die. That was done in what was lying on that white hospital pillow.

That we had come from the same country was no longer relevant. What of it! The same planet, solar system, the same galaxy. Suddenly the universe began to shrink. It closed in on us. There was no longer enough room. The third minute had passed, and what was inside that

15

head on the pillow was still alive. The air was stifling. Galaxies, I thought. There were millions of them. The chance that there is life elsewhere is remote. Are we alone?

I spent the next minute wondering about it. Alone in a vast, infinite void inflicted with a disease of energies rampaging, filling and emptying again, a vacuum beyond our comprehension.

You aren't really dying, are you? We looked at each other. His eyes opened a little wider, his pupils filled with an ocean of vision. He saw, we didn't. That happened during the fifth minute before the sister came back to tell us our time was up.

What about him?

The sister came to his bedside. She closed his eyelids with an expert's hand. It was as simple as that.

Or was it?

Laughter and Tears

When the laughter dies down
a hollow echo repeats it
then silence again

In a dark corner
someone is weeping

Our laughter was thunder
made by the waterfall
crashing on rock

The weeper's tears trickle slowly
the same distance

Pietro

Pietro
how small you are
your feet will never
reach the sky

you walk the earth
and leave no trace
the things you touch
will not be moved

Pietro
how small you are

but at the end of time
when all is done
you will be there

walking the earth
small as you are
you will survive

ALMA ALDRETTE

The Black Skirt

Mrs Castellanos had lived in the Valley for over twenty years. She was an illegal migrant who, like many others, had made her life in America. She had worked many years as a nursemaid for Anglo families prior to her marriage to Severino.

She still prided herself in the fact that her former employers used to tell her that she looked like a French maid. To her this meant that she did not look like a common Mexican.

Her skin was of a pale gold colour. She was of medium height. Broad shouldered, slim. Her hair was jet black and curly. Serious brown eyes, high cheek-bones and finely chiselled lips and nose appeared even more aristocratic set off by her haughty facade. When she was angry she could look as menacing as a serpent; ice-cold and dangerous.

She still retained memories of her life as a child in Mexico. Although her family had not always been poor, when the Mexican government seized their lands, the family was forced to flee across the border in search of a better life.

Now, she had that. But this also meant that she constantly had to be on her guard so that her place of birth would not be known. She was too proud to apply for American citizenship, besides, she didn't want it to become common knowledge. Wouldn't her neighbours love that bit of juicy gossip though! She still spoke only in Spanish, but she had consciously abandoned many of the Mexican customs so as to dissociate herself from her compatriots. God, how the peasants caused her shame when they let out a blood-curdling *grito,* the Mexican yell, in the middle of a song! And how her blood throbbed in response to the rhythm of their music!

'Ah, but our people have Castilian blood.' she argued with her daughter Anita. 'We are not of Indian blood.'

'But the Spaniards mingled their blood with that of the Indians. Our family couldn't have escaped that.' But Mrs Castellanos remained adamant. When asked her nationality, she always replied 'Spanish'.

Ironically, she was well versed in Mexican history and lost no opportunity to coach her daughter with these facts which inluded much Indian folklore, while her daughter was taught American history in school which depicted the Mexican race as consisting of pagans and dog eaters.

Mrs Castellanos read the newspapers diligently, especially the local events. The contents were enough to make her spine stiffen even more. During the summer months the Mexican migrants were more visible, as they flooded the Valley seeking employment. This summer there appeared to be more of them than usual. The newspapers carried articles almost daily which reported that a *mojado's* body had been found floating in the Rio Grande. Sometimes this was obviously a case of accidental drowning. At other times foul play was suspected.

When the Mexicans were unable to acquire a green card permitting them to work from the authorities in the United States, or time didn't allow for the application for one, many aliens sought an alternative. A *pato,* a 'duck', was contacted. This term applied to a man who could swim. He was contracted to swim and guide the *mojado* safely across the river, for a fee. Sometimes a *pato* would deliberately allow his charge to drown, and rob him of his belongings. Since the body was naked, and the man could have been a traveller from many miles in the interior of Mexico, the remains were not identified.

There were also other incidents of suspected foul play, as when decapitated bodies were found along the railroad tracks. Supposedly, the *mojados* had tired of walking and had fallen asleep with their heads resting on the rails.

Sometimes Mexican women and children waded across the river when it was running low. If they were in extremely poor physical condition they couldn't find employment even under the sweltering heat in the cotton fields. Then they relied on hand-outs. Barefoot women carrying naked brown babies with bloated bellies begged for milk, door to door.

The migrants who found employment and intended to remain in the States quickly altered their appearance. The *huaraches* were replaced by tennis shoes. Straw sombreros were replaced by baseball caps. The women replaced their luxurious waist-length braids with short permanent waves, transformed instantly to look like their American counterparts. The immigration authorities, the border patrol — or as the Mexicans referred to them, *la migra,* were kept busy picking up these aliens whenever someone called in to report a large gathering of Mexicans. They also worked in plain clothes. Boarding buses and trains, they'd wait until the vehicle was under way, then they'd flash their badges as they approached each 'suspect' and ask 'Are you an American citizen? Do you speak English? Where were you born?'

Many American-born Mexicans took to carrying birth certificates and social security cards as identification, to avoid being herded to a

detention camp awaiting deportation in case their answers weren't convincing. Any Spanish-speaking person was suspect, particularly those with dark brown skin, or those in clothing suspiciously colourful. 'Cut off your hair, Anita,' Mrs Castellanos pleaded with her daughter. 'You look like an Indian.'
'Don't go out in the hot sun. You'll get as black as a peasant.'
'So what?' answered her daughter.
'What do you mean 'so what'. You'll get as black as our newsboy — what's his name? Lupe. His mother insists on dressing the poor boy in white skirts and he looks like a fly in milk!'
'Lupe is a very nice boy. He's in my class, he's very smart too.'
'Es muy feo. Prieto. Uggggh,' argued Mrs Castellanos.

Mentally Anita disagreed with her mother. She much preferred Lupe's flawless caramel skin to her own freckled olive colour. Anita secretly adored Lupe, but she wouldn't reveal this to anybody. She knew her mother's opinion on these things; she detested the Anglo girls' freedom, the way they were allowed to say that they had boyfriends, meaning that they liked a certain boy. They were too young to date, being only fifteen years old. Mrs Castellanos thought that these Anglo girls were young and cheap. Mexican girls were expected to remain innocent and unblemished. So they only whispered to their best friends the name of the current boy they liked. Anita knew that many girls liked Lupe. Even the Anglo girls were attracted to him. Some of them were very brazen about their feelings. Lupe seemed to ignore all of this attention.

It wasn't safe to get involved with Anglo girls. In cases where a Mexican got friendly with a white girl, he got beaten up. It never was clear if Anglos or Mexicans had administered the beatings, but the message was clear; no mixing! He didn't have time for girls right now anyway. His two older brothers had already graduated from high school with sport scholarships. He intended to do the same.

As she grew older, Anita's restrictions in choice of friends were increased. Mrs Castellanos did not like her to have friends who were poor, too dark-skinned, or aesthetically unappealing.

Anita was torn between loyalty to childhood friends, and obeying her mother's wishes.

Some of her newer friends, girls who had lighter skin, but whose families didn't have much money were not entirely desirable either. Some of these girls had had more cntact with the Anglo world, could speak better English, but also had adopted their customs. This, in the eyes of Mrs Castellanos, was a drawback.

'Hold your head high when you walk, Anita. Don't look so timid, you're not a peasant.'

'Yes Mother.'
'Why must you always smile so much? Look at your school pictures.
'Don't laugh, it's not funny! Be serious, Dignified.'
'Yes Mother.'
'Anita, I wish you wouldn't whistle so much. Once I used to whistle a lot too, when I used to work for a Mrs Macmillan, years ago. I forgot what I was doing, one day Mrs Macmillan said to me "Mary, why do you people like to do that so much?" "Do what?" I asked. "Whistle. You're *always* whistling." Do you know what? I stopped whistling from then on. Imagine! Mexicans are always whistling.' Mrs Castellanos looked preoccupied. She very much wanted her daughter to understand how important it was to be *somebody*. To rise above the common peasant, to demand respect from the louts and the ignorant population. To be equal to or better than the Anglos. Ah! But would Anita understand? She was a good student, but she could be even better if she applied herself. Sometimes a teacher would stop them in a shop or grocery store and tell her 'Anita is very smart, Mrs Castellanos.' She felt very confused at these times. She didn't want to speak English and reveal her difficulty with the language. She would not be laughed at! So instead she would turn to her daughter and say 'Tell her that I think that you are too lazy. That you don't get enough homework.' She worried about the use of the word 'smart'. Didn't that mean smart-alec? Didn't it mean something bad? Precocious?

It was worse when a teacher told her that Anita had a good imagination. A frown would furrow her forehead. Didn't this mean that Anita made things up? That she told lies? My child is a known liar, she thought, will my worries never end?

Mrs Castellanos made all of her clothes and most of Anita's, although lately Anita was becoming very fussy and even refused to wear some of the dresses that she made for her.

One hot summer day as she added the buttons on the waist band of a skirt she had just made, she decided to put on the skirt on impulse, urged by the desire to dance in it, as the radio played a Mexican *wapango*. How she loved that music! She slipped it quickly over her head just as she heard her daughter close the front door, home from school.

As Anita entered the room Mrs Castellanos swirled around the room showing off the skirt, whipping up breezes, combining her own body scent with that of the new material. Only the hem needed doing, and she would do that by hand.

'How do you like it?' she asked.

'I *love* it. May I borrow it sometime?' 'As soon as she caught sight of her mother's demonstration she had matched the skirt in her mind with several blouses.

It was a full dirndl. Made from polished cotton. The background was black. The design of trees about twelve inches high encircled the border. The trees were poplar, pine, and maple. Each in a different colour. Red, lime, and emerald green.

Mrs Castellanos insisted on wearing the skirt first befor allowing Anita to borrow it, knowing fully well that once Anita took it, it would be difficult to gain access to the garment again.

Therefore Anita was very surprised when she returned from school one day to find the black skirt splashed like a butterfly across her bed. As she walked into the kitchen she could see that her mother was very agitated about something.

Her mother spoke first. 'That new skirt, that black skirt that you liked so much, you can have it. I don't want to wear it after all.' 'Really? Gee thanks Mother.' Not giving it another thought, Anita proceeded to make herself a snack while her mother prepared supper. Finally Mrs Castellanos released a jagged sigh. 'You'll never guess what happened today. I was so upset. I was furious . . .'

Anita finished off her sandwich with a glass of milk. 'What happened?' she asked as she opened one of her schoolbooks before her. 'Well, I starched that black skirt today, and put it on the clothes line to dry before ironing it. Then I got busy waxing the floors, when I heard a knock on the front door. I peeked through the window first to see who it was. Was I shocked! It was the border patrol. Two son-of-bitches stood at the door. One was a slender Mexican, the other was a red-faced fat-arsed gringo. I went to open the door.

What will the neighbours think when they see an immigration car parked in front of this house? I thought. Anyway, one of the men, the young Mexican, asked me who lived here. I told him that I do. Then the gringo asked "Who else?" I told him that a family lived in the cottage in the back. The men looked at each other, then one of them, the gringo, asked me "Who does that skirt on the clothes line belong to?" It was then I realized that they were after a wetback, presumably, the owner of the *black skirt.*'

'What did you tell them?' Anita's curiosity was aroused. Mrs Castellanos stirred the earthenware pot that contained the beans and lowered the flame under the pan of vermicelli as the aroma of garlic and cumin flavoured the air. She added a few sprigs of freshly chopped coriander to the beans. Then, with a face as mask-like as Anita's was animated she answered as she turned to face her daughter.

'I told them that it was yours.'

GARY CATALANO

4

What's happened to him
that old Romanian count
who kept home with chickens
and with cows? Every year
grandfather crossed the border

of blue metal and tar
and they swapped salutations
over the fence, two migrants
touching, with broken English,
on the weather and Parramatta

Georgescu and Catalano.
Each Friday he hobbled a mile
from the bus-stop, a cram-packed
sugar-bag of groceries
on his back, and a child's

mite-sized suitcase in his hand
— home to the house and land
he declined to sell.
In those pre-inflationary days
he knocked back two hundred

thousand pounds, leaving the grass
to the cows he never milked.
On school holidays
I biked up to Picketts
and got lost; and after boasting

of our growing pubic hairs
my friend and I dammed
the little creek with mud
like junior engineers,
or played with home-made bows

and arrows in the scrub.
With clubs on run-down water-tanks
we drummed those cows into a frenzy,
pretending not to hear the Count
when he protested 'Bastards.'.

6

A draft-dodger before his time
grandfather set his face
against the Italian army
in the First World War
by pretending to be deaf

— he thought of more important things
than politics and war
whose rumbles meant nothing
on the slopes of Etna.
A quiet uncomplaining man

he spent seventy years
entwined with the land.
I used to see him often
lying face-down in the grass
 — quite still! —

and always thought him resting
from the heat. A lonely
self-absorbed young boy
I never noticed any
of his heart-attacks

— he looked so calm and peaceful
in the grass; his small
unshaven chin and salty
old-man's smell
at home with worms and ants.

9

My old man used to say
'You'll end up in the gutter'
— I'd set my heart on being
an artist or a writer.
He said they always starved.

His one great wish was to see
a BA and an LLB
after the name;
in my unbending youth
I wanted nothing of the sort.

Tired, he left me alone;
his only intervention
was when he presented me
with two volumes of Nietzsche
and Rousseau's Confessions

for my sixteenth birthday,
oblivious to the queer
disruptive pair they made.
I read all three of them
beneath the mulberry tree

but preferred Jean-Jacques
— 'Why, he's just like me!'
and wondered who my
du Warens would be.
Unmarried aunt-type spinsters

urged me to paint
but poetry held me
even then. When I sent
sixteen items of juvenilia
to Douglas Stewart

I received advice and some praise
— though not the hot kind
I was after. 'You have a good feeling
for words and weather. By all means
keep writing.'

11

I haven't been back
for six years now. Then
the vegetable beds
grew nothing but weeds
and kikuyu grass

and the untended
prickly-pear had sown
its Hydra-head tongues.
The ghostly fig-trees,
eaten at the base

no longer bore fruit
and adjoining farms
had ripened into
greyhound studs, or tracks
for training trotters.

So much for progress!
Now I have no doubt
all chickens have flown
the coop: as Sydney's great
suburban claw takes

hold of the landscape
the young rabbits no
longer play leapfrog
on Georgescu's land,
ignorant of cars

and curious boys
— they have moved deeper
into this country
and I have gone South.
All the old landscape

comes back in a new
near-foreign city
where I eat the soft
and succulent food
the cucumbers eat.

MARIANO CORENO

You Can Go Men

I am not coming to the moon,
you can go, men.
I want to die here
where the tombs can be seen,
where the grass is green.
You can leave me,
you can go, men.

The War Stopped at Cassino

The war stopped at Cassino
with its wild dissension
slaughtering streets, people and houses.

Among the ruins,
among lime of houses and lost lives,
I remember an old woman
dressed in black
seeking her child.

'*Pietro, where are you?*
Pietro, your mother is here:
come, I have bread for you'

Near the monastery there was darkness
and the voice of a cannon
hammering the heavy air,
hammering people's hearts
hidden like animals in the ditches of the hills.

The moon was lost,
the stars were trembling
and the old woman's voice
returned to reveal its hope.

'*Pietro, where are you?*
Pietro, your mother is here:
come, I have bread for you'

For a Spanish Girl

Under the wounded moon
a Spanish girl is dancing
with her hands up
and with her eyes full of passion.

Colours, contrasts,
images in a broken mirror
that the emotional girl
is changing into flowers,
into red roses of love.

Absurd truth of my days:
I am listening to voices,
I am looking into the window's darkness
while the Spanish girl
speaks words of happiness
unknown to my heart.

JACK DAVIS

Urban Aboriginal

She was born with sand in her mouth,
The whisper of wind in her hair;
They washed her clean in warm wood ash
And wrapped her in loving care.

She lay in the mould of her mother's arms,
She suckled her honeyed breasts;
She grew and she watched day turn to night
When you came out of the west.

You came loud-mouthed, with eyes cruel,
You made her a concubine;
Then flung her into a wilderness,
That beautiful Woman of Mine.

With murder, with rape, you marred their skin,
But you cannot whiten their mind;
They will remain my children for ever,
The black and the beautiful kind.

The Girl in the Park

I had seen her walking in the park
Before today.
I watched her gazing at reflections in the pool,
Sad, alone.
Although she smiled a tiny smile,
I was not bold or brave enough to speak to her.
Then the chance had slipped away.
As stars that pass, blink out
And vanish,
She was gone.
Next day she did not come,
Nor in the days to follow.
Yet I know,
She was my lonely kind;
So she remains, one more regret
In the caverns of my mind.

Bombay

The taxi,
honking, weaving, swaying,
took us in our opulence
through the people-teeming streets.

An old man,
thin black,
shook the dust of night
from limbs made gaunt
by caste and Eastern ways.

A pig
sucked the street's grey mud
with slobbering jaws,
growing fat, no doubt,
as men died around him.

While we,
wide-eyed,
clicked our tongues
and made decisions,
arrived at, by what we saw
through Western eyes.

MARGARET DIESENDORF

The Escape

The atmosphere in the compartment had become tense when they came (two of them) to take the middle-aged woman opposite away for the search. Clearly, the black uniform and the silver Death's Head insignia were chosen for sound psychological reasons: Who would dare lie, or hide anthing, when confronted with such a stark threat to life? But the terrified look and the dishevelled appearance of those who returned, both 'Aryan' and 'Jew', were enough to make the air vibrate with the fever of fear. So the stories that circulated in Vienna about 'examinations in the nude' were true . . .

Yet, I remained unperturbed. Looking back from a distance of 37 years, I find it hard to believe that I could remain calm. I kept on knitting the long, pink, woollen underpants for my friend with whom I was to share the apartment and the Swiss village-school as a teacher. I had given up distracting myself with breathing on the frosted window to gain a view of the landscape. It was late November and heavy snowfalls had changed the Alpine scene which follows the tracks from Salzburg over Innsbruck to Vorarlberg, into Andersen's kingdom of the Snow Queen. In any case, passport control and the fetching of the passengers for the notorious search had indicated that the last stop was Feldkirch. We were approaching the Swiss border.

My suitcase in the net across the aisle swayed slightly. I got up to make certain that it was secure. A solid case, almost elegant; I had bought it at a reduced cost, one of my former school mates being the son of the industrialist-exporter of vulcan-fibre travelling goods. It looked plain and innocent. Who would have thought that it contained, besides the fashionable clothes, a death sentence? Not I. As to the expensive suits and dresses, they were not mine. All I owned at that moment was my purse and its meagre contents — less than Jane Eyre fleeing from her 'dear master' and Thornfield Hall. Ah! and the clothes? I was taking them out for a friend whose parents had been politically involved in the Dollfuss-crisis, on the Christian-Socialist side — an unforgivable crime in the eyes of the new overlords. Mercifully, my friend's father had suffered a stroke on one of those fateful days in 1938 when the German planes seemed to stand still over the city — the second Ides of March. But this had left the rather helpless mother and her only daughter, my friend Elsbeth, to face persecution on their own. They wished to leave the country, but had not yet been granted German passports.

I, who had nothing to fear from the *Anschluss*, was in profound sympathy with their plight. Having had to earn my living while studying fulltime, I had simply lacked the leisure to give thought to the threatening catastrophe into which the better part of Europe sailed blindfolded, thus supported neither left nor right. True, I had shared the dream of those who hoped for a union of all German-speaking peoples at the bosom of a Greater Germany, the realization of a Grand Design. Elsbeth and I had not seen eye to eye in this matter, but there were plenty of students nursing the Pan-Germanic myth: our detailed instruction in history had hardly helped to foster intellectual criticism and even in the young republic, teachers rarely got beyond the nineteenth century; if the odd one did, his bias would undermine the plinth of understanding. As to the socio-economic situation, it was disastrous. Only a few, privileged graduates could expect employment in keeping with their training and qualifications. The *Anschluss* then seemed a promise to both the idealists and the realists — so long as they had worked against the 'brownshirts', as the Nazis were earlier described.

However, living for six months under the new regime had totally changed my outlook, as it had changed the ideas of many others, even party members. We soon found Hitler's efforts at *Gleichschaltung* 'mere humbug', and the propagation of the *Herrenrasse* highly contradictory to Nietzsche's philosophy of the *Übermensch* which was said to be its source of inspiration; nor did the leaders of the party stand comparison with Wagner's heroes or the hosts of the Valhalla. The system of informers which soon sprang up, we found repulsive.

Several of my pupils were Jewish, or of Jewish extraction. Two of them, after years of sharing work and play, were as close to me as younger sisters. When they had to flee from Austria with their parents, I felt like an outcast among my own people. Twice already I had got into trouble for defending Jews in the street. The SA had come to fetch me from my rented room. I escaped with a warning, thanks to being young and (as they said) 'a foolish girls who should do her duty to the *Führer.*' My mother, fearing for my life, urged me to go to Switzerland earlier than intended, to take up the study of Rhaeto-Romanic dialects through which I hoped to gain my second doctorate in France. One day, after learning that a Jewish girlfriend's mother and father had been torn from their beds during the night and transported to a concentration camp, I turned the key on lived past and planned future. Saying 'adieu' to Elsbeth and her mother, I agreed to take a suitcase of her best clothes with me and to wear her beautiful fur coat. I was to leave these things with a friend of theirs in Zurich.

Thus I sat in the coach feeling as innocent as Abel in the field before the wrath of Cain, with no apprehension of doom. It is only when the door of the compartment opened with vehemence and the two SS-men approached me, one taking my suitcase from the rack, that my sixth sense flashed a distinct warning: I suddenly recalled the last whispered words of my friend's mother as she kissed me goodbye: 'Do not trust Elsbeth, she is my daughter and I love her but . . .'. At the time this had not registered among the many problems and decisions that were pressing on my mind. But if the warnng came now, it was too late to seek its meaning and to allow it to modify action.

As I rose to go with them, the first SS-man gave me an admiring glance which skirted my model-figure set off by the elegant fur. *'Wie hineingewachsen!'* he exclaimed. 'As if grown into it . . .'. The unintended irony of the remark made me burst out in gay laughter and forget my qualms.

We moved on, to the door of the coach: my admirer ahead, probably to hold it open for me, when the plump woman who had sat opposite, coming back from the search, rushed through looking petrified, eyes glassy, cheeks purple. In her obvious confusion, she threw the heavy steel-edged door into the lock just as I passed, catching my left hand. There was an outcry through the whole carriage for blood splashed everywhere. My delicate ringfinger had been crushed and my daintiest, carefully manicured nail stuck on the door. I stood pale but smiling, sensing that this strange incident had significance beyond my comprehension. I felt, of course, nothing yet, no pain at all, but those who looked on and saw the mess a small wound can make with that precious red juice were horrified. The two SS-men, and this was my luck, were quite human, had probably been drafted into the *Schutzstaffel* without knowing what it was all about. The one supported me while the other went off trying to find a doctor on the train. There was none, so I was taken to the dining-car for a hot drink and a lie-down. Someone applied an emergency bandage. By that time, I had begun to feel faint and seeing all the sympathizing faces above and around me, people in uniform, people in leather shorts, etc., I lost consciousness.

I came to, to hear the conductor's call: 'Buchs. Buchs.' Snow-clean air streamed in through the open carriage-door. We had reached the border. Swiss guards came on board. The accident was explained to them and I was left in their care. My SS-man, impressed with the 'Teutonic' pluck of the *Volksgenossin,* asked for a memento. All I had was a 'holy' picture showing St. Christopher, given me by the priest who instructed me in the catechism in primary school. He took it like an amulet, begging me to let him know the date of my return to the *Reich*.

In Zurich, at the doctor's residence where I was to leave the suitcase and coat, my bandage was expertly renewed, I was treated to an excellent vegetarian dinner and invited to spend the night in the family's comfortable guest room. The doctor afterwards went to examine the contents of the case. He returned pale with emotion. 'Tell me,' he asked, clearly with effort, 'did you look into the portmanteau to check what was in it?' I shook my head. 'I knew all Elsbeth's clothes and we take the same size.' He did not reply. His heavy breathing marked the silence. Then, in control of his feelings: 'You are lucky to be alive.' — I asked no questions. His wife came in and moved the conversation into lighter veins.

The nail did not regrow, the nailbed having been destroyed, and the finger remained mis-shapen. It is a constant reminder of those tragic years; a reminder too that the cry. '*Et tu*, Brute' has outlived the great Caesar.

Reading Akhmatova (and thinking of another)

There are no words to say what I feel
there is a 'tearing apart' for which
there is no vocabulary . . .
                        but my tears
are digging a bed right across the earth,
they have formed a river that will reach
your house;
                one day you will wake and find:
the water has reached your mouth,
then I shall hear you cry: 'Come!'
Too late! Too late! —
                By then,
I'll be deaf and dumb.

Woman Alone
(For Jenny Maiden)

That morning she rises subject to strong
internal pressures. The fried egg on her
breakfast plate has changed into one of
Picasso's raped eyes staring single from

the blank face without structural orbits; her
tea tastes the hemlock of Socrates'
cup; death's written up as imminent on
the cloud-burdened sky outside her window,

her inside torn apart like Dali's
'Premonition of Civil War'; only
the boiled beans are missing in the picture.
Oh, she feels ugly! Despair's breaking

up the roundness of her face in cubist
rhythms to triangle and square; where is her
fair cheek, where the meek smile, this grin could
belong to Medea murdering her children . . .

From Exile

Mother, I must not be sad
because I had to leave you
and could not come back
in time,
to be with you in your last hour
and hold your hand.

Here, at the other end
of earth,
in the land
of Namatjira and Rees,
I saw you walk into my room
from the hall
in your hospital dress,
the brown corduroy
with the tiny blue flowers
and the collar of ivory lace
they clothed you in
after your death.

And now — years later —
when I look in the mirror
on the wall,
you look out of my face.

JOHN J. ENCARNAÇÃO

Coming of Age in Australia

It has taken me 36 years, six kids, a divorce and a dozen jobs to come of age in Australia. It has taken me the last 20 years just getting over the first sixteen.

The first 16 years I belonged to my parents, the next 16 years to a wife and a bunch of kids — the last few years to no-one in particular — notwithstanding the 'for sale' sign, 'going cheap, runs well, body in need of some repairs, suit woman with hands, time and the inclination'.

The early discipline nearly broke me, but it's the only money in the bank I have today. I could have grown up a mongrel, but, instead, I just didn't grow up at all for a long time — then, all of a sudden.

I was not to know that Australia was growing up along with me; that it, too, was assimilating.

Although gregarious by nature, I had few friends. The 'eight ball' was taller and heavier than I and I didn't have the sense to walk around it — I had to *push* it, *lift* it, *fight* it! That ball was smooth — from where, then, did I get the chips? From the bigotry, antipathy, jealously and hate that was the pubescent fabric of Austrlia after war.

Physical survival was difficult in Australia then — both for Australians and the migrants. Fitness, cunning and rock-fast determination were absolute requirements, which, collectively, are called 'guts'. Those migrants who had guts were constantly called upon to prove them. 'C'mon, y'wog, dago bastard! Yer wanta 'ave a go, do yer? Oh, yeah!' Of course, you soon learned to say 'yeah' in the same drawn out, threatening way he did — thereby calling his bluff or, most times, finding yourself in the middle of a brawl.

No matter how god-fearing, placid, saintly or cowardly you might have been, you simply could not go through 16 years at the 'Loo without a fight a week.

The 'Old Barn' was within walking distance. And Monday night was fight night and you, and droves of migrants and Australians, would hoof it up to the Cross and down to Rushcutters Bay with just enough money for a ticket and a beer. You, the kid, had a milkshake from the fares you'd saved. (You did a lot of walking.)

Fighting was a part of life. In or out of the ring, with or without your parents' approval — you *had* to fight — and win. It was the only way of gaining respect. It wasn't respect really — what was happening was that you were building up a reputation, a name, that said 'Don't tangle with him; he mightn't look much, but, Jesus, he can fight!' This was the only thing that afforded you a bit of peace, bought you a bit of time in which to find yourself, rest and/or prepare yourself for the next fight.

In this I was lucky because I naturally loved to fight. I loved all sports and proved myself equal to my antagonists. I had to learn about them and they were learning about me. We didn't like each other but we were growing up together.

Woolloomooloo lay at the foot of St. Mary's Cathedral. The shadow of this massive temple provided the umbrage out of which flourished prostitutes and destitutes; fledgling gangsters and gangsters; galloping pauperism and pox; and death from consumptive despair, exposure, malnutrition and landlords.

Into this massive temple we would take our week's miseries and berate ourselves for our mortal sin of surviving, vow to punish ourselves more in the future and race home our hearts light and pockets empty.

The priest walks in his luscious garden, fumbling beads in his pocket, his breath still sweet from tea and biscuits, his mind poeticising the passion of his two thousand year old god. In his humble fantasy, he sees himself as a fisherman with hands calloused from fixing and hauling huge nets of silver bream. The sun on his face is brown and leathered from the sea and wind — and he is a contented man. He hasn't a wife or children — he was never inclined that way. The simple life was his calling — an open boat, a net and some buoys and god will provide.

This priest knows all my sins. I try to pretend he has forgotten them and I remember to call him father. He has never had children (or has he?), but everybody calls him father — maybe even his own father calls him father; maybe his father says to him bless me father for I have sinned and proceeds to tell his son his sins. Maybe the son then forgives him then says to his father go in peace, my son, and sin no more. Does this priest now know that his father did not marry his mother until after she was pregnant? Does he ever think of his father seducing his mother for the first time? Does he think that another priest knows of his father's sin and think that that priest might remember and realize that he is a bastard? Is this why this priest is a priest — because in his heart he always knew that he was a bastard? What sins does this priest confess to his father colleagues? Does he have to invent a list of sins so that he can go to confession and mockly beg forgiveness?

Religion and its inherent bigotry, imported from Ireland, left their mark in Wolloomooloo. Priesthood and teaching were the favoured professions — and who could argue that these were powerful positions from which to impose god's will? Who could argue that the insecure and impoverished children of migrants were not the most pliable material from which to make quick capital gains? The clash of cultures left me disadvantaged for many years. It was not the obvious shyness, nor an inferiority complex which left me lagging in matters academic and social — it was the double life I was living all those years — being expected to be Portuguese at home and Australian at school. Invariably, the exact opposite would occur. Being Australian in the home was interpreted as being disrespectful — being Portuguese at school meant you were weak, backward and therefore to be taken advantage of, to be exploited and abused.

My good nature and respectful demeanor, coupled with my foreign physiognomy — olive complexion, black hair, black eyes and slightness of build — did not promote many friends.

It was not until I was 15 and had won my first 100-yard dash in surprising time, had won many fights in the lighter divisions and was beginning to be thrown in with the heaviest and most feared fighters in the school, and beating them, that my companionship was sought. It was too late. I had been surviving on hate, isolation, duplicity and defensiveness too long by now. I had made up my mind about sadism in people of authority over me; about religion as the rock upon which the spirit and body of a man may be dashed. It was too late for my vanquished foes to extend their ungloved, open hands to me in, albeit, genuine friendship and admiration. My hands had been clenched into fists too long. I had equated my survival with winning — someone had to get hurt. I was impervious to hurt, to pain. How, then, could I lose? What had I to lose? Nobody ever stopped to think that I had *nothing* to lose. Fighting bigger and heavier adversaries, I had everything to gain and nothing to lose; same with other sporting events where I had to contend with older and established champions — I gained huge ground in winning; I consolidated myself in the eyes of younger would-be antagonists.

I still had few friends when I finally quit university — one of which I married — and she was Australian by the naturalization of her parents.

It was not until I had been married and had had a few children that I, by this time the only dago in my own family, decided that I should get naturalized. I became an Australian citizen — but that is only a piece of paper that is called upon rarely these days. The passport does for everyday needs. Naturalization may get you into jobs you might otherwise not have got, but it still doesn't get you your friends; it doesn't change your personality or change the past — it, unfortunately, does not cancel memory.

Your naturalization did not change Australia. It *could* and it *may* in the future — if enough of you get naturalized. Australians are aware of this too. A long time ago, they adopted the White Australia policy. It has never been rescinded and you have never shaken off your olive complexion.

Naturalization gave you a share in Australia's democratic processes. It afforded you a final retort. Now that you have become an Australian citizen, you begin to indulge in the Australian sense of humour and horse-play. (I don't mean that you begin to bet on the horses — some of you were doing that before you were naturalized). Now that you are an Australian citizen (and your children don't have a trace of foreign accent), you begin to speak up for yourself in the Australain bullocking manner. You realize that it is the only way that you can be heard in a bar room. Ears are pricked — some of the things that are hurting you now are hurting your mates too and they are pleased to see that someone amongst them is able to put it into words.

You are beginning to be accepted. You have wit (practised in silence up until now); you have yarns which ought to have been published; and, you're a good bloke.

You are different enough for women to raise eyebrows over, they may not bat an eyelid — that would be too obvious — but your foreign name now conjures up cultural conversations and awakens libidinous appetites. You revert to your naïve state temporarily and enjoy the new experience of short-term relationships. The first few smarten up and you realize that love is not easy to find — that it takes more than a good one-night-stand to form a relationship of half the stability of your now defunct marriage. You realize that almost all the guts you used to have been expended in the act of surviving and that your failure to form a new and enduring relationship with one other person is due to the galvanizing process which has been at work all these years on your feelings, fears and phobia.

The *you* in this story has been the *id* in me all along. Maybe it is pride that won't permit me to cast the whole story in the first person; maybe it is shame, fear or even arrogance. Perhaps this story is still premature, but it had to be written down before it was forgotten or drowned out with beer and laughter.

An Australian will still call me dago — but, most of the times, it is over a friendly beer — when we have forgotten whose shout it is and are testing the pokies for forgotten pays.

A jackpot is bound to come up soon — I'm hoping my kids will be around to collect it.

Football Like She is Played

We were all Catholics together. Not by choice, really. We were kids and our education was being paid for by loving, ambitious, Catholic, migrant parents — Maltese, Portuguese and Italian, mainly. Our parents had papal blessings framed behind non-reflecting glass so you could look at them from every angle. Rosary beads in our pockets made holes in them which our mothers blamed on other things but mended with the same love anyhow. Scapulas around the neck saved us from many an accident, some fatal ones, no doubt — Father Kelly was a good bloke and he sold them to us in the first place and he knew a thing or two about scapulas.

Religion was one thing, football was different.

We had never heard of rugby league. Our fathers were all captains of their football teams and, of course, were only too thrilled to buy us our first pair of soccer boots. The shorts weren't important — any old pair of shorts — khaki, grey, blue with pockets or no would do. The game was the important thing and the boots.

It wasn't hard to adjust to the oblong ball; the bounce was funny but once you caught it it was yours. If a fight broke out and the referee could not decide whose ball it was he would simply order a scrum and the whole thing would start all over again.

Of course, an Italian would never dream of passing the ball to a Portuguese or an Australian — that's not football. So you had to have at least two Italians in your team, two Maltese, two Portuguese and as many Australians as possible. That was the only way to get the ball moving. If you didn't have two Italians in the team, the idea would be to make sure that the Italian never got the ball or there was sure to be a lot of scrums.

Scrums were never popular because of the smell of garlic and sweat which no chewing gum could match. They were over very quickly because the referee wouldn't come too close and the players weren't keen on the whole idea anyway — they just wanted the ball.

You could always tell the new Australian footballers from their Australian mates after a game. The Italian, Maltese or Portuguese would spend the rest of the day boasting about what he had done with the ball and while he was boasting, the rest would be cursing him for not having passed the wretched thing. The Australians would head straight for the showers and dress calmly into their uniforms and polished shoes, fold their football clothes nicely into their bags which always seemed to have much more room than our bags. They seemed to take a loss much better than we did, too. They could start talking about homework and girls right there in the showers even. We never had girlfriends and we seldom did homework. And, if it *was* a loss, we always knew whose fault is was and would waste no time in bawling them out. It was never the Australians fault, rightly enough. After all, it was their game, they ought to have known what they were doing — and they did. Whenever there was a goal to be kicked, it was always an Australian who kicked it. We were too nervous and as far as we were concerned, the hard part had already been done — some fat Italian or long Maltese or speedy Portuguese had already scored the try. (There was no kissing done in those days — we were too young and hated each other and it was sissy at our age). We never watched while the Australian was kicking the goal — we were either too excited (even to watch) or were busy boasting or fighting.

Of course, when the match was written up in the school magazine, we were all mentioned — even if we had missed the game or hadn't touched the ball all day. The captain always got the best write-up or else what was the use in having an Australian captain. Next came the fellow who scored the most tries and the rest would be the same thing said in different words — but we loved them. We learnt a lot of English just from the football write-ups. We never accepted the bad connotations of a word — just the good ones. We would blame our silly dictionaries if we didn't agree with the given meaning of a word.

Our fathers thought we were all champions!

SILVANA GARDNER

Fox Fur

I found a black fur collar hidden
in a brown paper bag behind
the bottom drawer of the wardrobe.
Why all the secrecy I asked my mother
who replied it belonged to grandma
when she was young and must be preserved
from the moths in the years
that shred everything, even memories.

The fur could be a cat's
but the family insists that it's fox,
status symbol in the *belle époque*
and I see my grandmother carrying a dormant
animal around her shoulders, paws dangling
like plaits near the vixen head
flattened by the mallet of fashion.
She is dancing the mazurka
in a primitive pelt, barter for a gentleman
hunter with itchy fingers, the ladies
warding off the evil eye. The fox fur
is punched hollow with envy, a woman's head
nuzzling satisfied vanity.

Was it as simple as this or
did they sometimes cry behind it?

The Burial Dress

My grandmother keeps a black dress
hanging alone in the closet.
From time to time she leads me
to its shadows and points
'this is what I will wear
      when I am dead.'

A forbidden dress,
already flattened and thin
from years of waiting,
its consumptive lankiness softening
the droop from the iron shoulders
of a coat-hanger.

A touch of lace around the throat
scoops a modicum of coquetry
with death and I say
'you should add a brooch
      for the total effect.'
My grandmother is not sad;

she wants to be prepared
for one last modesty, she said.
Sometimes I go alone to her room
to feel this secret of hers
      with curiosity.
      Smell it,
      touch it
to get a clue
of the mysterious absent friend
      living in the dark.

Villa Gardone

The aristocrat's retreat opens
for the shelter of people in exile.
Servants proudly remind us
that we are in a famous place:
Mussolini slept here!
No one wants to remember
how he died . . .
I watch how the powerful live
with Greek statues whose power
is only beauty, Nausicaa's budding breast
filled with fantasy milk, bronze
cypresses fondling the curve
of her nipples. I take my fill
of the classical gardens, the order
of gravel paths (again, the milky whiteness!)
and ignore the empty palace.

        Louis XIV chairs
can be desecrated as much as Napoleon beds
so we sleep on mattresses in empty rooms
and taught to be grateful for half-hearted
generosity. 'Noblesse Oblige' can only last
for a few days and the gardeners mistrust me
when I embrace Aphrodite, searching her marble skin
        for bed lice.

GUN GENCER

Mekong

the victor's chopper amputates the victor's dreams
the blinding beam tears open his darkest wells
vomiting fire
'cause we disbelieve in different things
'cause I have my cross to bear
'cause Grade 1 weighing down the Air America
must cut through the eager vein
of the cut-throat muscles of masculinity

choppers in a surgical operation
of limited escalation
going high

the blade chops through pregnant saturation humidity
plump rice fields with mosquitoes
and their mosquito-like men
must wither
'cause we all die differently
me with my parched trunk like a carcass on a hook
of an overdose
or a cardiac
or neurosurgery
and you
in the inverse darkness of my chopper's shaft

Killer Prayers

I believe for every drop of blood that falls
faith bleeds
high heavens stink

every time I hear a new-born baby cry
of hunger
god sneers

every time all those prayers are handed out
as alms
to the mobs
Olympus grows
rarified more and more

I believe in the higher reason for things that rot
a human foot
a golden tooth
opaque lampshades in the sterile surgery
toothpick limbs there and there
slender and Gothic
uplifting the soul

I believe in pious paternal oppression
in Charlton Heston's weighty slate
the ponderous cross dragged
the bold swastika
a sea of black shirts
I believe him
for he doubts not
the Providence
or Descartes or Marx
or Christaan Barnard

I believe the American way must triumph
over the ruins and napalm burns
Stalin now, he was a believer
in the ultimate good
that you'd ultimately live

with bowed heads
incensed
freezing fingers clutched some faded icon
on the way to Vladivostok
they understood
'cause they too, were believers
followers of some other orthodox beard
dust to dust

KEVIN GILBERT

Baccadul

Baccadul baccadul chugar tea
This is the price you paid for me
Baccadul baccadul chugar salt
No meat come so soon I halt
A few lead bullets into tribe you see
This is the price you paid for me

Baccadul baccadul chugar flour
Missionary callin' the 'Golden Hour'
Then comes army when he get sour
This is the price you paid for me

Baccadul baccadul worthless beads
Poisoned water-hole fill my needs
Soon no black tribe will there be
This is the price you paid for me

Baccadul baccadul soon some wine
White boss soon think 'Jacky mine'
He says 'Hey Jack, I say there choom
I'm growing cattle but where I come from
We don't pay wages to boongs you see
We buy then with some baccadul, tea . . .'

Baccadul baccadul chugar tea
This is the price you paid for me.

Soft Sam

Times and people change —
Every mission once had hockey
Football teams and basketball
They'd travel in their sulkies many miles
To go home wreathed in sorrow if they had a losing team
Or if their team had won — wreathed in smiles.
I remember at Forbes Oval — not the game but picnic lunch
When 'Depression' families lived on damper/fat
My uncle bought some saveloys — a treat, a real feed then
A little black girl smiled at me and sat — quite near
The girl and I was five — while I'm alive I'll never forget
What my eyes saw when our eyes met — hounds of hunger —
Sorrow, plea — my mother understood my face —
I grabbed her wispy slip of lace to wipe the child's snot nose —
    her face
Then gave her damper, saveloys, oh Christ, oh Christ
    a thousand joys
Sprang from her eyes — I'll not forget.

LOLÓ HOUBEIN

Fighting for Peace

As she rounded the corner of Government Road, she found herself in the midst of the roar she'd subconsciously registered. She ducked stiffly to avoid a baton-wielding arm and was thrown breathless against a wall by a body that flew past. Hysterical shouts and screams exploded upon her eardrums. Her hand clutched the shopping bag with the food for her pension payday meal tonight. A massive man in uniform loomed up in front of her and bellowed: 'Get out of here, lady! As quick as you can — before you get hurt!'

Her eyes caught the banners at the rear of the seething mass of humanity. STOP THE WAR, they said. She ran. Along the wall, crouching, clutching, warding off.

The turmoil behind her now, she placed a hand on the right side of her body to suppress the violent stabs. She stood still, surveying the scene. The park was on the other side of the road. Far enough from the trouble. Too far almost to drag herself there.

When she reached the wooden bench her trembling legs collapsed under her thin frame. She was dizzy. She wasn't supposed to run. Hadn't run even for a bus since her early thirties. You only survived war at a price. She'd never had strength and only a minimal ration of energy. Never played sports. No late nights. And pain of course . . . but with that she could live.

The tree behind her cast a cool web of balmy air over her crumpled shape. There was a perfume in the air — boronia, she recognized. It calmed her pumping lungs. She closed her eyes against the glare of sunlight outside the canopy of dark leaves — closed her ears with effort against the sounds of violence in the distance.

* * * *

She sat between the other children on the wooden cart, the bland sun of early summer scalding their pale faces, skinny bare arms. The cart stood still. The procession had halted at the crossroads. Adult voices argued, shouted, accused and condemned.

The uniformed giants had come the day before. When she woke up in the attic that morning she'd heard a shrill voice outside, calling: 'Trudi! Trudi! We are FREE!!' It was the voice of midwife Kraal who lived next door.

She'd wondered first what the stern face of Aunt Trudi, her foster

49

mother, would show as she received this message. When imagination failed her, she tasted the word herself . . . slowly, cautiously.

'Free . . .' she whispered into the new day. She shifted under the blanket, turned to the small window between the roof supports. Blue sky. 'Free . . .' she tried again. She knew not what it meant. It felt like a great emptiness — an absence of all she knew.

People always said: When we are free again, we will do this, say that, eat as much as we want. She couldn't remember being free. She only remembered the outbreak of war, just when she was about to start school. This big event in her life had been postponed for some time because of the war, but otherwise little changed at first. Except that one wasn't free. It meant there were soldiers everywhere, speaking in a familiar yet foreign tongue. And there were tanks and proclamations in red letters on white paper pasted on public buildings. Only gradually did the meaning of not being free become part of her existence, as did the hunger and as did the constant danger of stray bullets, curfews, bombardments, taboo words, walls that had ears, secret radio sets, scabies, fleas, headlice, the disappearance of trees for fuel and cats and dogs for food and Jewish playmates for . . . what?

She couldn't remember being free. Midwife Kraal kept on shouting up and down the street that they were all free now. It tasted like nothing. She couldn't feel it.

'Nellie!' called Aunt Trudi at the foot of the ladder. 'Get up and get dressed. The porridge needs stirring.'

Same as every morning of the two months she'd been here. Eight times Aunt Trudi had recorded an increase in weight in a small notebook. Thirty kilos on arrival, a hundred and sixty centimetres tall. A skeleton in a skin bag. One dress that fell apart at a touch and couldn't stand being stitched up much more. Thirty-eight kilos last Saturday and almost able to eat anything now, except fat and butter.

She slid out of bed, pulled the covers straight and took soap and towel down to wash under the pump in the barn.

At breakfast Aunt Tudi's ancient father, whom she'd never seen without his black cap, prayed in unusually trembly tones. 'Dear Lord, our Father, Thou hast delivered us, our faith rewarded.' He quoted texts she hadn't heard from him before. Keeping her head bowed and eyes closed over folded hands, as he'd taught her, she waited for the requests which came always near the end. Requests for daily bread, an end to war, peace . . . Her only participation in his prayers was to echo in her head 'give us today our daily bread' in her head. If bread came from heaven and they had enough up there then it was worth asking for it. She could never get enough bread — black or white, dry, without butter, or with a crumbly patch of goat's cheese.

'And now we ask Thee to deliver our charge back to the fold of her family, if it so pleases Thee.' After a solemn 'amen' he placed his silvery-haired hand on her head across the table. Aunt Trudi looked very strange; a bit like mama when she held her belly in during her last pregnancy whenever she had to go out of the house, because she had no dress wide enough to cover herself.

It was school as usual. She dragged her ever-tired feet through the dust of the village. All the refugee children clustered in a corner of the playground around Mr Tromp. They pressed him for an answer. When could they expect to be sent home, to the western provinces?

'They aren't free there yet,' explained the schoolmaster. 'No one knows how long . . .' They tried to do their lessons. Mr Tromp walked out of class a dozen times. At eleven, the three classes combined and were taught a new song.

> 'In freedom, peace and joy
> we join our hands
> to build anew
> our fa-ha-therland.'

When they could sing it with eyes closed, not peeking at the blackboard, school was dismissed for the day.

The Great Liberation Procession was to be held next morning, starting at ten from the locks on East canal. There would be farmcarts to ride on and each child was to wear a flower garland.

She sat on a peat heap near the swamp that afternoon — that empty afternoon of broken routine — in her constant state of homesickness for the faraway family in the land of the dying, where war still raged.

She saw the green trucks come rumbling along the canal road, driven by uniformed giants. She cowered behind a neighbour's shed, clutching the blue forget-me-nots she'd plucked in the bog to make her garland. In the distance Aunt Trudi had yelled her name in a voice so changed, it frightened her. She came on feet prepared to die.

'Nellie! Quick! Come to see our liberators! They're here!' Aunt Trudi laughed as tears ran down her ruddy cheeks and she flung off her apron to run around the house to the road.

The soldiers came from an unknown land called Canada. Their voices were fearless and frightening. Their barbed laughter clawed playfully at the people's incomprehension of their foreign words. Their mouths were caverns, booming coded sounds. They stood as tall as their trucks. They gave away cigarettes and chocolate and they wanted eggs guessed Aunt Trudi when one flapped his arms crying 'Tock-tock-tock-tock' and another crowed like a sick rooster.

Eggs for chocolate. Chocolate was a well-remembered word. Was this it? This hard brown square melting in a hand cold with dread at the smell of soldiers? All soldiers smelled the same. No soldiers were like other men. The men of the land were either old or mere boys.

'Eat it, child!' shouted Aunt Trudi with that never before seen laugh, that reckless uncontrolled hooting noise.

She ate it. It tasted bitter after a first promise of sweetness.

In the dark of the attic she cried effortlessly that night, while the voices of adults droned on below, still excited about freedom. They seemed to know what to do with it. Every house in the village bustled with discussion over cups of ersatz coffee.

* * * *

The forget-me-not garland hung limp around her sweaty neck by ten thirty. Her bones ached from being jostled along the uneven road on a cart with twenty other bony children, behind a brass band come from nowhere. Tri-coloured flags also appeared miraculously, draped with orange rosettes along the sides of the cart which stank of manure.

Proud old men she'd never seen in the village, strutted alongside in black suits with tails and rosettes in their buttonholes. Behind the cart a group of women carried banners: FREEDOM * PEACE * OUR FATHERLAND ADVANCE *. The band struck up the new-learnt melody and the children sang from dry throats, the words already part-forgotten, substituting la-la-la or mixing up the order of freedom, peace and joy.

When they sang the refrain for the second time with still one verse to go, the band stopped in mid-tune, the cart came to a creaking halt, the children tumbled forward, grazing knees on rough planks and shouting abuse at those who fell against them.

The crossroads had been reached. To the left and right, dirt roads led to other villages, whose inhabitants participated in the procession. The road ahead led nowhere.

The old men gathered up front, their black tails swinging. Voices cut the hot air, mouths were wells from which sprang streams of words in argument. Rosettes trembled on hollow chests as arms cleaved space and stubby fingers pointed in different directions.

She felt dizzy. Her eyes stung from salty sweat dribbling down her forehead. Rubbing made it worse. Her dress tore again, the second time today. Her bony backside ached on the hard wood. The sun burned. The children smelled of violence. The boys were pinching any girl they could reach without being seen by the women, who talked angrily in the vanguard. Amongst old men and boys the women were like men in their vexation.

Her arms were showing an angry red hue by the time the final discomfort assailed her. She had to urinate. The cart stood at the crossroads near the rickety wooden bridge over North canal. The village lay far behind them. There was no tree nor other cover in sight. If only the procession would move on to the next village, east or west. She could hold herself until the next church hall.

But the air was rent by rasping voices. The old men had doubled in number. The women called them names. The musicians rolled and smoked their home-grown weed. The air was foul with sweat, manure and violence.

With bursting bladder, parched tongue, bony buttocks pressed together in despair, her thoughts fought clear and pounded inside her burning skull: THIS IS PEACE. THIS IS FREEDOM. THE WAR IS OVER. THIS IS PEACE. THE WAR WILL NEVER END.

She had never believed she would die. Other people did. Her girlfriend was cut up by flying fragments of a crashing war plane. People died in the streets at home because of hunger and disease. But she'd never thought of her own death until now. She felt she would die on this cart in this procession celebrating peace.

* * * *

The young man hurtled across the green grass with hands covering his face. Blood dribbled through his fingers, spattering his torn tee-shirt.

She had not been conscious of her eyes being open. She had not seen anything until now.

'Why don't you get off y'r goddamned arse and help us stop the bloody war!' the young man shouted in her direction. 'People are getting bashed up over there because the like of you are too bloody apathetic to care!'

He tripped over his own feet. 'Do you know they're killing children in Lebanon and throwing gassss . . .' He sprawled down on the grass, his head just in the shade of the tree's canopy, which rustled fiercely though there was no breeze.

She gasped for breath. Her body jerked upright.

'I have . . .' she began. But her voice buckled and she started crying with long, whistling gulps as she shook her head wildly from side to side.

From the green grass the young blooded face raised itself, showing dumb illumination. The young man dragged up his feet and sat crosslegged in the shade.

'I'm sorry, lady,' he said and waited.

She opened her mouth again between the horrible sobs.

'I was . . . going to . . . shout at you! Tell you . . . t'go to hell . . . because you . . . know . . . noth . . .ing! Nothing!'

She groped for a torn tissue, blew her nose, drew air and shook her head again, though very differently from before.

'But I never want to fight for peace . . . again — d'you hear me? Never fight for peace again!'

A large sob escaped from her throat. She held out her hand and the young man took it, tears washing his dried-up blood.

'I only want to *be* peace!' she added and closed her eyes.

* * * *

Police mopping up, saw them from a distance. An old woman leaning back with closed eyes on a parkbench, her hand held by a boy seated on the grass with bowed head. They just sat there, not moving at all.

The men in uniform moved on. One glanced back over his shoulder. As if he wanted to join them.

JURGIS JANAVICIUS

Morning Frosts in Dungog

The morning frosts remind:
Boy's memories are always there
embedded in man's mind. (Father still sees
the slowly circling fish he once observed
during the summers of the 1890s.) Here
in Dungog it's wintry. The afternoons
are short. The days are fine.

Land of Mark

Orange and fading gold
— dienos skaidriu tarpudebesiu —*
pictures of little Paul
wading warm, shallow summer streams,
my Redhead when she falls asleep,
Francisca when she wakes,
the brass French Horn,
the winds in spring in '48,
all this:
The Land of Mark,
silvery meadow flats, the plains
where I am growing middle aged,
my father — old.

* days of brightness between the passing clouds

Silver Plains

Glimmering eyes of wakes still watch us,
sunsets are holding us up and mounted
> men,
also ramparts across our own hearts.
Today we are in the midst of the plains
— all silver: cumbungi marshes.
And whilst we are here all we have lived
> so far
we are to live again and yet again,
and seasons, frosts and thaws, men's fits
> and women's fancies,
all kitchen gear, purses for items useful but
> so very small
will ride and drag and crawl with us no
> matter where we go
or what the ground we shall be treading
> on will be.
And then the past, the names of all our kin,
and of all those accepting them and us
— zmones zemaiciu zemes po Tavo, Vies-
> patie, akim —*
still being branded upon our foreheads,
> jaws,
and limbs. And far into the plains
obscured by tall cumbungi reeds the amber
> coloured
flags already flutter in the future winds on
> all
we shall disclaim, or claim, or dream, or
> think.

* people of Samogitian Lands under Your watchful eye, oh Lord.

MANFRED JURGENSEN

object-lesson

i trace the aim of your design
with new-found patience and respect
for all the meanings that define
themselves, as their own truths reflect
the nature of life's mystery.
in you i touch the sacred heart,
the absence that evaded me
in my part's reckless counterpart.
how to describe you, how to name
an object that proclaims the law
all beings are one and the same — .
the thing itself exists in awe
of matter. it is created
as one innumerable part
to which all parts are related
as wholly as a work of art;
the beauty of a measured rule,
the splendour of pure craftsmanship,
the use of a discovered tool,
the missing word within my grip — .

(for loló houbein)

bonegilla 1961

the heat of burnt grass,
impotent anger
at an english class,
men getting younger
by each disciplined day,
till they are school-boys
again, told to pay
attention, roll-calls
into another
life, how to translate
the humid weather,
the shame and the hate —
at night, the huts throb
with desperate love-
making, young men sob
in darkness, dreams of
childhood call them home,
twilight rains set in,
morning builds its dome,
the snake sheds its skin.

ethnic food

the brotherhood of man
in an imported can,
history's grim lesson
as delicatessen — .

conscience trading on doubt,
the jew serves sauerkraut.
outgarlicked, we at last
are swallowing our past.

hamlet's blue cheese prices
mark an all-time crisis
in the growth of profit.
death thinks nothing of it.

VASSO KALAMARAS

Mademoiselle

The tall, dull-coloured buildings of the big city stood out, severe and ugly, silhouetted against the cold grey sky. People hurried with a desperate sad urgency along the footpaths. A general heaviness, together with their everyday worries, was mirrored in their faces. Today! — always today! They must hurry — to pass the man in front — the business colleague — the competitor — today — and then bring the whole thing back full circle, meaninglessly to the beginning again — an end with no result.

Mud had collected along the edges of the dirty asphalt street, lying there with no escape. Unheedingly the passers-by dragged their weary feet along, splashing their neighbours in their haste. Unbearable cold, dirt, dampness, and dejection.

Mademoiselle Katerinoula ran to get to her last lesson on time. Her pupils' homes were separated by great distances, but goodness, with fares so expensive, how could she ever afford to use the tram or the buses fecklessly, or as often as she wished? She was always working out arrangements that involved her strength, her money, and the length of her journey. She came up with strange solutions, and often made brave walks to save the pennies.

Life was hard for Mademoiselle Katerinoula living with her aged mother. For 35 years she had no father nor any male protection. Poor little thing, she seemed so tired that afternoon as she hurried down Hermes Street towards Monastyraki. Her patched up shoes with their dilapidated wooden heels clicked noisily as she hurried along. She was very conscious of them, and ashamed to be wearing the same pair again this year — but there was no alternative.

Passing the little church in the square, she made the sign of the cross and pushed on uphill into some narrow street in the Plaka, hastening her steps.

'Goodness me, I'll be late!' she kept thinking.

Finally she arrived. As she tapped on the bronze knocker of the front door, her little nose, very red from influenza, started dripping. Her gloves were worn and a few still undarned holes betrayed her to the cold and to the eyes of the world. Nervously she gave her ringlets a hurried once over. Fussily pinned with countless hairclips, they had remained obediently in place.

As the front door opened, the lively heads of five little boys could be seen at the top of the staircase. They noisily greeted her arrival.

'Mother, mother, it's the French teacher, mother!' They could all be heard shouting together as they ran to hide inside the house. From the long dark hall the untidy head of Mrs Evanthia, the confectioner's wife, appeared. Her husband had a big sweets shop with all kinds of goodies. The family was in very fair circumstances. Personal extravagance, however, didn't interest Mrs Evanthia. She had no time for that sort of thing, with all the little children and such a big house. She did find time, however, for a certain amount of leisure. There was always a young servant girl. It wasn't such a great expense to employ a maid. A few worn and faded cast-offs for clothing — and of course, her food. And quite enough too! The food she ate, the little devil! It never failed to amaze Mrs Evanthia. She always found time to voice her complaints to the schoolmistress.

She saw her now and ran to welcome her. She took her into the dining room with the big walnut table with its dark-red velvet table cloth.

'Sit down, Mamouasel, sit down. You must be freezing in such frosty weather!'

She gave her a chair and called loudly, 'Thymioula! Where are you, my bright girl? Put some more coal in the stove. You know Mamouasel Katerinoula always comes at this time. Go and get the children.'

The maid emptied the whole bucket of coal into the huge square belly of the stove. Bright red flames, strong and friendly, could be seen through its glass window.

Mademoiselle Katerinoula came closer, and holding out her gloved hands, numb with cold, warmed them at the fire. Then one by one she began to take off her things — the scarf, gloves, bonnet, overcoat. She waited for Mrs Evanthia to start up as usual on her husband's relatives, and all about people whom the poor schoolmistress had never seen and would never be likely to know — it was as if it were some clause in her teaching contract. She endured it all — she had got used to it.

From the other room the peevish shouts of the children could be heard, abuse and loud noises. The frightened little voice of Thymioula was repeating over and over. 'Your mother told me to, your mother. Go to Mamousella to learn your French. Oh, oh! It's not my fault! Your mother told me . . . Oh, oh!'

Mademoiselle Katerinoula was surprised that Mrs Evanthia had waited so long to begin her chatter. She turned to look at her, and found the woman observing her closely as if she had never seen her before. She blushed, pretended not to notice, and again remarked, 'My goodness! what freezing weather, but what a lovely fire.' She wanted to be the first to speak, but Mrs Evanthia was serious, very serious. She seemed altogether different, more square and flabby and even more foolish than usual.

The children rushed into the dining room in cheeky disorder. They quarrelled about who should have the red chair, and who the high leather one, and who the others.

Mrs Evanthia drew near Mademoiselle Katerinoula and whispered to her hurriedly, 'Please Mamouasel, don't leave when the lesson is over. We have something to discuss between us.'

She left the room quickly, closing the door so that the noise wouldn't worry her.

The little schoolmistress took a ruler from her worn black leather handbag and threatened the children, *'Silence! Bon soir mes enfants.'*

'Bon soir Mamouasel,' shouted the five youngsters in unison.

'Oh pauvre! non Mamouasel! Mademoiselle, s'il vous plaît,' she sighed with disappointment.

The lesson commenced, but the poor little schoolmistress's mind had become very unsettled by Mrs Evanthia's last words. Whatever would the two of them have to talk about? What meaning could the presence of an insignificant schoolmistress have in the life of this noisy, well-to-do family? Surely they didn't want to lower her salary again? Only the other day one of her pupils had done that. It was not as if it were a princely sum — a few meagre drachmas, so very few! My goodness! She became pale with fear, and began to tremble secretly. Her eyes filled with tears. Her head began to ache.

In the middle of all this, towards the end of the lesson, someone knocked timidly on the door. Thymioula entered shyly, and left a silver tray with coffee, two small fresh biscuits, and a crystal jug of water on the table near the teacher. Her expression was abject, full of awe, with such a truly deep respect for this very learned schoolteacher! She even trembled slightly — it became ludicrous. One of the children sneaked up and pulled at her untidy plaits from behind. Another stuck out his tongue in front of her. The little maid blushed. She became terribly embarrassed and rushed away precipitously.

It was past seven by the big clock on the wall, and there was still no sign of Mrs Evanthia. The schoolmistress was fearful and impatient. The lesson was over. Everything in the room remained in disorder. The stove no longer burned brightly as at first, but now emitted a quiet and pleasing warmth. The room seemed so very quiet without the children. Unconsciously she realised that this was giving her some confidence. She scratched at the velvet table-cloth with her fingers and gazed at the plaster decorations on the ceiling. When she heard the footsteps of Mrs Evanthia in the passage her heart began to beat.

She came in very changed — for the better, carefully groomed and powdered.

'Oh!' the schoolmistress opened her eyes wide in surprise, but she tried not to show it. She smiled as agreeably as she could, and assumed an air of pleasant nonchalance.

'How beautiful you have become, dear Mrs Evanthia, like a young girl! You must surely be getting ready to go out somewhere . . . and me so late! Goodness, my poor mother will be worried!'

The fat hand of the confectioner's wife enveloped the delicate refined little fingers of the schoolmistress in their plump palms, as she implored her with much tenderness, 'Please sit down Mamouasel Katerinoula. Sit down for a little while. I want to tell you something — very seriously!' Her voice seemed to tremble a little as if she were frightened and as if beseeching her from the depths of her soul.

'It is, er, it is about my brother. My dear brother who lives abroad. Ah, if only I could do something for him! He is always my secret sorrow. He is the only one who remains of my father's house. Do you follow me, Mamouasel Katerinoula? You're such a well educated girl, with so many languages . . . and you are so very worthy . . . you must understand me . . .'

Two blurred and heavy tears, oozing from the large colourless eyes, hung on her fat and swollen cheeks, glistening like silver sequins.

The luckless little schoolmistress in her confusion was deeply moved. She fluttered her eyelashes very amusingly, half opening her mouth as she nodded her head up and down. 'Yes, yes!' reassuring her companion, as if she already knew and understood everything. But the ill-fated girl understood nothing. Neither on that particular evening, nor weeks and whole months later, did the poor thing realize what had happened.

What is the meaning of 'Fate'?

It was as if she had lost her speech, as if her reason had been blotted out. You might say her advancing age was to blame; perhaps a weariness in waiting for her future lot. She seemed so sympathetic, so soft; or perhaps, better to say she was so hard on herself; or so improvident. She left her mother behind her, deserted and without any other company. The afflicted old woman threw her many and varied hopes into the hands of the Virgin Mary — and the good graces of Mrs Evanthia. How deeply earnest were her private entreaties!

'Oh sweet Virgin, let a bright day dawn for my Katerinoula. Let her know the sweet . . . light of life. Let the day dawn for her, my beloved little daughter . . .' Yes, it was necessary for the girl to get married. She was already well on in years. But how would the old woman fare, left all on her own? Well, it would only be for a little while Katerinoula would send for her as soon as she had exchanged wreaths with Panagiotys, the brother of Mrs Evanthia. The man had a shop in Melbourne, one of the most important big cities in Australia! In her reveries the poor old mother used to imagine all sorts of good fortune for her grown-up daughter, the poor orphan who had suffered for so many years, going from door to door for her living!

Her Rinoula had been the first girl student at the Academy. She was proud of her. She deserved such good fortune. She deserved to see all the best things in the world, all the riches and luxuries which foreigners enjoyed. For this the mother was prepared to turn her heart into stone. She tied her handkerchief in knots so she wouldn't cry too much; she wouldn't worry her beloved Katerinoula.

Ah, what sorrow was in store for the poor soul! Whom would she wait for at the window in the evenings of the days to come? For whom would she prepare warm food? Whose little hands would enfold her old palms and bless them with their warmth? And at night, who was there to see that she was covered up again when the blankets slipped away?

'But now my Katerinoula will have a fine husband at her side. He will look after her. He will shoulder the worries of making a living. She will be so fortunate and so happy with him. It must be so, it couldn't be otherwise. Lucky girl!'

The old woman would think about herself. What did she have to fear? She only had to arrange for her own meagre requirements. Besides, how many times had her son-in-law written, 'As soon as we can, we will bring you to us . . . so you won't be lonely, so your daughter will have you for company, and won't have to worry . . .'

Katerinoula was so sure that they would send for her mother after two or three months, that in order not to weary the old woman, she collected all her belongings privately, and arranged everything for the long journey. She took only two suitcases, with only the really indispensable things. The rest her mother could bring — it was all the same.

* * * *

'Hey! where are you, you stupid bitch, blast you!' the heavy angry voice of her husband bellowed from the shop. His tongue dripped venom and betrayed his irritation.

Only seven months married, and now all this had happened to darken and weigh down her life. The nightmare was choking her. 'Oh my God,' the unhappy woman whispered, starting up from the bedclothes which reeked of male breath and cigarette smoke.

'I'm coming, I'm coming,' she called out half in her sleep, groping for the switch to turn on the light. It was still pitch dark, as you could imagine in the middle of winter. She looked at the tablecloth and shivered in the chilly dampness. How had she possibly overslept? It was past six o'clock! She rushed to put on her calico dress, and her kitchen apron. This was becoming more difficult to manage these days, now the little one was beginning to hamper her movements. She could feel the tiny creature very much alive, growing and demanding more and more room under her cheap dress. Her hand instinctively caressed the swelling in her belly with a special tenderness. She always seemed to be on the verge of tears, and now her eyes moistened and shone sadly. Going to the dressing-table she cast a disinterested glance into the mirror. She stuck a couple of clips into her neglected hair, and fastened it back in an ungraceful pony tail.

Panagiotys was working in the kitchen. The hot stove, smeared with fat, reeked of beef and fish. 'Welcome to our studious one,' was his ironical early morning greeting. 'Useless bloody thing, you've been looking at those un-nailed boxes since yesterday, and you still haven't put any oranges or lemons in the window. Do you expect me to do everything, Mrs Schoolteacher?'

His wife lowered her head in silence, and with tearful eyes started in on the work — work which really called for more endurance and stronger arms than even those of her husband Mr Panagiotys. She tried not to think or reflect on anything. She had extinguished her past; she trembled for her future. Her husband was in one of his fearful moods. He had been playing cards the night before till 2.30 in the morning, and had obviously lost.

'I expected to get a woman who would be a standby in the shop, but instead of that up comes a half-dead cat. Bah! talk about touchy! . . 'I'd rather not, if you please . . . I can't do it . . . I don't think I can manage' . . . 'ph! — to hell with such a woman! Ha! look at her, sleeping in till 6 in the morning like a duchess! And who, I'd like to know, is going to clean the potatoes? Who's going to fillet the fish? I'm asking you. Have you been struck dumb?'

'Dear God, have pity on me,' sighed the afflicted girl, unable to restrain her tears. They fell, salting the endless stream of potatoes passing through her chapped and dirty hands. She experienced queer fits of dizziness. An unbearable dullness continually clouded her thought and her will to react. If she could only defend herself, even slightly, even on one single occasion!

It only maddened her husband to see the decline into which she had fallen. He raged from the depths of his soul, and despised her more and more. He provoked quarrels one after another.

'I feel I could rip you in two, you dumb clot! Do you think I don't know that you want to send money to that wretched old mother of yours? Hgh? You won't get a bad penny out of me— I'm not going to roast and fry in this kitchen here for the sake of you and her ladyship. Just for you to sit around and do nothing. Not a bad penny — do you understand? Come on, if you've got the guts ask me for it and find out who's the boss around this place!'

His wife had heard the words so many times that you'd think they would have lost their power to worry her any more. But what would you wish? That she had never been born? That no one had reared her with a fine and gentle nature, in poor circumstances it's true, but with such love, so full of solicitude and devotion?

'Oh mother dearest, what will become of you, my darling?' She whispered in a sort of feverish delirium. She felt tired out, unimaginably exhausted. The fate of her lonely mother in her advanced age, with no hope of assistance from anywhere and no close relations, was all an unsolved and tragic problem for the unhappy girl, on top of all her own troubles with this intractable husband of hers.

His hostile malicious words were a burning knife thrust deep into her heart. They drove her mad. She stood up in an attempt to react. She could bear it no longer.

'Let me breathe, Blessed Virgin,' she shouted in desperation.

What darkness, what icy frigidity! 'Mother, dearest Mother, hurry I am lost! Your ill-starred daughter is lost. Run my dearest.' She shrieked like a mad woman, and fell in a heap on to the dirty lino of the kitchen floor.

'Hysterical bitch!' shouted her now infuriated husband. Snatching up a slop bucket, he threw out the mop and emptied the filthy water over his wife's head. He rushed madly out into the yard making straight for the garage. He started up the utility and set off for the vegetable market. He was very late.

Ah, what an eternity all those months seemed to her! Entire months with their immeasurable days; and nights that seemed to know no dawn, strung like a black rosary, repeated endlessly over and over, as they had been since the first day she disembarked.

What bitterness! How could such a fate have been in store for her, this girl who from her childhood had always been so diffident and so reserved? Her timid existence would have been lost and annihilated in the face of some much less dangerous male. Believe it or not she was a girl who had grown up untouched, undefiled and unmolested. Perhaps some deep fear or perhaps from some unusual mental sensitivity and perception, she had lived to that time an almost unbelievably chaste life. Her character was as delicate, fragile, and transparent as fine clear crystal!

She awoke, confused from chloroform, and aware of an extraordinary pleasant numbness in her body. If it were possible, she felt she would like to spend the rest of her life sunk in this half-drugged state, without pain, indifferent to her misfortunes. She tried to collect her thoughts; to remember where she was.

'Mother dearest, mother dearest!' she whispered, reaching out in the darkness for her mother's hand. They always slept with their beds side by side. They had done so since she was a little child. How else could her mother be near to cover her again if the blankets slipped from her?

'How poorly you are sleeping, Katerinoula dear,' her mother complained tenderly. 'You are all uncovered again, you'll catch a cold.'

'Mother, have you put out the lamp?' Katerinoula asked loudly.

The beam of a torch fell on her face. Someone approached, stood at her side, and put the light on at the bed. A beautiful young girl in a white cap bent over her. She asked quietly and sweetly in English, 'Did you call me, Mrs Panagiotys?'

The woman came to her senses. It all returned to her. Her time had arrived, she had become a mother! She had had a child, her own baby child! She should be so proud, so happy . . . But no! that was strange, she had lost the sweet drugged feeling. Fear and misery crept into her soul once more. The disillusionment of harsh reality rose up and suffocated her. Ah, so she was not back in her home after all, close to her dear mother. The dream had been so sweet! Reality became a nightmare for her. She looked at the nurse with an uneasy pained expression.

'Don't worry, Mrs Panagiotys. She is so pretty; such a lovely little girl!'

'Girl, girl? *Koritsaki,* ah yes, I know,' whispered the woman wearily. She closed her eyes, but not in sleep.

The lighly-tapping heels of the nurse faded away into the darkness, leaving her on her own again with all her scattered thoughts, and a bitter taste in her mouth. Her tongue was dry. She was burning all over with fever. What despair she felt! Ah! was this the fruit of that hideous marital experience? Perhaps on that very first night — the very evening that she disembarked. What a frightful recollection! How could she ever forget it? . . . The humiliation . . . the coarseness . . . the violence . . .

'A little girl! I've got a little girl . . Ah my God, what we will have to suffer together!' For the first time she was thinking in the plural.

'What we will have to go through! Ah, my child . . . Where is my child? No, no my little daughter . . .'

Her sobs shattered the silence of the hospital. Worried nurses ran and turned on the light. She was crying; loud, poignant sobs. Her breast was bare and her hands tore at her clothing and anything they encountered. She was transferred to another room on her own, with a nurse to watch over her. She had become very sick, dangerously so, but she would be cured. Modern science had such powerful and sophisticated drugs! How could they fail to cure her?

Her husband came next day. He sat in a chair looking at her seriously, absentmindedly, with colourless eyes. He resembled very much his sister, Mrs Evanthia. The sick woman with the pallor of death on her weak and sunken cheeks slept uneasily, breathing with difficulty. From time to time she whimpered and raved in her sleep in indistinguishable words. Some time passed and Mr Georgiou lost his patience. It was very busy at the shop. Just the time the bulk of his customers were arriving. He couldn't remain here stuck in a chair with his wife asleep. What about the shop? Who knows what would go on there without the boss?

'Katerinoula, come on, it's time to wake up. You've had enough sleep. I've waited long enough.' He pushed her shoulder.

Startled, the woman opened her eyes and looked at him wearily. He turned away to avoid her gaze. He snorted, but restraining himself said curtly, 'I expected as much; I expected it would all be a ridiculous mess. You never were what I wanted. How can it ever be any better now? We could well have done without being overrun like this with females. The business will go to pot. It will be ruined. Ask me what good you've been in all this. It's the finish of us!'

Her pillow was soaked with dumb tears. As she listened to him, she felt their burning drops wetting her cheeks and running from her ears into the roots of her hair. Her eyes were smarting and her breasts hurt her with an unbearable pressure. His malicious tongue went on and on, exuding its poison drop by drop. You would think he was experiencing some unnatural pleasure, some blind, wild joy. He realised her torture and it stirred him up even more.

'Hm, where in hell did Evanthia dig you up? You know my cousin Michael? He's only three years younger than me, just turned 42, and he's got himself a real blossom for a wife, only 22 years old! And what a girl she is! Something like a woman. Stretch out your hands and you can grab arms worth cuddling. The thighs she's got . . . the buttocks . . . breasts like mountains! You call yourself a woman and you deal me out another female like this. It gives me a pain in the guts. I told you I wanted a boy. I'll never forget this . . . A dirty black snake can eat the two of you. Besides . . .'

In the doorway appeared the sweet face of a nurse with bright carefree eyes, and cheeks pink and white like a spring rose. Light chestnut curls hung artfully down from her starched white cap. She entered, gracefully smiling, and holding in her arms a tiny babe; a red-faced mite with black hair and a big half-open mouth like a newborn sparrow.

'Mr Panagiotys, look how lovely she is! What a charming little girl you have!' She held the child out in her arms towards the father.

'Oh my God, don't,' the sick mother screamed wildly. Mad with fear she jumped up and snatched the baby into her embrace.

'No, no, not my child! Dear God protect my little daughter! Ah! where can I hide my little one?' she screamed despairingly. Barefooted, clasping the tiny newborn creature to her breast, she made one confused circuit round the bare room before rushing into the passage. There she began to run with all her might.

She had only one thought, to escape, to get away from this tyrant; from her loneliness; from this foreign country with its strange language; from her fate. Where, dear Virgin, could she allay her fear? How could she even admit to this torture of her soul, her hatred for this entire foreign world, and above all for her husband?

'She's gone mad, the crazy bitch,' grumbled Panagiotys, 'that sister of mine really caught me out with this bookworm for a present. They tell you to go and get married! . . . hgh, and at a busy time like this! I'll lose all my customers! How did I ever come to get mixed up with a thing like her? Bugger me dead! A man ought to be pitied!'

A Christmas Gift

A modern industrial city — one of the more recent, carefully planned and well laid out. Each separate house, beautiful as a toy, was surrounded by its little garden and ample greenery.

Department stores stretched along the main streets, displaying in their huge windows every variety of luxury and comfort. There were refrigerators, electric stoves and expensive motor cars with glistening exteriors. How brilliantly they shone, side by side, with furniture of every kind, laminex tables and elegant television sets. Then again, other huge show windows seemed as if they were adorned with flags, with their fantastic range of materials, fashionable dresses and every style of clothing. These all bordered on heaps of indescribably varied merchandise, from screwdrivers, saws and stationery, to confectionery or jewellery. A brilliant, dazzling array, producing at every turn some dizzy excitement, bearing down on one's will and weaknesses with all the force of a steel press.

What an ant-like world! The heat was unbearable. It was two days before Christmas. All dry and yellow in the country paddocks, the grass had begun to smell like tinder while in the city, life became ever more hectic. Policemen on their motor cycles edged their way with difficulty through the dense traffic. In the general disorder motor cars with noisy horns crept along, slow as tortoises, at the cross streets. Pedestrians like leaderless animals stood mechanically in groups with eyes rivetted on the traffic lights or jostling each other as they tore in opposite directions along the footpaths.

Swarms of people; every kind of countenance. The well-fed with their expensive clothes; the miserable with their bargain-basement cottons or denim jeans. Eyes that were weary or joyful, tired or indifferent.

High in the air shone the imposing trade names of some giant emporium. It was one of those buildings which occupy an entire block, from one street to the next. Inside could be found everything, from bootlaces or vegetables or fresh bread to the more luxurious and expensive accessories of our modern and extravagant age. Its wise directors, despite having such odd and uncountable masses of merchandise in their labyrinth of a store, knew very expertly how to advertise it, each item separately and in its place. In one of these departments, look! a huge glass show window. It seemed to reach to heaven, and inside, what a collection of the very latest models! Bicycles of every colour, some small, some big, all decorated and turning slowly on their revolving pedestals. Bicyles! How they would fill you with envy if you were a 12-year-old boy who had never owned one. The headlights, the metal accessories, the spokes, all sparkling under the electric floodlights. And look at those tyres on the wheels. Just to touch them would give you goose-pimples!

The management had arranged for a show girl, a charming little model with a soft alluring voice, to repeat over and over the same refrain, 'Parents! Look! The best and most practical gift for your deserving children. See! What more beautiful bicycle could you buy. Just a minimum down-payment with easy instalments, and it will be yours.'

The crowd surged past with the noise of countless footsteps, nameless and unknown. Only at the very edge of the huge window, like a tiny dot on a sheet of paper, had stopped one very small boy.

How to describe him? Uncut, uncombed hair, dirty bare feet,

wearing a faded check calico shirt and worn-out blue jeans that were so tight his little backside looked like two apples in a handkerchief. His gaze had an unusually bright hypnotized look — the expression of a hunted animal in the face of its captor! So alive and real can something become when it touches on the desires of the soul.

'Do we have to take so seriously every demand of a child?' The irritable voice of his nagging mother still rung in his ears from the day before. He had been eavesdropping outside her room while she was scolding his father.

'Stavros had better take a different road from you, you waster. You only worry about pleasing yourself. All that remains over for us is debts. Debts, debts, and *you* stinking of sour wine.'

The father bellowed. Something sounding like a punch was heard and something broke at the same time.

'You bitch,' the man roared like a wild beast. 'You've lumbered me with seven of them in a row, you rabbit — you bloody great rabbit!'

'Take that and that,' screamed the infuriated woman. She must have struck him a couple of heavy blows, because he groaned drunkenly and shrank back for a while.

Stavros held his breath. The baby was probably asleep, but Nickie, his little two-year-old sister, was screaming fearfully in the other room. The little boy's inflamed cheeks burnt as if he had a fever, and his chest swelled fit to burst . . . The more he heard, the more his eyes flooded with tears. Trembling, he rubbed and wiped his wet cheeks with his dirty open palms. But the tears only wet them again. Gerasimos, Novos, Savas and Rinoula lay on a mattress on the floor in the adjoining room where he too had his pillow and shared a little of the mattress. The neglected children, tired out from their play, were all sound asleep, but Stavros was so upset and nervous, and his will had been so shattered. Where was there any room in this place for him — where could he ever get any sleep?

'Huh! So he's been at it again, eh? Well, let him go to the "Premier" and collect rubbish if he wants to — that's what he wants — you don't understand, he's a boy,' his father stammered drunkenly. 'He'll save something in time — The instalments . . .' But his voice had lost all its authority — it wound down like a hoarse trumpet.

'What?' she snapped at him again, 'the grandson of Signor Giovanni to collect rubbish? I spit on you, you embezzler, you thief, you sneaking rat! You're the one that brought us down to this crowded hole. Look at you ! You'd send a child of mine, a grandson of Signor Giovanni, to collect people's rubbish round a picture show?

Never! Get lost.' She shrieked hysterically, out of her wits. The big nose in the middle of her angry face was threatening him like a bent finger wagging to put him in his place. Her lank dull hair, half undone, hung in straggling whisps from an untidy bun, and her unkind eyes glowered from under a high, wide forehead, robbing her of any trace of womanly grace.

Signora Victoria was the daughter of an Italian father and a mother from Kephalonia. She had met her husband at the height of his glory, some dark and dirty business which Signora Victoria was prepared to overlook; but she couldn't dismiss the money involved! He had a fat wallet . . . He was a man . . . A friend of her father . . . A Kephalonian . . . He had plenty to offer. Besides, she was getting on in years, 28 in fact, yes, fully that. But the Kephalonian with the wild adventurous eye regarded it as a good match. He gave a hand to her father and helped in the mysterious business which they carried on . . . golden guineas! In due course they were married, never expecting what was to follow; all that litigation and ignominy. He up and went, secretly and stealthily; but on the downgrade, slippery and inevitable. What a debacle!

Outside the noise of locomotives started up again, shunting backwards and forwards. Whistles, nerve-wracking and prolonged, drowned out the voice of Signora Victoria. Little Stavros could no longer hear what they were saying. The trains were grunting and manoeuvring about close to the ruined picket fence of their wooden house. They had lived long years in this black hell of smoke, coal dust and fearful noise. A door with a filthy grease-stained curtain joined the kitchen to their shop. Cool drinks, cigarettes, matches, withered oranges and some lollies — it was a miserable business — a miserable life — general wretchedness.

Little Stavros loathed the unforgiveable deadliness of it all. The noise, the misery, the nervous miserly Signora Victoria, wiping spilt sugar or drops of milk from the floor with her fingers; his wreck of a father with his swollen watery eyes, fat ugly lips and broad unsympathetic nose.

'I hate you, I hate you!' he cried, hitting his little fists angrily on his bent knees, as he squatted behind the closed door, listening in the darkness, suffering dumbly, with no hope of finding any solution.

'I hate you!' he hissed unheard, in ever mounting anger. But within his own soul he was shouting madly.

'I want to die! I want — I want —' With his dirty uncut nails he tore at his arms in rage.

This day amid the dazzling lights, the showy advertisements and those prohibited heavenly enticements — all well locked up, of course, in shop windows, according to the proprieties of our particular civilisation — the small boy became numbed and bemused, like a little snake in the heat of the sun. He allowed his dreams and desires to coalesce and become a reality. Oh, what moments of madness! What joyous pride!

'Just look at it — that blue bicycle with the red handle grips, its revolving spokes, its shiny handlebars, the beautiful seat, the flipping pedals like little angels' wings!'

In the intensity of his imagination, Stavros felt it was already his. This illusion, which happens so often even to grown-ups, has a magic and solemn force in the little soul of a child . . . it can go beyond the tragic. Little Stavros was living at that moment in a private world all of his own.

See how easily one could throw one's leg across the saddle. How quickly one could steer it, according to all the rules of the road, turning into some great highway with boundless fields and farms to left and right. He was doing clever tricks like Mack when he got close to school. And Georgie Stamatiadis would turn pale when he saw him. He would know for certain that Stavros's bike was more beautiful than his. No longer would Thanasis, whose father owned the big cafe, poke out his tongue mockingly at him as he passed by riding his bike, while he still had to go to school on foot.

How delicious it felt! Surely some silent music was flooding his senses with a strange magic! A delirium of happiness carried him along. Immeasurable happiness sweet as a mother's love. But a mother who would share his troubles, who wouldn't scourge his sufferings . . . Not one afflicted with unbearable meanness and crazy, grandiose ideas.

Gaily whistling some school ditty, he would go first to the little faraway milling quarter, to the house of Costaki, Mr Lefteris's son. Mr Lefteris had worked on the saw in the mill there for years.

'Costa, Costa, get your bike quickly and we'll have a race to the paddocks.'

People came and went around him. It was two days before Christmas. Everyone was so busy. Everybody was on the move. Time was running out for them all. They must make the most of it for their last-minute requirements. Night was coming on. They must get back to their homes to take stock of the goodies they had purchased. But Stavros mused on. With wide-eyed surprise, he imagined he saw another of his friends.

'Hip, hip! Now we'll have a super wonderful game — and a useful one too,' Stavros concluded, 'because I won't have to make that three-quarter of an hour's walk every morning to school.'

'Hip, hip! Look at this, Costa — look at me — no steering! Look at me! Both hands crossed on my chest!'

The shops were preparing to close their doors. The time had come. The crowds were thinning out.

Pale and tired from his long day, the little 12-year-old boy dragged himself away from the big display window with slow despairing steps. He felt that his little body was a heavy bundle of useless old rags which he could only pull along with great difficulty. He found the return road, and went back home.

The yard door creaked as, with heavy head slumped between his shoulders, he crossed the grass-covered yard. He entered the shop. There behind the dirty, grease-stained counter, his mother was serving a small urchin. The customer was picking and choosing some chewing gum from coloured cards. Finally he selected one and ran off. Stavros stood there half looking at them with a surly expression on his face, and with his hands in the tight pockets of his trousers. His mother carried on as if she had not seen him, opening the till and putting in the couple of coins from the small customer. Then slowly and with hostility their eyes met.

'And where have you been all day, you good-for-nothing,' his mother exploded, full of exasperation and anger. 'A busy time like this and everyone disappears. The devil only knows where your father is, and now you — where have you been?'

Stavros became even paler than before, his weak 12-year-old back was gathered into a premature stoop. His frightened expression showed his presentiment of punishment, but he summoned up all the strength he could from his miserable experience of life, his own private unhappiness and his exasperated existence. With a formal seriousness, and in a voice hardly audible, he asked again the same question.

'Will you let me go at night to the "Premier" to collect the rubbish? I still have three pounds left from the lottery. I'll get the bike on instalments. I'll be able to pay it off. I'll pay for it in instalments. I'll work in the evenings at the "Premier". They want me there.'

'Ha. So you're a waster like your father! You want to sweep up rubbish round a picture-theatre, eh? You, the grandson of Signor Giovanni! So this is what you've descended to! No! You don't realize what an aristocrat, what a business man you had in your grandfather — and what a distinguished family you come from — not a run down shambles like this one, with no self-respect, no pride in your origins. If only I could knock some sense into your head.'

'Will you let me?' the boy asked with impatient fervour, and contempt for all she had been saying.

She felt the provocation in his reply, the defiant attitude. His contempt for her great patrician family bit deeply into her soul.

'And what if you do go,' she shouted angrily, intent on wounding him. 'Suppose you do go, you'll bring the money back here, piece by piece, to the till, to help feed you, you lazy good-for-nothing; not waste it on bicycles and your own amusement.'

'Ptoo, on your Signor Giovanni!' the little chap spat impudently, 'blowing us up with talk of your fine ancestry.' He stamped his foot on the floor as he'd seen his father do.

The infuriated mother rushed behind the counter with all its cheap articles. Her awkward rubber thongs caught on the corner and she nearly collapsed sprawling on the floor.

The child laughed mockingly, with deep new-found malice, and with a hatred which strained his throat and choked him.

The sight of this sudden cynicism in her 12-year-old son stirred his mother up till she was blind with rage. The fatigue of her trying day; the other smaller children; the untidiness of the lot of them; the babe; the husband never at her side, but who left all the business worries to her; everything; her aristocratic background; her sick pride; the general misery and chaos; it was all too much for her. The small shop seemed to shake around her. She lifted her arms into the air. Calling on God and the devil, she cursed bitterly everything that came into her confused mind — the house, children, husband!

Snatching up a worn-out broom, she gave Stavros a mighty whack in the ribs. Panic stricken and in pain, the boy started up and took to his heels. He jumped over the broken fence in a trice and was lost amongst the old abandoned railway carriages. In the half darkness his panting nostrils sucked in the coal dust and blackened his lungs.

The shrill angry voice of his mother could still be heard threatening him. 'Come back here, you worthless good-for-nothing or I'll tear out your bloody little tongue!'

But Stavros didn't go back home. They all waited in vain for him that evening. As usual his father was in a drunken stupor, with his wife quarrelling and raving at him with ineffectual words.

The boy was hungry, but what tormented him most was the breakdown of his whole inner world. He could put up with the other things, tolerating them with hatred and loathing; but they were habitual. To find the same evil in himself was something else again. This he could never accept nor get used to. Inside him something had collapsed.

The whole order of his consciousness had been broken down by this wounding of his will. He could find no balance.

The most serious, the most fearful thing that could happen to a child occurred. He was in revolt against himself. The dark chaos of his inner world shuddered with sick explosions. Fear, humiliation, misery, poverty, lack of sympathy — where could he go?

Time slipped by unheeded and with no ordered purpose. He was hungry. He had two shillings and eight pence in his hip pocket. He entered a nearby cafe and stood timidly on one side counting his money with trembling fingers. He bought a pie. He put the change back in his pocket and closed the zip. Going out into the darkness, he devoured the hot food ravenously.

He felt more comfortable now, and jammed his hands into the pockets of his trousers while he sauntered along the road in an unknown neighbourhood.

In a side street near a house with flood-lit windows where some cars were parked, laughter and a merry din could be heard. With nothing else to do, he leant against the trunk of one of the trees on the opposite side of the road, staring at the merry-making. Young men and girls, some in charming dresses, others in tight provocative jeans, were dancing rock and roll. A radiogram emitted the jarring modern sound of guitars and drums, followed by the voice of a singer, harsh, staccato and passionate.

With loud laughter, shouts, and sidelong glances, they were swinging their hips this way and that in swaying movements. (How the dark cheeks of savages would be inflamed acting out the same movements at their religious ceremonies or love feasts.)

At the far end of the room on wide buffet, lines of plates were set out in rows, with sweets, cakes, savouries and all kinds of goodies. There was beer galore. Most of the young men held a brimming glass with one hand and a girl with the other!

A gay party indeed! but its noise now only served to wound the wandering boy. The laughter, the half-intoxicated voices, the flirtatious movements, struck him like a personal affront, a real mockery. His suffering went beyond imagination. He felt a chilling pain in his body. It had been a sweltering day under the hot midsummer sun, but the night was cold and damp. The boy clutched at the thin trunk of the tree as if it were someone he knew and loved, hugging it desperately, spasmodically, with his little arms, demanding from its dumb presence, from its wooden heart, some measure of understanding and protection.

The lights went out in that section of the city. Half asleep, Stavros pushed in behind a wall where, in a heap of fire wood and empty cans, he slept till dawn.

Early next morning the husband of Signora Victoria recovered enough from his drunkenness to go to the nearest police station to notify the authorities about the disappearance of his son. His wife, with her dismal appearance, and her long hooked nose more prominent than ever, was quite sure the prodigal Stavros would soon turn up. She was awaiting his return to make sure his bold disobedience got the full attention it deserved — the little scoundrel!

The police didn't take the matter too seriously. This Greek stood anything but high in their estimation, and his son, considering his upbringing, would probably be in trouble with the Department from then on. But they did search. They searched all Christmas Eve. They put a notice in the special announcements on the local radio: 'Attention! The police request anyone seeing a 12-year-old boy of such and such an appearance to report immediately to the nearest police station' etc. etc. . . . .

And so the day passed, as all days must, and Christmas dawned!

Think! Who can imagine the mystery of the soul of man? Behold it, unknown and shadowy, with depths that we shall never fathom; neither shall we ever make rules for its containment nor set limits to its scope. No matter how many the discoveries and inventions of our wisest men, or to what heights of civilization and comfort they may aspire, still, darkness lies before us. In front of the soul's mysteries, a curtain hangs forever in its place. Our fate remains unknown, our happiness is always independent of our will. How frightening when life in its urgency opens its iron maw to crunch the soul of a 12-year-old child.

Christmas Day! Down in every other street the Christian churches hymned their 'Hosannas'. There the fair, new-born Christ with rosy hands and shining eyes bright as stars smiled in the manger's warmth. Avidly, drop by drop, he was drinking in the milk of tender solicitude and life from the white breast of his mother!

Such a sacred day! From a rafter jutting out at the back of his parents' tumbledown house, suspended from a half rotten rope, swung the bruised body of the 12-year-old child. His bitten tongue protruded from his mouth, and his huge, childish eyes were opened wide, as if the better to see and understand in this strange world, the reasons of our just society.

ANTIGONE KEFALA

Parish Church

Alive, she said,
all around you
the ancient saints.

Pray, and you will see
how they will step out
and the lady herself
the all blessed
and all the others
out of the painted wood.

Now and again
a passing car disturbed
the burning heat of the day
and from the ceiling window
the gilded light
floated soundlessly down.

The Old Palace

The winds blew restless
through the empty grounds,
as always in my memory,
this accursed landscape, —
now orphan girls in uniform
were playing in the tall grass,
the Sunday afternoon settling
wet and forsaken over the
dove grey walls, the long facade
with all the shutters closed,
the chapel, ochre yellow, —
their thin voices flickering
in the wind . . . lady . . . lady . . .
whom are you looking for . . .?

Family

The garden full of trees in bloom,
spring scents, angelica, birds
crying in the still, clean light.

In the dark house behind the shutters
they were waiting
with the bread and the olives.
Marble dusted, ancient faces
with eroded eyes,
shell eyes of statues bleached by time.

At night, their shadows
on the white washed walls
breathing in silence
the scent of the white lilies
blooming in the moonlight
as if consumed with longing.

STEPHEN KELEN

The Intruders

Mrs Johnson, as was her custom every morning, scraped the food left on the plates by her two sons and a daughter into a newspaper, wrapped it up, went into the backyard and placed it in the garbage bin. Having replaced the lid she would turn around and go back into the kitchen, to do the washing-up. But this time, her routine pattern was disturbed for she heard a slight rattling. She froze still. Who was the intruder? The Johnsons lived in one of the fashionable outer suburbs, on the top of a hillock, in a rather isolated position. She was all alone in the house, and her neighbours, people without children, had already left for work.

Mrs Johnson's first impulse was to rush inside, lock the door and ring the police. Her nerves on edge, she trembled and listened to the slight sounds of the lid of the garbage bin being placed on the concrete, she could hear papers rattling, as if . . . but no, that was impossible! Who would want to fossick through rubbish? For what reason?

Curiosity nagged her to turn around. Terror prompted her to make a dash for the kitchen door which she opened and then, feeling a little safer, she turned around.

She looked and looked again. Her fear transformed into amazement. Never in her whole life had she seen such a sight. She had read about it, yes! Occasionally she saw it on the TV screen, leaving a passing tinge of unease in her mind, quickly followed by the assurance, 'Yes, it does happen in other parts of the world, but here? Never!'

It was only nine in the morning, the temperature was already nearing the century. This was the worst heatwave to ravage the city in living memory. Yet, the small, dirty boy, raiding the Johnson's garbage bin, and just finding the paper containing the left-overs of the breakfast, was clad in heavy rags. It was a patchwork of dozens of different materials, sewn or tied together . . .

'How can he stand the heat with all those rags on him?' Mrs Johnson wondered. The boy was deeply involved with his find. He smelled it, smiled, made a hesitating move to open it. Clearly, he must have been ravenous. But then stopped himself. He went on with his search, diving in the bin. Suddenly he stopped, looked up, and saw Mrs Johnson watching him.

He smiled at Mrs Johnson, a timid, rather apologetic smile, bowed slightly, replaced the lid, and before she could call him, he ran away.

Dumbfounded, Mrs Johnson stared at the spot where she last saw the boy. In her mind lingered the pitiful little figure, really a bundle of rags, and the face that looked and smiled at her, the slightly Oriental slant to the boy's eyes, the button-nose . . . it would have been difficult to say just what race he belonged to . . .

Mrs Johnson looked around the empty backyard.

'The heat is playing tricks on me,' she tried to set her mind at ease. 'It must have been a mirage . . . ' Didn't she read in the paper a couple of days before, that passengers of a ship a few miles off the coast had seen a mirage of a ship travelling upside down, with its propeller revolving in the air? So why shouldn't this be just another illusion? What else could it be? But she saw the boy so clearly! How could she forget his pathetic smile? And another thing! She saw him taking the food-parcel away.

Fighting off her nausea, Mrs Johnson started to search the garbage bin for proof.

* * * *

'Take it easy, Alice,' said Mr Johnson. 'It was the heat and nothing else. I don't blame you. The whole city was boiling. Not a breath of fresh air. You should have seen the boss,' he laughed 'he looked more dehydrated than ever. I thought the air-conditioning wasn't working till I stepped out of the office. What we need is a long, cold drink.'

'You think, Mark, that what I saw was just a hallucination?'

'What else? In this country there are no young boys running around raiding garbage bins for food. I remember, during the Depression years . . . yes. But we have never known more prosperity in all our history. And you say he was dressed in heavy rags?'

'Yes, in heavy rags. I saw him, Mark, I saw him.'

'In this heat? Now really, Alice.'

'He looked like a foreigner to me.'

'I don't care what he looked like, I'll tell you — it was the heat and your imagination.'

'Then how can you explain the disappearance of the left-overs I wrapped up in paper?'

'Maybe you didn't put them in the bin at all.'

'And where do you suppose I put it?'

'Then you didn't look for it properly.'

'Would you care to convince youself?'

'In this heat? Now really Alice. It might be a good idea if you take a couple of weeks' holiday. Go to the Mountains. I can ask Grandma to come and look after the kids. Now how about that?'

* * * *

The following morning, after her husband left for the office and the kids for school, Mrs Johnson wrapped up the food remnants, just as on the previous day, placed the parcel in the garbage bin, which had been emptied at dawn, and waited.

Maybe the urchin would turn up again? She feared and hoped for his appearance. If she could only talk to him.

Mark's attitude irritated her. She wanted to prove him wrong.

She stood in the kitchen door left ajar, watching — waiting.

When the unsuspecting boy appeared, Mrs Johnson waited till he lifted the 'food parcel' from the bin, then she rushed out. The boy looked at her alarmed. The he turned around, and ran away.

Mrs Johnson went to the bin — it was empty!

* * * *

'Well,' said Mr Johnson, after the children went to bed, 'I hope you had a better day, Alice. It is a bit cooler — such a relief.'

'I wasn't seeing things, Mark. The boy came again. The food scraps I wrapped up was the only parcel in the bin — there's no question about that. He took it with him.'

Mr Johnson looked at his wife. Alice was never the hysterical type.

'Well, then' he said 'Maybe you are right. We'd better tell the police about him.'

'No,' Mrs Johnson protested. 'I don't think we should do that. He's quite harmless.'

'Harmless? He is trespassing, stealing . . . '

'He is only taking things we have thrown away . . . He must be wretchedly poor. Please, Mark! Give him a chance. Let me talk to him first. I have a plan . . . Besides, he may not come again. I know I frightened him this morning.'

'You think you'll be safe alone, or do you want me to take tomorrow off?'

'Don't worry, I'll be all right, Mark. If you stay home we might frighten him away for good. And I would like to know this boy, I would like to help him.'

* * * *

'Are you sure you don't want me to stay home?' Mr Johnson asked.
'No, no, just go. Let me do it my own way. Please, Mark.'
Following her routine, Mrs Johnson wrapped up the food remnants, placed it in the bin, which she transferred into the laundry. Then she returned to the kitchen, prepared a good plate of food, made up a parcel of the boys' summer clothing, a pair of half-worn, outgrown shoes, shirts, singlets, took up a strategical position, and waited.

Mrs Johnson knew it was ridiculous, but she trembled in her excitement and fear that the boy may not turn up.

But he came. Quite suddenly he appeared, as from nowhere, looking with dismay at the empty spot. He raised his head, like a hunted beast, when the door opened, casting a suspicious glance at Mrs Johnson. Then he saw the plate of food, and the glass of milk she carried. Her intent was obvious, assuring. He smiled. Mrs Johnson felt her heart thumping as she approached him. Now she'd be able to talk to him, find out his identity, his story! How did he get here, why does he wear rags, search rubbish bins for food in this land of plenty? Where did this terrible poverty stem from? The very presence of this miserable little creature now created a feeling in Mrs Johnson that her own prosperity, her own happiness was threatened. Could this abysmal poverty strike her own children?

* * * *

There was a bundle of waste papers in the backyard, packed up, ready for the collectors who worked for the hospitals' appeal. As Mrs Johnon tried to entice the boy to accept her offerings, he pointed at the newspapers and showed that he would rather have it wrapped up, and take it away.

'For your family?' Mrs Johnson asked.

The boy nodded eagerly.

'So you speak English?!' Mrs Johnson exclaimed.

The boy smiled, put his hands together — was he praying or begging?

'All right then just wait here, I'll put some food in a container, and give you a lot more. But you eat this,' she offered the plate.

But the boy just shook his head, and smiled.

Mrs Johnson hurried back into the kitchen, and packed up as much food as she could spare. She returned with her gifts. The boy looked at her gratefully, then, before she could resist, he kissed her hand. He made a little bow and gestured that he had to go.

Mrs Johnson was disappointed. She had made her contact, but knew nothing about the boy.

'Name? Name? Your name?' At least that would be a little help to find out his origin!

The boy smiled, nodded, signifying that he understood the lady's question.

'Mirki Jelaschitch, Hrvatska.'

* * * *

Roger Smith, head of the Department of Immigration looked at the reports on his desk — dozens of them. The country was invaded with wretched beings, raiding garbage bins, rubbish dumps . . . Young children, men and women belonging to all nationalities . . . apparently harmless, even polite, some spoke a little English, others only their own language . . . They belonged to all nationalities. Mirko Jelaschitch came from Croatia, Kati Ember from Hungary, Daya Mantrian, an Indian, Tanzen Tashiro a Japanese, a little boy named Jesus Sebastian Rodolpho Ramirez, had travelled the long distance from Chile in South America . . . Names, hundreds of names, reported . . . And there might be others harboured by migrants formerly of their own nationalities. Not one of them had entered the country legally, yet they willingly gave their names and countries of origin to all who inquired. There was only one hitch in getting to the bottom of this peculiar invasion. Not even the most intensive official search could trace a single one of them for departmental interrogation . . .

Mesmerized, Smith stared at the list. The opening door disturbed his unpleasant reverie. The Prime Minister entered. He carried a batch of newspapers under his arm, and threw them on the table.

'Did you read the papers, Roger?'

'Yes, sir.'

'Well?'

'I have everything available on the move. The Police Chief asked for the full co-operation of the civilian population. There is the closest possible watch on all incoming ships, airports . . . we are doing everything possible!'

'And what is the result?'

Smith made a gesture, very much on the verge of surrender.

'Now,' the Prime Minister went on, 'you have quite a list of the names and countries where these illegal immigrants came from. It is rather unusual, I know, but I would suggest you write to the respective governments, and try to find out the identity of our 'uninvited guests.' Surely, they will have some information at least about some of them.'

*　*　*　*

The countries of origin were only too willing to co-operate. Replies came rapidly from all places ravaged by wars and poverty.

Smith read the letters written in English, and translations of others. He couldn't help noticing that there was a sharp note of irony in all of the information he received.

He picked up at random some of the communications and read them over and over again. His eyes read the lines, the names, which exactly tallied with those he had sent away, stating age, in some cases even descriptions of illegal migrants, but his mind refused to believe the information received.

He brought out the extensive list of strangers who specialized in raiding garbage bins, the waste of the country . . . Again he compared the names and descriptions with those contained in the letters . . . There could be no doubt about it — they were the same persons. The same persons!

The reports had been coming in for a week. The first ones he refused to believe, but now that all the countries concerned had supplied the information requested, he had no choice but to ring the Prime Minister and tell him — tell him and all his countrymen that every one of these mysterious people, seen, heard and spoken to by responsible citizens, was dead. They were all dead, and they died in their many countries of origin at various times, and the cause of death, in every case — starvation.

RUDI KRAUSMANN

The Art Critic

C., art critic of a daily newspaper in S., carried in every pocket of his suit a small reproduction of a masterpiece. Today, for instance, in his inner breast pocket beside his wallet, a self portrait by Rembrandt; in his breast pocket, instead of a pocket handkerchief, a nude by Modigliani; in the left side pocket of his jacket a chair by van Gogh; in his right side pocket a landscape by Monet; in his left hip pocket a clown by Soutine; in his right hip pocket a still life by Picasso; and in his back pocket a bird by Braque.

This armament gave C. assurance and he walked like a sovereign through the art galleries of the city, not to be fooled by anyone, least of all by the new exhibitions. Certainly, equipped as he called it with 'inner weapons' it was easier to keep distant, or, if you like, to look at contemporary art as an uncontemporary. C. was aware that nobody was in a more dangerous position to make false judgments than the critic himself, because of the position he occupied between the artist and the audience. And contemporary art at this moment, he thought, was not only questionable — as art indeed always is and has been — but moving to a point of self-extermination. Not only that, art — rather the value of art — in present society was in question, but was there still a point in asking questions?

Fortunately, for C. the past had supplied us, thought C., with some 'fixed stars', which shone as brightly now as they did when they originated, while the present was mainly producing 'artificial lights', which, without doubt, will be extinct in future. But how to bring this across to audience and artists alike, and how to become immune, oneself, against this coming darkness, this future age without illuminations and perhaps illusions, dragging not only the man in the street, but the artists and critics as well into the abyss? Because, thought C., there is only a real future, if not only the past, but also the present can produce masterpieces.

Apart from such thoughts, which didn't occur to C. too often, he went about doing his job like everyone else, wearing a suit in the top price range and unfortunately not looking very much different from the people of the same income level. When writing a review he was mentally and emotionally elastic enough, to be either enthusiastic, respectful, cynical, negative, nauseated, positive, etc., in short, to act out some kind of response in words even when he was essentially bored. Certainly he was not such a fool as to tell in his articles what he thought was the truth.

Much harder, of course, and finally much more important was C.'s position in life. There, without any cultural guidelines whatsoever, one could get lost really. This afternoon, for instance, after C. had visited four major galleries in the stretch of one hour, letting the taxi driver wait. It was the approaching evening which would be most difficult to deal with. After C. had changed into a kimono and had cast a quick glance at the various artifacts decorating his modern flat, he found it most difficult to decide where to sit down. Should it be on the couch or the rocking chair or perhaps on the Persian carpet? Having decided finally on the rocking chair, C. noticed that the movement of his body, although he had caused it himself, made him nervous. Also he found the wood hard and pressing against his tender back. He moved over briefly on to the couch but settled finally on the floor. Once this problem was solved he was confronted immediately with another one. What to smoke? A Russian cigarette or a Dutch cigar? He was longing to smoke a cigar but even before he had it lit he remembered that it could, as it often did, ruin his appetite for dinner. A dry martini with a sobranie was the present answer. Yet soon he had to tackle a more fundamental question. Where and what to eat tonight? Of course there was still time to decide that later. But what could not be postponed was the decision to eat or not to eat in company. For the moment he preferred to be alone, but to remain alone for the whole night was another matter. That would be difficult, to be precise the difficulty of being not by but with himself would intensify with the passing of the hours of the night, at least that he knew by experience. And C. thought cleverly: to be alone is like a work of art without a public. That made him decide instantaneously to dine out in company. What remained was the difficulty in choosing between male or female, as C. liked, or disliked, both sexes. In his position as an art critic for an important newspaper it was easy, all he had to do was to make a phone call. In this respect the technical age, although responsible for so much confusion, destruction, bad taste, low standard and declining artistic values, he thought, offered advantages. Or was this advantage another trap? How could he choose so quickly, when his nerves were still on the edge from all the trash he had seen this afternoon in the art galleries.

Unfortunately, confronted with the demands of his physical desires C. felt disarmed. The knowledge of the history of Western art, which he knew from back to front — not to mention the works of Sigmund Freud, Andre Gide and others — were of no use to him in that decisive moment. Am I, thought C., although professionally efficient, privately a neurotic? As a result, he made no decision. Nevertheless, the evening and the night, stretching in front of him like a gloomy landscape, had to be filed somehow, enjoyed, possibly made a success of. But how?

Am I the victim, C. thought sadly, of the power of my profession, — which he had used occassionally for personal pleasures, — or am I only a child of the malaise of the times? To that, he certainly had no answer.

C. looked at his watch. It was nearly 6 p.m., still time to ring someone. But when he touched the phone he felt that he really didn't feel anything for anyone. He decided to leave everything to chance and to dine out alone. But what to do with the two remaining hours, before it was possible to turn up in a restaurant? He could either write his review for the newspaper — a routine job offering no satisfactions — or have a bath and read — supported by another martini — a detective novel. It was with the second choice that he spent the remaining hours.

When C. left his apartment at 8 p.m. he felt some kind of excitement, although it was not directed at anything in particular, and at least he knew where he was going. It was to the 'Happy Joe', a fashionable restaurant frequented mainly by male customers.

Walking through the restaurant C. noticed some inviting glances and smiles from not very attractive customers, which he ignored. He chose a small, isolated table in a corner of the balcony. From there he could look at the lights of S., which were the more glamourous the further away and protected he was. Even a passing drunk who was also in a deplorable state physically and who had stopped under the balcony grinning up at him rather strengthened than destroyed C.'s opinion that he had chosen the right spot. Unfortunately the meal and the wine did not bring the expected results. Instead of increasing his well-being and his spirits and perhaps giving him the courage to a little adventure, he felt drowsy and dull. Was he getting too old already — not yet having reached 40 — to go out without a nap. And sentimental, romantic memories — although in his art criticisms he liked to attack sentimentality and romanticism — suddenly crossed his mind. But worse than that. Whenever he looked from his balcony inside the restaurant — these happy smiling faces, well dressed and familiar, now looked grotesque — in fact more ugly than what he saw passing in the street.

He couldn't understand what was happening to him. Was he going through metamorphosis? Had he been living in illusions, and in aesthetic illusions at that? Whatever the case, he had to leave the 'Happy Joe', before having eaten his favourite cheese. C. threw a 20 dollar note on the table and headed towards the door. At the exit he hesitated for a moment. A pale youth with long black hair was staring at him. A wink from him would have been sufficient and this young man would have followed him. But C. didn't dare. Would he, from now on, ever dare anything again?

On the street he looked at his watch. It was only a quarter past nine. Although he had not exactly made any mistakes, the whole evening seemed wasted in advance. He didn't know what to do from now on, except that something still had to be done.

He stood under a balcony, where he had tried to dine just a few minutes ago. From here, the city looked less attractive, but perhaps more real. Opposite, in front of a shabby terrace house he saw a young, female prostitute, and further down, another one was sitting on the doorstep, her pale face lit by a street lamp. Glancing at these figures he was thinking of the pale youth with the long black hair who was probably practising the same trade under more favourable circumstances. And he thought, not really knowing why: how little life had changed compared to art. Indeed, on the street it looked as if life does not change at all. How absurd the efforts of the artist to create new perceptions.

And now — this surprised him most of all — C. felt some kind of longing for these prostitutes — who in the past only had repulsed him. He played with the idea of crossing the street and taking one of them home. Some people from the restaurant would of course notice. About that he no longer cared. But he was afraid that a close contact with a prostitute would annihilate his vague desire.

So C. stood paralysed on the pavement for a few minutes, incapable of any action. A taxi passed. C. let it pass. Had he reached the state that he could not lift his arm? Then he walked slowly up the road, not looking at anything.

The Poem

A. had, even before he left school, what he considered a marvellous unique aim. His aim was to write the perfect poem. This unfortunately led not only to the alienation of his male colleagues but also to the distancing of his female acquaintances. Where A. lived, to write poetry had always been considered ridiculous, to write the perfect poem more or less insane. Soon A. had not only lost his friends, but was hardly able to date a girl. Yet A. was determined to have a definite aim, when everybody else knew hardly what he was doing, made him stick to his decision. What he had not realized was the difficulty, if not the impossibility of his intention. How long would it take him to write a poem, a poem of average quality let's say, and having once achieved that, how much longer would it still take to write the perfect poem. Could it be done by work, method, discipline and knowledge alone, or was genius a necessary attribute. What was genius? Hard work or a gift of the gods? Maybe both.

By the time A.'s doubts arose, it was already too late. Not only had he found because of his poetic preoccupations that he was unsuitable for a job, but also for marriage. In other words A. was unemployable and incompatible. Also A.'s parents, sympathetic at first with perhaps having a son with higher aims, could not understand nor support him any longer. A. had to survive on the dole, alone and alienated from the rest of the world. When A. was 30 he was thin and sickly, by 40 undernourished and mostly bedridden.

By then A. had read most of the significant poets of the past and present including the most significant critics of the past and present. None of them had either discovered or written the perfect poem. When A. was 50 he had already written a thousand poems, probably superior to the poems of his contemporaries, but far from perfect.

When A. was 50 he finally was ready to write the perfect poem. Poetry, of whatever period, of whatever form had nothing to give him anymore. The most ambitious poetry of his time he read like the newspaper, the most acclaimed poets of the past bored him. Poetry reviews or poetics in the fashionable literary periodicals were chit chat to him.

In short, A., was ready. He was convinced that within the next ten years he could write the perfect poem. To what purpose? First to fulfil his adolescent dream, his marvellous unique aim, as he called it, and secondly, to make an end of poetry altogether. Once the perfect poem is written, no more poetry can be written. Perfection attained annihilates imperfection. Every poem before or after would consequently be superfluous.

At 58 A. was feeling fine. The perfect poem was already drawing to its close. In one year it would be finished and the last year he would reserve for correction. It was by chance that he came across a thought by Robert Graves, which was published in an interview Graves gave, on his 80th birthday. Graves had stated: 'When the perfect poem is written, the world will end.'

This poetic truth discouraged A. to such a degree, that three days later he committed suicide. As a result the perfect poem was never written.

YOTA KRILI-KEVANS

On The Other Side

Refugees
    saturated with guilt and hate
    for being on the wrong side
    or just spectators from behind
    the shield of prosperity
    for being trapped
    for having suffered in a land
    where the monster
    vomited 30 billion bombs,
    spewed tons of vermin and fire
    poisoning the earth
    murdering the trees
    destroyng life.
Where the anguish reached the sky
    and its echo cracked the hearts
    of people around the world
    driving them into streets
    crying 'stop the war!'

Victims of war
    fleeing from a waste land
    from suspected fears
    from responsibility
    to build a new life,
Where the wounds are like craters
    and the spilt blood
    a bleeding rose
    sapping the dreams of justice.

Children from Vietnam
DAO flowers of spring
    faces of the early morning sun
    your growing youth
    by-passes the traumas of war
    the horror voyages in dinghies
You spread your aerial roots
    absorbing life in a new land
    protected by the counter-rays
    of your love and sensitivity
You watch on TV
    the Battle for Dien Bien Phu
    your hated brothers
    fighting like David
    against the plundering Goliath
    and your bitterness mellows.

To The Adopted Mother

I came to you without knowing you,
but I held stored within me
the strength of love and of dreams,
and a chest on my shoulder,
full of choice possessions
heirlooms of a long tradition.
Full of light and songs,
songs of joy and sorrow,
sweet-scented from love
gold-embroidered with the toil of life.
Full of dances that soar in the air
and spread fires in the heart.
Full of dreams thirsty for life
all expectation and certainty,
for a house bathed in the sun
for a piece of honest bread
and with reverence I placed them
in front of you, my adopted Mother,
but you did not feel for me
only with words you praised my work,
the treasure of my heart you did not desire
— I'm only the adopted child of your necessity.

Together with my other brothers
Salvatore, Hermann and Nazim
and your own children of the working class,
who talk to us with their eyes
and we with smiles,
we bent the iron, we drilled the earth,
we turned the rivers back
and built the dams.
In the scorching sun we gathered the fruits
and harvested the fertile vineyards.
On the line, standing without relief,
we fashion your machine-made products
and on the air like eagles
we build your skyscrapers.

Many of us never see the sun,
in the factories and the mines
from dawn to dark,
for the profit of bitter work.
Our dreams are gnawed by the gloom
and the horizon has become very small.
Many of us are maimed,
victims of toil and progress.
Many of us have buried the treasure of our soul.
In the nights drowning in our fatigue
we grope among the secrets of your language,
we stretch out our hand we open our heart
but we cannot articulate your words
and we remain marked in our exile,
branded by the sting of the wasps.
Our children do not know us,
they talk to us only with their eyes.
Circe has set a spell on them
and they don't learn our secrets.

It is time to open your heart,
for the wasps to be redeemed
for their sting to become perfume
and the darkness, light.
For us to build together in the fountain of love
And in the mulit-coloured waters
to baptize our dreams again;
to build the tower of justice
that this land too may become a motherland.

Migratory Birds

(translated from Greek)

— dedicated to migrant students I taught as an E.S.L. teacher in my first year teaching at an inner-city school in Sydney.

There was no time for you to build your nests
on the crystal mountains near the mother-springs.
There was no time to enjoy
the music of your own speech,
to suckle the secrets of your own language.
Mulit-coloured and carefree fledglings,
your mothers carry you in their warm embrace
to the distant summer lands of their dreams.

In the dark cells of the light-cloisters
where the owls hold the wires,
frightened and bewildered
you forget the signs of your own voice,
because the birds here sing differently,
and kookaburra-laugh
at the sounds of your song.
They don't understand the rhythm of the migrant —
Narcissus is their Idol.
With the scales of superficial logic
they measure the cells of your brain
and mark your wings.
The pharisees of Minerva
make steps to the light —
barriers for your young mind.
And you gaze with awe
at the rope-ladders of knowledge
and you don't dare to step ahead.
My heart breaks when I hear you say:
'Never mind, Miss, it is easier for us
not to climb.'
And you don't realise that everything is a trick
so that only the cuckoos may perch on the apple tree.

Ivan, they took away your voice
and you always stood speechless in front of them.
You believed that it was in your nature to stammer.
Ah! what a consolation to see you
engraving in wood the dreams of your soul.
And you, Aristides, with the proud eyes
you wanted to be a surgeon,
to salve pain with your slender fingers,
you used to say as you looked around in despair:
'I'm stuck on the last step, Miss,'
and only your imagination soared unbound.
And Nebil who wanted to be a pilot
— and the owls chuckled at his innocent dreams —
now with clipped wings he clips tickets
for a measured distance.
Boris with his golden hair
and his heart a rose,
who could heal sorrows with his smiles,
roves the streets now and begs for work.

Tender swallows of dispersion
in the markets I greet your smiles,
your early-wakened eyes
red from lack of sleep,
the despair that hangs from your eye-lashes.
And from speeding wrecked up limousines
your eagle-eyes greet me.
Caught in the glittering net of the spider
on the poker-machines
and in the dazzle of the nightclubs
your hearts flutter.
And I who administer the pharisees' charity
and teach you how to parrot,
I gather the griefs of your lives
and your eyes' warm tears
— pearls of your tender souls,
and your amptutated dreams.

MARIA LEWITT

Refugee 1944

Fritz was his name. I couldn't help knowing it.

The screaming order *'Raus, heraus'* came at the same time as the banging on the door. My aunt's hands lost their steadiness and it seemed like eternity till she finally unlocked the door.

They burst in pointing guns at us. They rushed through the house shouting, knocking whatever was in their way and when the young one said to my mother *'entschuldige',* the taller one roared at him. *'Das ist eine Evakuierung, verstehst?'*

The young one saluted, or rather half saluted. *'Jawohl* Fritz.' This is how I learned his name. This is how I learned that we were still under German occupation and were forced to obey; the guns pointing at you are very persuasive.

They marched us away. My aunt carried a suitcase. Somehow she had managed to pack it during those few chaotic minutes.

It was a crisp, autumn morning with sharp, long shadows and swallows sitting on the telegraph lines yet undecided if the time was right to migrate.

Last night it was great. We saw German tanks and the army retreat, we were sure that in a day the occupation would end.

This morning Fritz and his men combed their hair, buttoned their uniforms, polished their boots and checked their guns, ready to take us with them. I was frightened to speculate what our destination was.

We reached the roadway. Storm-troopers emptied methodically house after house and the country road, uneven and dusty grew denser with people, constantly prompted to walk faster by barked orders and the occasional jostle of a rifle butt.

I heard Fritz's voice in front of me, behind me, and whenever his voice levelled with me I froze inside and quickened my steps. His helmet was slightly tilted and his oval number-plate shone to perfection.

I thought that somewhere there must have been girls who wanted to be photographed with him and maybe even now were looking at his photo saying: *'Das ist mein* Fritz.'

I thought: it's warm, why don't the birds sing, I am thirsty, my feet are hurting, what am I doing here, why war? I walked within myself.

My aunt breathed heavily, her whole face sprinkled with a dirty mixture of perspiration and smudge. I took the suitcase away from her and almost fell to the ground. 'What on earth have you packed?'

She stopped for a moment. 'Refugees. Who knows, must have them.'

My mother and sister disappeared somewhere. The artillery thundered and periodically Fritz fired his gun, just in the air. Around us the cottages and haystacks were in flames.

And we marched. Peasants leading cows and children; goats; and old people pushing wheelbarrows, carrying huge loads on their backs. For a moment I saw them as second-rate circus clowns, walking on a tight rope and that comparison made me feel small and ashamed.

Clouds of smoke shifted, dimming and tarnishing the sky and the sun.

'Schnell, schnell', our escort urged us.

I lost my mother and sister, my feet were blistered, I wanted to drop the suitcase but my aunt didn't allow me.

'Matulu' cried a little girl, 'matulu!' Mottled, almost whitish hair. She was pressing her fingers to her eyes, wiping the hands on her once white, sun-bleached linen caftan. Her face smeared with tears and dust, her nose running and her sobs sporadic like the artillery fire. Her eyes were cornflower blue and there was such a depth of pain and bewilderment in them that I couldn't stand it any more and turned my head away.

'Holy Virgin, Mother of the Polish crown' someone intoned.

'Have mercy upon us' invoked eager voices.

'Halt' snapped Fritz. 'Five minutes rest.'

People squatted where they stood. An old man kept on standing, petting his cow. He was as scrawny as his animal. What was he doing here? He should have been somewhere in the field together with his cow. Both of them should have been warming their old bones and chewing the cud.

My mother and sister, I was sure I spotted them. My aunt was safe. She held to her suitcase like others to whatever they possessed.

'I'll be back with you soon, stay where you are' I instructed her. She lifted her head and nodded.

I stumbled over legs and heads, over children and dogs and pushed my way disregarding whomever I hurt, ignoring curses and abuses.

But on the way back, holding hands together, my mother, my sister and I, we trailed back slowly and carefully. I tried to locate the little girl and couldn't — there were so many children crying 'Matulu'.

My Aunt was in exactly the same position as when I left her. The tears carved straight, clean lines on her dusty face; she was glad to see us and smiled but cried again when I suggested leaving the suitcase behind. I made up my mind not to carry it any more and not to allow anybody else to carry it either.

I opened that wretched case.

'Don't throw the things away', my aunt begged. 'We might need them all.' An iron with two cast iron heaters — absolutely necessary in case we wanted to freshen up our clothes! My uncle's portrait, well . . . Toothpaste, a wall mirror, a cooking pot, some old potatoes, a crystal vase; badly needed, who knows, we might feel like throwing a party for Fritz & Co.

The shouts and then distinct *'Schnell, marsch schnell'* put everybody on a go. We were pushed, I picked up a few pieces of clothing, left the rest and with the help of my sister dragged my aunt forwards.

'Schnell, schnell!'

There was no plane in sight but their vibrating drone made everybody nervous.

'Quiet, calm yourselves folks', shouted a young, one-legged man. 'They are ours! On reconnaissance work. Don't panic. They have better things to do than waste munition on us.' He lifted his crutch up and waved at the sky. And he laughed gaily, joyously.

'Verfluchte Schwein', Fritz knocked him down. I didn't really see it, it happened so quickly. But I saw the young one trying to get up, swaying and wiping the blood off his face. He looked a mess but forced a smile.

'Bloody bastards. Desperate, that's what they are . . . Their breeches full of shit . . . What else is left for them to do? Won't be long, folks!'

The sun was getting hotter and the plane above glistened from behind a smoke screen.

Fritz's parents, I was sure, must have his photograph, somewhere in their house. In a place of honour. Dusted every day, standing on a hand crocheted doyley. *'Ja, das ist unserer Sohn. Gott mit Ihm'*

'Schnell, schnell, schnell.'

Deafening explosion and the guards running and screaming, forcing us to hurry, pointing the guns at us with more urgency.

'Apparently a goat . . .'

'No, not a goat, it was a dog . . .'

'Ran away, followed by its owner . . .'

Nobody knew who it was though swore on their lives that it was a child.

'Not a child! That old man got bashful all of a sudden; went to have a leak. Saw it with my own two eyes, so help me God. Stumbled over a wire and . . . phewt, straight up to Heaven.'

A mine they said.

A woman dragged her feet in front of me, her steps mechanical. Couldn't guess her age. Head covered by kerchief, ragged, long dress, full at the bottom, barefooted. She carried a clay statuette of some saint — brightly painted, and she prayed incessantly, calling on all saints and calling to God for guidance. Left her shoes at home, purposely. So one day, when she will return to her place, together with her saint, she will put her shoes on and go to church again, to thank God for all His mercies, dressed properly.

Her feet were rough, her steps automatic and I had a feeling that she was capable of going on like this to the end of the earth, as long as she was holding to her breast her only trust.

I staggered behind her to a constant barrage of artillery and human voices. People kept on going, some exhausted, some full of hope, some reduced to nothing. Dry-eyed, passive, nameless, grey mass.

I was taking in only what I could. The burned out houses were ugly. I hated seeing the fields ploughed by tanks and explosions.

But mostly I hated an old tree which had withstood it all. It shouldn't have been there. Red and green. Yellow, gold . . . beauty.

SERGE LIBERMAN

Envy's Fire

My father was a little man, with little ambition, little talent, little initiative, little achievement. While he remained a small-time shoemaker, his landsmen, ship's brothers and friends had become manufacturers and builders, and while he sat day in, day out in his little shop, they took vacations for months on end, sending him picturesque postcards from the beach at Surfers Paradise or from overseas. His shop in Fitzroy was a narrow dingy place with a grimy window looking in upon yellowed newspapered shelves holding a half-dozen pairs of dust-laden women's shoes and two or three outmoded handbags, while inside, the walls were a dirty leaden grey and the floor, whose bare boards were smeared with black and brown polish, was strewn with remnants of leather, bent nails, some with their heads snipped off and bits of string. It smelled fustily of leather, lacquer and dust.

He had few customers and these mainly from among the poor — pensioners, sales girls, labourers with large families, and a few Maltese, Italians, Greeks and Turks who lived in the commission flats that rose high and box-like in the street behind his shop. To them, he sold his labour cheaply — often giving credit — and if my mother had not worked as well, serving in Koppel's grocery five-and-a-half days a week with the self-denying dedication she gave to everything she did, there is reason to suppose that even the rent towards the flat in St Kilda in which we lived might not have been met. Certainly, despite my scholarships, I would not have been educated towards the lectureship in English I was in time to attain. Most of his time, my father spent in the doorway of his shop, without particular expression, watching the passing trade of Smith Street — young mothers wheeling babies in squeaking prams, old men with walking sticks, housewives in a hurry, businessmen emerging satisfied from the corner hotel, migrant children chattering spiritedly as they idled to and from the nearby school. To everyone he nodded, bowing his balding head ever so slightly in deference to all and sundry who came by his way. At other times, when he was not bent over his last, humming an obscure unrecognizable melody in a droning monotone as he glued down a fresh leather sole or hammered with quick, deft strokes a rubber heel, he sat on his stool, reading, nearsightedly, by whatever light entered through the grimy window. He read a lot — the daily *Age,* Friday's *Jewish News* or a Yiddish book

— but for all his reading, he held few opinions of his own. He was more given to agree than to dispute and if a customer or a friend made an observation that instinctively ran against his grain, he would nod, smile meekly as if embarrassed and say in a hesitant but conciliatory tone, 'Yes, I see what you mean; there may be something in that.' Sometimes, he took out the stub of a pencil from his smeared grey apron and on a paper bag or along the margins of a newspaper, jotted words which struck him as he was reading or gazing blankly out of the shop. On occasions, in the evenings after returning from work, he would enter my room where I was studying, he would run his eyes over the titles that were accumulating on my bookshelves and nod approvingly — he was always nodding — saying as he pointed first to his temple and then to his heart, 'In the end, the real world is in here and here.' He would then leave and while my mother prepared the next day's dinner or ironed the clothes or chatted with our neighbour Mrs Fainkind in the kitchen, he would retire to the lounge room where he would read sometimes until midnight and make notes in Yiddish in a little notebook that was curling at the edges and dog-eared in the corners. Seldom did I have much of importance to say to him — I whirled in my own livelier orbit of student life, parties, concerts and football matches — rarely did I intrude upon his privacy and for that, I often felt, my father who held himself shyly remote, was not entirely ungrateful. I shared his roof, his food, even his ties, but, unlike other sons, not his being.

I was not particularly proud of my father whom, in a phrase I gathered first from Steinbeck, I came to see as a mouse among men, so reticent, acquiescent and colourless was he. In the fourth form, I envied Mark Wechsler his father who told lively humorous sometimes bawdy stories by the yard and later Paul Kagan, my classmate, whose own father, a coin and stamp dealer, was a man of the world, much travelled and articulate, a huge imposing man always smartly-dressed, with a broad sturdy brow, white elegant hands with long fingers and unchipped nails, deep wrinkles of mirth alongside his all-comprehending eyes and abundant hair which rode in rich silvery-white waves vigorously swept back in all its fullness. And there were other fathers I came to know — men of substance and opinion, of ambition and achievement, immigrants too who had come with merely a suitcase, like my father, but who were laden with mines of initiative and forward vision that seemingly put behind them the past of a Europe destroyed and buried that past under the more durable and securer concrete and steel foundations of flats and factories and supermarket chains. If in the new land, there was gold to be had, my father, though not blind to its relfection in others, never touched it with his own fingers, clinging instead to what I saw as the dress of a quaint old-fashioned vanished past peopled by naive *rebbes*, naive socialists and naive visionaries alongside little tailors, little shoemakers and little saints who held a tenuous and — as the reality of history was to prove — a precarious foothold in the wider world of men. To my ever recurring dismay, whenever I thought about it, my father was cast from the same mould and, circulating by predilection in the sphere of more sophisticated friends and their worldly-wiser fathers, there were occasions when in his presence I was, even involuntarily, ashamed. His stunted English, as he asked for a packet of cigarettes at the milk bar or for three tickets when I still went with my parents to a picture show, jarred my ears and my sensibilities and I would at such times sidle away from him and pretend preoccupation with whatever distraction presented — a poster, a bill-board, or the traffic outside — the less to evade that jarring than to publicly deny any kinship or connection with him. It hurt him, to be sure. But this I learnt not directly from my father, who when wounded silently nursed his wounds in private and unfathomable retreat, rather, I learnt it from my mother who, noticing, would say with a sharply-honed penetrating barb in her tone, 'Are we giving you the right to study and be somebody so that you should be ashamed of your own father?' I protested and denied and, however reluctantly, returned to the family shadow by way of proof, but had to acknowledge that my mother certainly knew how to rivet a nerve with the truth. I would then walk beside or behind him, already at 16 a head taller than he and sturdier, and promise myself — vow — that I would be different from my mouse-like father, that I would be like other ougoing, articulate, clever, achieving fathers, and attain to heights where a man did not live and die without a ripple in the waters of life but when he stirred the currents and waves himself with the full force of his gifts.

And I had gifts. Quite apart from the praise and prophecies lavished upon me by my teachers and my parents' friends, I recognized my own worth and felt, indeed knew, my potential to be unlimited. Where my classmates wrestled with a problem in maths or agonised over the interpretation of Chaucer or Keats, to me they came like breathing. In my final year at high school, I was leader of both the school's chess and debating teams and contributed amply — a story, a poem and an essay about non-conformism — to the school journal. My mother fretted that these diversions might stop me 'getting on', as she termed scholastic success, but by year's end, I could present her with a string of honours and two scholarships that would enable me without excessive hardship to my parents, to pursue a university career. Their one disappointment was in my choice of courses. Inclined towards literature and sociology, I enrolled in the Faculty of Arts. They — particularly my mother — would have preferred to raise a dentist or lawyer, an architect or engineer. These they understood. My own choices left them bewildered. 'What can you *do* with other people's scribblings?', my mother asked in a harassed display of philistinism, 'and what is this sosho . . . sosho . . . logy?' My father, however, became more easily reconciled. Bowing his small balding head as he scrapd with the tip of a knife the grit from under a chipped thumbnail, he said simply, 'What goes into a man's head is never lost.'

Entering university, I came to nurse and nurture another more edifying ambition: to write. And more, to have my own writings known, or rather to become known through my writings. I dreaded littleness, anonymity and, at life's end, oblivion such as that towards which my father, sequestered in his dingy shop for days, months, years on end, was heading. A man was born for greater things. It was true, I knew, that opportunity had cruelly eluded my father. Born at the wrong time in history, the third son and sixth child to an invalid asthmatic father, he had lived in Warsaw, become apprenticed to an irascible punitive shoemaker upon completion of primary school, and in later years had been driven, upon the German invasion, from that city to wander about the steppes and forests of Siberia before returning west to the devastated city that had been his home. Thereafter, he drifted along currents not of his own making and coursed through a series of byway stations — through St Ottilien where he met and married my mother, through Paris, through Marseilles, through Genoa — before arriving with his battered suitcase at the remoter, quieter, more mysterious shores of Australia. I often wondered whether he took time to look around. Within the first week, he was settled as a process worker at Julius Marlow's, barely raising his eyes to the wider world, it seemed, until much later — some ten years — when he purchased, with whatever copper he had saved, the narrow mouldering shop in Smith Street from a recently-bereaved widow who needed the money. That money, had he been a different man, he could have invested more wisely, more profitably, as his ship's brothers had done, but the scope of his lateral vision did not extend beyond the pavements that lined his daily route between our St Kilda flat and his shop and it held him within the strait confines in which was harboured the stultifying fate of mediocrity, insignificance and littleness which I came to despise. It was that insignificance, that littleness and that narrow vision that I sought above all to transcend.

Academic success, as before, came easily. I completed my honours degree within the minimum four years, embarked on a Masters thesis dealing with changing social movements as reflected in English literature since Chaucer, and obtained first a tutorship and then a lectureship in English in the Faculty of Arts. Along the way, I had written articles and book reviews for the campus magazine and for two years headed the university's debating society.

These years were not, however, free of their disappointments. I came to collect a veritable treasure-trove of rejection slips for my creative work. Under the influence of Camus, Kafka, Eliot and Beckett — all of whom were in vogue at the time — I wrote in my spare time stories, verse and one-act plays which I typed, bound and submitted with almost loving solicitude and heady confidence, only to see them returned to my letter-box with little more than appended preprinted notes regretting their unsuitability for this, that or other magazine. Failure — a novel pill too bitter to swallow — drove me harder. That I possessed creative gifts, I did not doubt, I could not doubt. But what lit the trail to mere dogged, and sometimes frenzied work was the desire, or need, to have them publicly acknowledged. Thus driven, I wrote; wrote between lectures, between reference work, late at night, in the early mornings; wrote about alienated professors, hallucinating students, incommunicative couples, remote fathers, rebellious sons; wrote about nature, fate, godlessness and chance, and wrote about futility, absurdity, emptiness and death. The ideas came readily enough — but not, to my growing chagrin and frustration, the success.

In the year that I completed my Masters thesis, my father fell ill. He was then nearing sixty-five. He was totally bald, had become short-sighted to the point of relying on a magnifying-glass for reading and had developed high blood pressure and heart disease. As long as he was able, he drove to his little shop every day, returning home towards late afternoon too weary to eat or read or scribble notes into his dog-eared notebooks. He spent more time in the kitchen, stirring his spoon in successive cups of black tea, his face dark and wrinkled like a winter leaf, listening absently to my mother and to Mrs Fainkind as they chatted, as ever, about recipes, their husbands, their sons or the price of tomatoes. At such times, he seemed to me more pathetic than ever and his littleness in the world struck still more forcibly as an affront to all that I believed a man should be. And seeing him wither and wilt within a shrivelling shell, my own dissatisfaction with myself mounted as did my apprehensions that I, too, for all my academic attainments and success, should, in that one pursuit that had come to matter most, make no ripple, no mark, and like my father be consigned to that ageless anonymity and oblivion that enveloped his existence. If I wept when, in the end, my father died — he had suffered a stroke and lingered without dignity for three weeks in a coma before dying — it was less because he was my father, I knew, than because of the irrevocable ugly waste of a life that he had come to represent. In keeping with custom, I recited *kaddish* after him, sat *shiva* with my mother for a week and let my beard grow. But, within, the acts were hollow and, to my nagging shame, insincere.

For more than a year I had been living alone in a flat near the university. Upon my father's death, to keep my mother company I moved back home.

One Sunday evening, disinclined for any particular activity, — another story and a poem had been returned in the preceding week — I sat in the lounge-room gazing idly over the Yiddish titles in my father's bookcase. My mother was ironing in the kitchen and every so often I heard from there the hiss of heat upon moistness. Languidly, I reached out for one and another of my father's books, flipped through their pages, and returned them to their shelves. In some, I noted my father's pencil markings — words, phrases, sentences underlined, and brief annotations made around the margins of the pages. This held no surprise for me. My father had never been able to read without a pencil stub in his hand, a habit which I, who seldom took voluminous notes, regarded as quaint but also reflecting a distrust in his own capacity to grasp at first reading an author's meaning and intent, a limitation which confirmed me in my long-held opinion of him. On the bottom shelf of the bookcase, I saw a pile of uneven newspaper cuttings, already yellowing from exposure, with the same now-fading markings in the margins and on top of that pile an open shoebox containing a score or more of those cheap dog-eared notebooks with which I had seen him occupy himself in the evenings after work. Although they had always lain exposed in that box, I had never taken interest in them until now when idleness and vague curiosity made me reach out for them.

I had, despite many years of growing up in Australia, retained a good knowledge of Yiddish, and to my astonishment which made me sit up as if thunderstruck and which brought creeping tingling goose-pimples to my flesh, I realised — such a thing had been beyond conceiving — that my little baldheaded wrinkled reticent colourless unambitious unachieving father had also been a poet. One after another, I turned over the pages of his almost mangled notebooks to discover in his script, minute and cramped, verses which in their Yiddish rang with a rhyme and rhythm more lyrical and moving than anything that I had ever written.

Quivering with the unexpectedness of my discovery, I read:

> I fiddled away my dreams on strings unseen
> Playing silent song on surfaces serene,
> While coursing deep in the crypts of being
> Cadenzas crashed in torrents streaming.

Turning the weathered page, I came across a simple quatrain that surprised me, my father never having been a paticularly observant man.

> Pure the dawn as is the dew
> None so homeless as the Jew,
> Strong the sun and mighty the sea
> None that yearns so strongly after Thee.

And towards the end of what must have been his last notebook — his writing had become uneven, jagged and spidery — my father emerged, uncovered, in a guise unexpected because never sought.

> Sweet summer once shone in the face of my son,
> My silken-haired, my wide-eyed child
> Transforming my wasteland into a kingdom splendid.
> Remote now our souls, touching but rarely,
> In his breath the chill of winter,
> In my own that of abandoned dying.

There were more, many more — entire poems, fragments, single lines — contemplative in the main, depicting at times in almost tactile forms the broader gamut of his experience, ranging from the close warm tradition-bound existence in his old Warsaw home through the years of uprootedness to his brooding sense of homelessness in the new land, of crumpled dreams, abandonment and isolation.

My father had never read Kafka, nor Beckett, nor Camus. Where I — as I recognized now — wrote my stories, poems and plays about futility, absurdity, emptiness and death in vicarious imitation of my mentors, myself living a life of comfort, companionship and outward success, my father had written out of the depths of personal pain. *He* had dreamed, *he* had experienced, *he* had suffered uprootedness, abandonment and isolation. And he wrote about what *his* soul had known and comprehended and felt. Where I had been derivative, he had been honest; where I had been hollow, he had been pure.

And in that moment, I came to hate that honesty and purity that mocked my own work; I came to hate, despite myself, that little man, my father, who had in all past years been bigger than I; and I came to hate the poems, the fragments and the lines that were in my hands, branding into my flesh and my brain my own dishonesty, my lack of creative gifts, my failure in that which mattered most. And I could not contain my hatred, could not subdue it, as hand over hand, I threw all my father's notebooks into the shoebox, carried them under my arm to the backyard outside, where, with a motion that would allow no retraction I thrust them into the incinerator in which a dying fire left by my neighbours flared as little tongues of flame leapt up to lick and embrace the curled dog-eared pages of the notebooks. I watched, watched, with fascination and trembling and abhorrence. I saw the pages glow, blue, orange, crimson, saw them shrivel into charred blackness and saw them crumble into grey ash which fell and settled on the amorphous glowing cinders in the incinerator's depths. Above, a handful of stars towards which isolated ephemeral sparks flew appeared through the clouds, the air was still and all about there hung the concentrated silence of entrancement.

At that moment, my mother, holding a pile of ironed clothes in her hands, looked out through the bedroom window and asked, 'What are you burning at this hour?'

And hunching a shoulder and raising a palm as though it were nothing, I said 'Rubbish', knowing — realizing, too late, too clearly — that it was my little father's soul that was burning there, his life after life that was dying and his stature that was crumbling into oblivion everlasting.

UYEN LOEWALD

Nightmare

The dull pain and nausea keeps Pao awake again. Now he understands why people say Asians are yellow; they belong to the Yellow Race. His skin becomes yellower every day. Perhaps the Vietnamese gods are punishing him for having taken advantage of their princess and abandoning her. He tries to push the face of that toothless prostitute out of his mind; her tears keep haunting his sleepless night. He wishes he were not curious; there can never be anything to gain from raking up the past. He cannot understand why he keeps remembering that trip to Hong Kong after he became a millionaire. He wanted to know what happened to the family who had refused him charity. He had had to walk all the way to Vietnam instead. Perhaps all happened for the best.

Pao remembers that dark alley, that woman who shyly put her hand over her mouth. Casually he ordered her to follow him into a cheap hotel. He expected a virgin girl in semi-darkness. Excitedly he turned on the light to undress her. The woman's face became distorted by fear. He removed her hand with anger; her denture fell out; she looked the same age as his mother. Pao ordered the women to get up from the floor. 'Why do you do this?'

'My daughter is desperately ill; I swear to God I have never done this before.' The way that woman spoke Cantonese indicated she had come from his home town. 'Take the money and get out of here.' He threw a pile of notes at her. For the first time, he did not count the money before spending it. The woman stood like a statue, then bowed her thanks. 'You are very kind, Sir. Your goodness will be met with goodness.'

He hated her ugliness, her wrinkled age, everything about her. 'Go to your daughter.' He threw some more money at her.

Hot blood rushes through his body to his cheeks. He wonders why he still feels guilty whenever he thinks of that woman and why he still hates her. Numbness spreads to his heart; nothing works anymore. Despite all the virgins he has had and the thousand eggs his wife has distributed to the poor on his birthday for wealth and longevity, Pao knows that his days are numbered. At least the most unpleasant business for this month is over; he has faced Mrs Van Anh, the Finance Minister for the National Liberation Front. 'You must know that even your own people hate you. You buy and sell everything and betray everyone. You exploit people and create misery. That's why you have to pay taxes to me in antibiotics and rice if you want your gold trade in the Delta and other businesses to be safe; you have to return some of the things you have taken away from my people.'

Does Mrs Van Anh really represent the Vietnamese people as she says? Do the communists really represent Vietnam? He cannot help admiring her; she collects a million a month without ever spending any on herself; she wears the same simple clothes every time he sees her. It would be wonderful to find someone like that; Pao would even employ her as his manager. She is as tough as a man. 'In a way, you help me recruit officers; all the slave girls you brought from Hue and virgins you raped for good luck have become active members of the National Liberation Front. There is no such thing as being apolitical. People like you are the worst traitors.'

But how can business people afford to be political? He is Chinese, Vietnam is not his country. People who don't live in their own country have to get along with everyone. Pao feels proud of his heritage; Chinese people can even get along with people who are enemies of each other because they are apolitical. They can deal with two opposite forces in the same country because they don't mind paying for their security; they look after one another; they have an old, continuous, and homogeneous civilization.

Pao cannot concentrate on his bank book. He looks at his wife smiling in her sleep; she must be meeting Buddha in her dream; she has had the same smile since Tuyet Lan's mother left; she has eaten vegetarian food three times a month ever since. It's enviable; women have such simple desire: a home and children. But she has become strong lately. 'We should sell our business and retire in France. We need a good life now to save happiness for Tuyet Lan. I know you love her more than anything else in life; you love her mother. I love her as much as my own flesh and blood. Do it and offer yourself to Buddha's gate; we have made enough money to spend for generations'.

Part of him welcomes the end, even cancer, to escape pain and uncertainty. Pao wishes he could share with his wife his loneliness, his fear, his pain. But she would never understand; she was born in power and affluence; her father had been the governing mandarin. Pao had known but poverty and humiliation. He wants to be respected, his parents revered; respect is more important to a man than love or understanding. He used to hate his wife; she never had to pretend she was superior; she treated her servants with equality; she entered palaces as if they had been her home. She never feared losing status; she seemed to have no fear. Her ease became humiliation; the gulf between them was the same as that between him and the toothless prostitute. He suspects one kind of loyalty and rejects another. He feels glad they have become friends although he cannot expect them to be lovers.

Pao puts the book away to relieve its weight on his tired hands, then turns to his wife as he switches off the light. Perhaps he could become potent again, or even virile, if he could feel the way he did about Quit, before Tuyet Lan was born. Pao stretches his body beside his wife's. She was a picture when they got married. Even in darkness he can see their wedding portrait on the night table, what a perfect display: She still looks better than most women of her age, her unwrinkled stomach, her firm breasts, her shapely body. Pao feels sorry he has beaten her. He was angry. Barren. The word explodes in his mind. Pao shrinks away from his wife; milk has never flowed in her breasts; life refuses to grow in her womb. Marrying her has wasted his life. The curse goes on; he has been denied the son with Quit, the chance to blend his blood with that of an emperor's although he has saved the emperor's granddaughter from starvation, restored her dignity, helped her mother end her life in comfort. Pao has built schools, hospitals, orphanages. Hardly any Chinese in Cholon doesn't owe him favour; hardly any Vietnamese doesn't know his power and charity.

The bedroom is as quiet as a cemetery. No noise to disturb his sleep any more. No life is left in his property. No mosquitoes, no butterflies, no rats, no cats, no birds. Only four Dobermanns to guard his fortune. He has given orders to spray the house once a month. American insecticides work wonders. That's the kind of intelligence worth having. As soon as there is peace in Vietnam, no matter what government is in power, which side wins, technology is the thing to get into. Science and technology are to serve wealth. The shares in the *Banque Marseillaise* must amount to some 20 million by now. That should buy quite a few scientists. The shares in the Swiss banks should buy quite a bit of technology. And the gold in the shops, the pharmacies, underground gambling (it can hardly be called underground any more; the government is paid enough to not only keep their mouths shut but also their eyes), opium dens and pleasure houses. Pao really needs Quit to feel better. His passion for her has become pain.

He cannot keep his eyes open any more. Quit comes to him in an exquisite white gown made of the same material as the pink one he bought for her after their first encounter. What a moment that was. Her shyness, her innocence, her youthful soaked excitement . . . But why has that dress become white? Is she still mourning her mother?

Her mother did die just before Tuyet Lan was born. Pao wishes Tuyet Lan were a son; they would not have been separated. But it doesn't matter any more. Quit is here right now, with him. Quickly he walks to her. She looks angry, but the same face, smooth and pale, with the same haunted look in her eyes, the look after Tuyet Lan's birth. Quit withdraws as soon as Pao touches her. He pulls her against his excited body. 'You have no idea how long I have waited for this moment. Please, turn to me. Don't tease me any more. Let me show you how much I love you, how much I need you.' He turns her head to face him; his body is burning with desire. But Quit still looks angry. She has not unfolded her arms. Pao can barely contain his excitement. 'I know you are shy because we have not been together for a long time. But I love you the same as always.'

Quit remains silent. Pao tries to arouse her; he lifts her hair to kiss the back of her neck. That kiss has always made her squirm. But she remains still. Her hair becomes black clouds; he can no longer reach her neck; it moves farther and farther as he moves closer. There is always a distance between his lips and the part of her he wants to kiss. Finally Pao holds her shoulder. 'I know men like shy women, but we know each other well. We used to do all sorts of things together. I still remember the way your tongue feels on my body. You don't have to pretend you are indifferent to me. Please, please come closer.' Pao puts one arm around her back and the other under the bend of her knees to lift her. The same firm thighs and round buttocks, but they suddenly become as cold as marble. He no longer has the strength to carry her to the couch where he first made love with her. He wants to start everything from the beginning again. But where is the leather sofa which was specially made by the best furniture company for his seduction? He can smell her teenage fragrance.

But they are in the open air. How can he be so forgetful? He takes her to the highest spot on the meadow. She becomes as light as feather but remains silent and motionless. She is still angry at him. He strokes her hair. It feels like air. 'I did not want to abandon you. I thought it was for the best; you were so young: You could be my daughter. I had nothing to give you. When we had Tuyet Lan, I felt I had been punished; God had refused me a son; I wanted to free you of the curse on me. You must believe me: I let you go because I love you. My wife and I have looked after Tuyet Lan with the utmost care; she has given up every profane activity to accumulate happiness for our daughter. She even urges me to retire in France. But you understand me better than anyone: to settle in a new country at my age is an exile. I am too old for that. But if you want me to, I'll do it. You must come along with me. I can't live without you any more. I have advanced stomach cancer; it has spread to my vital organs; I am dying. I am glad you have come back to be with me.'

Quit stops frowning and stares at him. He puts her down on the furlike grass, her knees raised. He lifts her white dress past her knees, her womb, her waist, her breasts. The same firm breasts. He parts her legs to feel the fine soft hair, her silk-like skin, her flat abdomen. He waits for excitement to bathe her. The memory of hot velvet comfort tightens his body.

The ground shifts away from under his feet as a stream of blood flows from out from her body. He cannot see Quit's face any more. The ground on which her body lies becomes an island moving farther and father. Her body grows. Her hair expands to become angry clouds darkening the sky; her eyes brighten as they become stars; her legs become a mountain; one breast becomes the sun; the other becomes the moon. Her mouth moves to the sun as it smiles. The sun rises as the moon disappears. Her thick pubic hair becomes a fertile valley; her blood changes colour as it spreads more widely. Its pink colour gradually fades. Then bright light from the sun makes it look orange. The sun keeps rising until morning governs the entire valley. The spread of blood loses all colour to become a stream of crystal clear water. Pao feels thirsty; he walks to the stream to drink. Each mouthful strengthens him a little. He keeps drinking until his virility full recovers. The mountain becomes smaller, the size of a tomb. The stars, the clouds, the valley, the grass, the sun, and the moon get together and reassemble to become Quit again. She smiles as she becomes thinner. Something seems to pull away. She becomes invisible.

It was a strange dream; the room is pitch-dark: Pao goes to the ensuite, walking carefully without switching on the light. He flushes the toilet twice: he refuses to see his body wasting away. Although Pao found no satisfaction in his dream, he feels better. Perhaps his stomach will be able to tolerate some tiger bone gelatine and ginseng again. Wise ancestors can't be wrong; tiger bones must be good for his back. Maybe he can go to Cholon in the morning to eat elephants' feet, buffalo penis, and deer's tendons again. Pao turns on the light in the living room. He should send that set of elephant tusks to California before it becomes too late. He should send that statue he took from the Cham ruin in Phan Rang also. Some museum in New York will be interested in it and pay a fortune; there aren't any left. French and American diplomats have taken them for their investment. Pao opens the antique chest of drawers to admire his collection of jewels: red jade, diamonds, rubies. Then he counts gold nuggets in the second drawer. Quit did not talk in his dream; she was weightless; it means that she must be dead. She still wore white. So she must have died while she was still mourning her mother. The doctor had said she was unbalanced. Pao expected her to be depressed but he never thought she would end her life so young: She looked angry in his dream. Did she blame him for what happened? Pao changes into casual clothes and goes to his study.

Light escapes the curtain to fall on the bed of roses in the garden below; Pao can see the same perfect rose he gave Quit after he first made love to her. He has given her innumerable gifts, many precious things, but that rose remains the perfect symbol of their affection. 'It is the first rose any man ever gives me. You give me. It is our love.'

Pao picks a bunch of roses and takes two Dobermanns with him. He walks in the quiet streets. The night belongs to him alone. He feels sure Quit is buried in the Chinese cemetery in Cholon, remembering her words. 'We live together and will die together; whoever goes first, will wait for the other.' She must be waiting for him. A taxi stops at his feet. 'The Chinese cemetery in Cholon.' Pao hands the driver twice the fare. 'Go.' He can understand, no Vietnamese wants to visit that part of the town in darkness. Pao has no worry; he has paid for his protection. They have helped him and he has helped them. He wished the Americans and Vietnamese understood business as well as the communists. More Americans and Vietnamese would become millionaires overnight. Pao feels angry. Education only hinders understanding of human nature. Everyone likes money; it's as simple as that.

Pao knows that cemetery well, from the low tombs in the charity lot to the highest part of the ground reserved for the rich, where people with wealth are buried in ostentatious mausoleums. His family lot faces South East for moderate temperature and the preservation of family power and prosperity. He must cancel the ads in Indo-Chinese newspapers tomorrow. He wonders why Quit did not go to Cambodia as he had suggested. 'With this necklace and the money my wife and I gave you, you shouldn't have any trouble finding a good Vietnamese husband. You are King Thanh Thai's granddaughter; you must never forget that. Live to honour your grandfather. I have not been able to give you a son. At least I feel pleased to have restored the Emperor's granddaughter. The necklace made for King Minh Mang's concubine is yours now. It will remind you who you are and to marry the best suitable man.' Quit did not seem to hear him. The doctor said she had post-natal depression. Maybe he should not have let her go. Maybe she smiled in his dream because she has forgiven him.

The taxi quickly turns into unlit streets. Darkness brighten the stars. It is a cloudless night. If there were moonlight, it would be perfect. Pao remembers his walk with Quit in the Forest Of Lovers, counting the stars together, her head on his shoulder, her finger pointing to two stars which were so close that they looked 'as if they're ours.' Quit smiled. 'The brighter one must be yours because you're stronger.' She moved closer to him as he drew her body to press it against his. The pine trees sang with the wind. She chanted Nguyen Cong Tru's verses:

Next life, I beg not to be human,
To be a pine singing in freedom.

They walked from Rose Street to Gladioli Street, past the Pasteur Institute, toward Cam Ly Stream. She smelt and caressed every flower on the way. The next day, he ordered the Palace Hotel in Dalat to fill their room with fifteen kinds of orchids and every kind of rose to contemplate her nakedness enhanced by nature's vivid colours. The following day she led him through streets lined with cherry blossoms. 'Cherry flowers are to be admired from a distance while peach ones are to examine closely.' Quit gently brushed her cheeks against the flowers. Pao made acquaintance with peace through her love for simple things. 'You see how the earth is bursting with life. I feel I could hear those cabbages, onions, tomatoes, and lettuce joyfully stretching if I listened carefully. I like the smell of cow dung, the smell of fertile land. Land is so rich in Dalat: When I was living in the North of Hue, the land was so poor that it had no smell. I think I see life everywhere because I am conscious of life growing inside me.' They found a patch of clean grass and sat leaning against each other. He touched her stomach as she turned to watch for passers-by. He wished he could feel at home the way she did when they visited poverty; his movements became awkward; anger choked him. He wished he could trust people who shared the same status. Wealth had rendered him discomfort and isolation.

Pao remembers the time they visited Miss Phuong Thao's tomb near the Lake of Sighs in Dalat. Quit's eyes were filled with tears. 'I promise myself I will never interfere with my children's happiness. Poor Miss Thao to end her life because her parents refused to consent to her marriage.'

'But sometimes parents have to intervene if their children make foolish mistakes.'

Tears streamed down to her lips. 'All mistakes are foolish, but you learn from them. I hope I have the strength to stop you if you are reasonable.' Quit smiled. 'I am sorry; I said that because I thought of my father. I did not know who my father was until the day I left my mother. She could not stop me from becoming your servant. She was worried because of the slave traffic from Hue to Saigon. She did not want me to become one of those girls in the Saigon brothels. Their employers cheated them, exploited them, then sold them to brothel operators. I must confess I was worried too. But between risking my own life and ending my mother's, I had no choice. My mother told me then, that my father was one of King Thanh Thai's three sons. Unfortunately, unlike my grandfather, his sons were slaves of carnal pleasure, gambling, and ostentatious living. One of them had taken my mother, a beautiful country girl, to the citadel to be his concubine. My mother hoped to help my father restore my grandfather, the King she much loved and respected. Vietnamese people were behind him in his uprise against the French.

'When my father ran out of money to gamble, he sold everything, including his concubines. I was a baby; my mother took me away to escape humiliation. We joined her father and brothers in the Vietminh controlled zone. My uncle was killed in 1946, when the Japanese helped the French return to power, in a battle North of Hue. Shortly after that, my grandfather died, then my mother contracted malaria. For my protection, she took me back to Hue. We became destitute when your wife found me. I would like to know why she got me while she could have had anyone else for that money.'

'It doesn't matter now. I am glad she found you. Maybe it's fate.'

Pao wishes he could have given her a son. He wishes he had told her the truth: his wife knew about her father and other royal bastards. She had searched for a genuine one to blend his blood with the Royal family's. She had rejected many offers before finding Quit. It was fate that he could not have a son with her. He wishes he had learned the insignificance of having a son sooner. Tuyet Lan is really all he needs and has ever wanted. It is always too late for happiness.

Pao remembers that day in the Saint Paul Hospital, when they were expecting a son. All the vivid flowers could not remove Quit's fear. She was seized by expectation. 'She had become catatonic; I have to deliver the baby by forceps.'

'How long will it take for her to recover?'

'It's hard to tell.' The doctor seemed to understand Pao's worries. 'It's really a simple operation and the baby will be safe. I will have to make a small incision.' But Quit did not recover from the shock; she was not aware of his presence, paid no attention to her daughter, left her food untouched. Pao could not bear looking at her. She seemed to be seized by evil spirit.

Pao cannot remember when he left the taxi. As the Dobermanns leap away from him, Pao notices a shadow in semi-darkness. They must be graveyard thieves. He has read about them stealing gold teeth from Chinese mouths in new graves. But he has never seen them before. He gives order to the Dobermanns to attack. Chinese people should protect one another in life and in death. Saigonese people are most unprincipled; they even disturb the dead. Perhaps that's the reason for their suffering.

Two shots. 'Your dogs are dead.'

Pao feels a cold metal ring against his chest. The shadow is now an arm away. 'I know who you are; Mrs Van Anh has told me everything about you. Unfortunately you have seen: yes, we're emptying fancy graves to store our weapons inside them. You, backward and superstitious people, worry about souls. Everything is over when you're dead. You are not going to tell anyone what you've seen. We are keeping arms in the graves in the Chinese cemetery, not souls. You must discourage nuts like yourself from visiting this place when it is dark, if you want to see 1969, if you want to celebrate Tet with your family. We even know about your favourite mistress, whom your private detective has failed to find. She is living in Paris with her French husband and two sons. Yes, two sons . . .'

Pain increases in Pao's left arm; his chest feels tight, as if a strong and narrow belt were around it. He cannot support his body on his feet any longer. The ground feels like fists against his aching bones. His chest hurts. Quit comes back, the blood in the stream he saw earlier is the colour in the National Liberation Front flag in her hand. She is followed by other women, the virgin girls Pao has had and the ones he bought in Hue for his pleasure houses in Saigon. He cannot stop them; they march on his chest like a bulldozer. He must try to breathe.

ANGELO LOUKAKIS

Being Here Now

I sit outside the theatre and can do nothing but exercise my memory. As I wait to see if he will live (they tell me this open-heart stuff has a 95 per cent success rate), I make him young again. I find him in another life. The late 1950s, early 1960s were really his salad days.

Say Christmas around 1960, an even 20 years.

My memory lets me down on this bit, but I would have said that this was a week of heat. There were always heatwaves in our little Arncliffe, weren't there? I'm pretty good at remembering things.

He comes up from the yard behind the shop, in his singlet. It's soaked in sweat.

'We can do nothing about this heat. We have to live with it. Open the doors, close the doors, what's the difference? We are baking in hell.'

'Doesn't matter,' I say. 'Christman is soon. Aren't we gonna put up decorations? All the big shops have decorations, why can't we have some?'

'*Kala. Pare* six bob from the till. Six bob only. Go up the paper shop. But listen, don't bring me back rubbish.'

I take at least eight bob and go via Frank's milk bar so I can play the pinball first. The Hawaii machine, two games for one shilling, replay for lucky number. And only then do I go, two doors up, to the newsagent and buy glass baubles and tinsel and a cardboard Santa. Mrs Mack wraps it up in brown paper, and after that, I start back to our mixed business.

I always hated the bits of footpath with no awnings in the summer because it was always so stinking hot. And so I'd run the last little bit to our place, and finish up red and panting anyway. But I had to get inside quick, didn't I?

He is wary of looking in the parcel. I mean he half-wants to, but my past form when it comes to carrying out instructions suggests to him he would only be disappointed. So he just asks, and I tell him. He looks blank, so I must have done right, more or less.

'But still we have to get the trees don't forget,' I say.

'Tomorrow.'

The sister comes and calls me, because they are wheeling him out of the operating theatre and into intensive care. How is he? Reasonable.

It was a bit complicated. A couple of things the surgeon wasn't expecting. He is stable, however.

When I see him, he doesn't recognize me. He is doped up and will remain that way for a couple more days, they tell me.

The next day when I come to visit he is asleep, and I wait in a chair by his bed. Where was I? I was going to go to the markets today, to buy the trees.

I had this pet thermometer which I bought at the chemist and carried around with me everywhere. No doubt I had that in my pocket this morning. I put it in my shirt pocket so it doesn't get crushed when we push the Renault around the corner. I help him do this every day so it can roll down the hill and get started. There's something wrong with the battery. There's always something wrong with the battery.

And it's hot again today. In the car, I look at the temperature on my thermometer. 80 at 9 a.m.

I loved it at the markets, the Haymarket, the way he knew everybody, their names, and everybody knew him.

'We go to the Chinese man for Christmas trees. But first we got to get fruit and vegetables.' He sends me to get a trolley. Then he lets me wheel it to the first stand, and as it gets full, he takes over.

A box of lettuce, a box of tomatoes, a half-case of cucumbers, a sack of onions. Salad days indeed.

'Enough until after Christmas,' he says. I know we don't sell much. He pushes all the stuff back to the car and I help him put it in. I watch the muscles move on his arms. He's got big hands too.

I look at mine and compare them to his as he lies there, still groggy, 24 hours after they slit his chest open. His hands are still large. Mine are still small. Except for his hands, every part of him seems wired to something, and there are drips in his forearms.

Then he says —

'Go to the Chinese man, you know the one, and wait. I'll be there in a minute for the trees.'

I know what he does. When he used to send me to wait somewhere at the markets, it was so he could go to one of the pubs and have a couple of quick ones. I didn't care. Only I wasn't supposed to tell my mother what he did, he told me once.

When he comes back, he's smiling at me, looking as if he's done something wrong, but not really wrong, and we're both in it together, aren't we? He kisses me, even though he knows I don't like him doing it when anybody is around.

And now, and 20 years later, he's lying in this hospital bed. He's been coming around for the last hour or two. Finally, he moves his arm, meaning I should come closer.
 'What time is it?'
 'Two in the afternoon.'
 'I woke up so quick,' he says slowly.
 He is thinking it is the afternoon of the day of his operation.
 'It's not the same day. It's two o'clock the next day. It's Wednesday today,' I tell him. He nods and then closes his eyes again. He seems so incredibly tired. I stay a little longer, then leave to go back to the office.

Today, three days after his operation, they tell me he is going to be all right. I settle back to pass the time while he sleeps, playing my game, putting it all back together again. There was a once when he wasn't such a mess. I wish it were still here, that once.
 Mr Chin, a skinny little guy whom I still see as clear as anything, Mr Chin used to start something like this —
 'Is he a good boy?'
 'Yes, he's a good boy,' my father answers.
 'Help his father?'
 'Yes, he helps his father.'
 Mr Chin smiles at me.
 'Help your father, son. Jackie here works hard. I work bloody hard myself.'
 Mr Chin called everyone Jackie. My father's name is Pavlos. 'Help your father son', I keep thinking as he picks out three small trees. I take out my thermometer as we head back to the car. 90 today. How are we gonna get the trees in the car? The ends will have to stick out the window, he says.
 We pull them out of the car first when we get back. One is for us one is for Mrs Riley, and one is to put in the shop for sale — only one because our customers usually get their trees from the big fruit and veg. up the road.
 Christmas Eve? I would have delivered the tree that was ordered like I always did. My father puts our own tree in an old five gallon ice cream tin with some water, and carries it into our living room behind the shop. He puts some Christmas paper around the tin to hide it. Then I'm allowed to put the decorations up.

Christmas morning 1960? Presents. Some clothes, a model aeroplane kit from Phil, son of the lady who cleans the shop once a week. And I get a Meccano set from my parents. This part I like. But then my father says Kosta and Maria and Dimitri and some other friends of my mother's are going to come around in the afternoon — same as every Christmas. They'll make Greek food, which I like, but they'll play records on the radiogram too, which I don't. Her records are always whining ones, and everyones is always singing high notes. And that's how it was.

And I'm thinking maybe after lunch I'll remind him of those times. He likes to hear stories about the past, not much less than he likes telling them.

I watch him eat, slowly cutting up his cottage pie and piling small amounts of potato onto his fork. I know he doesn't like this sort of food. He likes plenty of *salsa,* lamb and beans done Greek style, everything juicy. He pushes the bowl of custard with half an apricot on top to one side. He does like tea, however, which he eventually drinks leaning back against the pillows.

'Almost Christmas . . . Are you feeling sentimental?' I ask him.

An ironic smile, and he points to the dressing on his chest.

'Here is my present,' he shakes his head, and then tears well in his eyes.

'I've been thinking of Christmas when I was a kid . . . Do you remember when I was always making trouble to buy the decorations? And I came to the markets to buy trees? Remember? Every year I used to . . .'

'Not *every* year,' he says. 'You come a couple of times.'

'I used to deliver them to your customers.'

'Sometimes . . .' He smiles again. 'You didn't like to make the deliveries. You complained. "I want to go out! I want to ride my bike!" . . . You forget.'

'Remember the trouble we used to have with those old Renaults? Trying to get them started to go to the markets?'

He grins again. 'The Renault was a good car.'

'That's not what I thought,' I say, knowing that when he interrupts me like this, I may as well give up. He's not in his listening mood. Anything you say he just takes as a cue for himself.

'The doctors say everything is OK, you are going to be all right.'

I hold his hand but he doesn't seem to notice. He seems to drift off for a few moments, then he says —

'Yes. The surgeon come to see me before. Same thing, he said.'

'It's a pity you won't be out for Christmas.'

'Pah. I don't care about Christmas. You know that.'

'Not even if you were in Greece?' I say, trying to get him onto his favourite subject.

My old man lives in his mind, and always, for as long as I've been aware of these things, has done. It's the only way he can cope with his life, which he hasn't liked for years, but hasn't been able or willing to fix either. In recent years I've spent plenty of energy trying to find things we could talk to each other about — although he himself has never bothered to do the same. I haven't been able to find too many. My father is a very selfish man.

'If I had stayed in Greece, I never would be sick. In Australia everybody gets sick, doctors, hospital all the time.'

'It's the change of diet. Too much animal fat. No exercise. Too much stress. All those things have . . .'

'No, it's the water,' he says. 'And the climate. All my life here, 40 years, I never had a drink of water taste good. Clean water. From the mountains, and cold. I remember still the taste . . . You telling me before about Christmas when you was a kid. When I was young, not just 20, but 50 years before, I can remember, and I can tell you.'

'So tell me.'

'We had plenty holidays. St Nicholas Day and Christmas and New Year and *Ta Fota*. We play cards, everybody get together and we play cards on the eve of New Year — *ti Kali Hera,* we call it. In winter don't forget, I'm talking about. In the village we kill one or two pigs and make sausages. Only one time a year we had sausages. That was Christmas time. And the smell, and the taste, mmm . . .'

'Did it snow where you were?'

'Yes, sometimes it snow too.'

The nurse comes to take pulse and blood pressure readings, and while she's doing that I go for a walk down the corridor.

I am so tired of humouring him, even as sick as he has been. I've humoured him for years, although he doesn't seem to realise, or want to acknowledge the fact. I've arranged for this operation. I'm paying the bills. And what's my return? Nil. He doesn't really care about me.

He switched off years ago. When he decided that Fate had dealt him blows he just hadn't deserved, he cut everyone out. My mother, myself, everyone. He couldn't cope, so he made life a misery for everyone else.

As I walk back towards his part of the ward, I see the nurse exit.

'How are they, Mr Krinos' readings?'

'They're fine. He's doing well.'

When I get to his bed he says —

'You didn't go. I thought maybe you go back to work.'

'No I'm still here.'

'I remember some more. You talk before about Christmas, what you did. And I tell you about snow in the old country?'

'Yes.'

'I remember something more . . . One time, near Christmas, or end of the year — I'm talking maybe 1927-28 — my father tell me he have a job for me — to take some potatoes, a sack of potatoes he grow himself, to my uncle up in Varvisa. Varvisa is the village high up from us in the mountains. I was twelve, thirteen *chronos*. I never been to that place by myself before — but I know where it is. That's what I say to myself. The donkey I've been riding everywhere else, so my father said, take the donkey, put the potatoes in the pack, and take him up to Varvisa.

'It was afternoon when he tell me to do this job. Really, it takes one day to go up to Varvisa and come back down. He gives me only half-day. But I love my father and do what he say. I take the donkey and start to go to my uncle in Varvisa.

'The road is very long. Ten kilometres. Twelve kilometres, maybe more. And . . .'

He can't find the word, and tilts his hand upwards instead.

'Steep,' I say.

'Steep. Yes. Steep . . . Only times before I went to this village I went with my father. And this time I think to myself, I know how to go there. So, I'm going. One hour. Two hour. Should be about three hour. But three hour pass and no *horio*, no Varvisa. Then four hour. It's after four o'clock. It's late. Then I see I am lost. I am lost. I have to think what to do. What can I do? I turn around and come back down.

'And I am very upset. All the way I come back down I think how stupid I am, how every time I do the wrong thing. My father send me to do the job, like man, and I can't do it.

'Anyway, I am back in Ritopolis, oh, after dark, and I put the donkey in the shed, and quietly I take potatoes and pack off him. I am doing this and my father hear the noise and he come to the shed. He has the lamp with him, because it is dark in there, and he sees me. Me and the potatoes.'

'What did you say?'

'I say nothing. I am very upset. I remember even now. I start to cry. He say to me "I send you to do job, to your uncle, and you come back like this. What's the matter with you? Where you been?" He ask me questions and questions and me, I am crying.'

And my old man's eyes, which had been welling up as he was speaking, finally spill over.

'It's all right,' I say to him, 'It's all right. That was a long time ago. It's all over now. All over. Come on. You're all right.'

I take his hand, and the tears start to subside.

'You've been through a lot,' I say. 'The operation was hard, I know. But you're going to be better now.'

He nods hopefully. He just nods. Looking like the kid he really is and immediately succeeds in turning me off again. He is so self-indulgent it is unbelievable. How I am going to put up with his old age is beyond me. There's no-one else to look after him. He's only in his 60s and already he's a fond old fool. I don't know what the answer is. I know I can't go on resenting him like this, I'll finish up with some disease myself.

I think there's nothing I can do but just put up with it. Depressing as that prospect is. I decide I should leave him for today.

'I'm going now,' I try to tell him, but he's so tired, he's already falling asleep. A meal and 15 minutes talk is enough to wipe him out at this stage of his recovery.

I walk away from the ward. The answer is to try not to think what things might be like tomorrow. Being here now is what I should be aiming at. Great.

DAVID MARTIN

Letter to a Friend in Israel

You write the *khamsin* blows from Sinai
Fierce as a storm at sea. The land is brown;
You long to leave the desert for a day
To see again the hills of Galilee,
Green fields and settled country.
Yes, I recall the Negev after drought,
The loneliness, shirt sticking to the shoulder,
The water tower glaring at the sky,
The Arab sand that drifts under the door
Like the eighth plague of Egypt.

Dick's gone from the kibbutz and Miriam too,
But you could no more think of living where
The taxis honk than Father Abraham
Could think of leaving Sarah, though at times
You dream of Haifa and Jerusalem
As David dreamt of naked Bathsheba.

Remember me to pioneerhood, Sam,
And to the tea-urn in the dining hall
Around which watchmen gather in the night
When guard is changed, if guard is changing yet,
To the red cactus blossom that the camels eat,
To children singing in the children's house;
Or if by chance you're travelling north please give
My greetings to the little fish that swim
In the cool water of Beth Alpha's pool —
Beth Alpha where I had a girl.

                          What news
Of Melbourne, Sam? Well, Essendon's on top,
Carlton lies second, and a lad's been jailed
Who broke a bottle on the umpire's head.
The wattle's coming out at Ferntree Gully,
The pubs are coming down in Swanston Street,
And on a fine day, from the Trades Hall roof,
The class struggle can still be clearly seen
Beyond the university where, lately,
The dogs of Patrick White made love off stage.

Fondest regards to Mara and yourself:
I'd bridge this chasm if I could, but since
My heart is drying on a laundry hoist
Far from that other Israel of my youth,
You'll understand the problem that we have,
You there, I here . . . and over us together
The neutral sun, the smiling renegade.

Gordon Childe

From this far, late-come country that still keeps
A primitive and ancient dream he drew
That which is name- and changeless. Here he grew
And, all his work accomplished, here he sleeps.

Scholar and man, his road lay straight through the time.
With rational affection he restored
From shards the road by which the race explored
Its world and heaven, risen from the slime.

Not on the wings of mystery but through shared
Dread and experience. Ranging free he saw
The gods, with Caesar one before the law
Of birth and death, decay, and God not spared.

Our prehistoric father who was sent
To his last journey with an axe of stone,
With this same axe cut through the dark unknown
The road on which Saul to Damascus went.

And so, come home, he closed the book and cast
Upon the fertile wind his unwrit page.
Dying, the hills stood round him, age on age.
Man makes himself. Each crest out-tops the last.

The Turkish Girl

Fatma Akalay's trouble was that she was a girl and that her grandmother had been left behind in Izmir. Had she been a boy she would have gone to school, like her brother Osman, who was 12 — one year older. But there was also Levent. Levent was getting on for three, and someone had to stay at home and look after him while their parents were out at work.

This was Fatma's job. At the age of 11 she was substituting for a grandmother.

She hated it. In Turkey she used to go to school, and since she was lively and intelligent she had many friends. From morning till evening there were people to talk to, but now her days were dull. Cleaning the house and preparing the vegetables, feeding Levent, taking him for walks and sitting him on the pot — these things bored her. When she had had enough of listening to the radio she played Turkish hit-tunes on the record-player, but she liked them loud, and then their neighbour would come and bang at the door.

In their street the Akalays were the only Turkish family. Mr Akalay was a car assembler and his wife worked in a factory where they made children's slippers.

Not only was Fatma bored, she was scared as well. One day a young man had come wanting to sell her some books. He asked to see her mother, and she told him she was asleep, as she had been ordered to do. He soon came back, to the kitchen door this time — some half-wit had told him there was only the girl in the house. He pushed his way in, got his hand under her blouse and squeezed her breasts, which were already filling out. This was all he had done, but it happened only a few weeks after she had begun to menstruate. She had been too frightened to scream, and almost too ashamed to tell her mother.

When Mr Akalay heard of this he said he would go to the police. But Fatma knew he would keep well away. For one thing he was never out of trouble over his car, and for another they were bound to ask him why his daughter was not at school.

On balance she was more afraid of the police than she was of being pawed by men. For this her brother Osman was to blame. He never tired of painting for her, in the most lurid colours, how a black police car would arrive one day, how two beefy constables would get out, and how they would grab her as a truant. They would drag off Levent too, perhaps in his blue-striped pusher. They wouldn't let them go until she explained why her mother as well as her father had to earn money. She would say: to pay off the house, the furniture and the Volkswagen, and to keep her grandparents alive in Izmir.

'What, isn't there anyone who can stay in during the daytime? Is there no night-work your father could do?' 'Not anymore.' They would spit in disgust and rush her straight off to school. To Osman's school, and they would march her into class in front of 30 jeering kids.

Mr Akalay discovered what Osman was up to and gave him a thrashing. From then on his teasing changed. He took pains to describe to Fatma all the marvels of Melbourne school life: swimming lessons in heated pools, visits to the planetarium, sports days and country outings. If she only knew what she was missing! Fatma was innocent enough to believe him.

One afternoon, when she was watching Levent, who was scuffing the autumn leaves on the nature-strip and kicking them into the air, a red van stopped at the corner of their street. Two telephone linesmen got out. They expertly removed a slab of pavement and erected a tentlike covering over the hole. She took her brother's hand and crossed the road to see what they were doing.

'Hello, little boy, what's your name?'

The men were jovial. Not getting a response from Levent they began to joke with Fatma and, English failing, tried out the four or five Italian and Greek phrases which they had picked up. She managed to convey that she was Turkish and pointed out the house where she lived. At first Levent was fascinated by the canvas structure, the rods which propped it up, the little celluloid window, and the profusion of wires and cables in the pit, like cords in many colours. But he soon lost interest. Fatma, however, was completely absorbed. At last, something entertaining! The street's grey hide had been stripped away and before her, as under a surgeon's knife, lay the riot of veins and muscles. One of the linesmen, seated at the edge with his legs dangling in the hole, was talking to a distant office with the aid of his portable instrument. She strained to understand what he was saying, but could not.

Suddenly she was aware that Levent had disappeared.

She had let go of his hand and he had quietly wandered away, a trick he had recently acquired. She looked about anxiously. The elder of the two linesmen, a man who wore woollen mittens and who had a fatherly face, thought he had seen him toddle back from where they had come.

Fatma ran to the house. Since the wire doors were shut he could only be in the yard. But he was not there, nor in those of the immediate neighbours. She asked, but they had not seen him. Thinking that by now he must have returned to the repair team and its tent, she dashed back, but the two men were no wiser than she.

'Now, keep calm, girl! His little legs can't take him far.' With his hands the fatherly one indicated how short they were.

Where could he be? At the tram stop most likely, the shelter where they often went to wait for Mrs Akalay. It was much too early and she would still be at work, but Levent's ideas of time were strange: he could wake from his afternoon nap and demand to be given his breakfast. The tramline was only a short block away, easily within his walking range. To it she raced, but could not see him. The bench he liked to jump from lay desolate in the shelter's dusty depths.

Three shops faced the tramline. The first, a delicatessen, was Levent's favourite, for there he could expect to be given an olive or a slice of sausage. The second was a plumber's and the third a newsagent's. Levent had not gone into any of them.

In the newsagent's shop the clock showed half-past two. Osman would be home soon after three, and Mrs Akalay at about five. Fatma galloped back, forcing herself to imagine the two linesmen waving to her that all was well. But the stares which met her were a mute question. She shrugged her shoulders, a gesture which the younger one copied without malice.

Once more she rounded the house, and then went in to search each room. It was senseless, since the boy could neither reach door handles nor climb in through open windows. The good order of smooth-drawn bedspreads and puffed out cushions accused her with its unfeeling sterility. She had longed so much to be free of her servitude, but not to be free of it like this.

She must ring her mother. She had promised that if ever such a thing happened she would tell her at once.

Clutching the coins which were kept for this purpose in a jar, she hurried to the telephone box. It was only a few minutes away. She had used it twice before: once to let her father know that a telegram had arrived, and once to report to him that a policeman had called about something to do with his car. (Policemen were a nightmare to which there was no end.) Each time a passer-by had helped her to make the call. Now she was alone, but Osman had taught her how to do it.

The telephone box stank of urine. She tried to hold the door open but this barely left her any room. She unhooked the receiver, heard a sound which seemed to her the right one, and dialled the number which she knew by heart. A voice came into her ear. She made the coin roll down the groove.

The voice was a man's. He seemed to be repeating the same words over and over, as if talking to himself, or praying. She broke in.

'Mrs Akalay! I speak Mrs Akalay!'

The voice went on disregarding her. Then it stopped. A toneless hum replaced it, as if from a record asking to be turned. Then it started again, passionless, unvarying.

'Mrs Akalay. Mrs Akalay, yes?'

It went on and then it stopped. On, stop, the humming, the voice, until at last it cut out altogether.

Fatma hung up, dialled again, heard the voice, the same voice that came from no living mouth, rolled another coin, and it happened as it had before. On, stop, humming. On, stop, on, stop . . . finish.

She had no more coins. She left the box. The street was empty.

She wanted to cry. What can my mother do? she thought. Who lost Levent? I lost him. Who must find him? I must find him. Then she changed her mind. Ask the man with the mittens! He understands telephones, he knows all about them. Perhaps, if he hears that voice . . .

The linesmen had gone. Two red lamps had been placed on the footpath, unlit, one on each side.

She went to the five houses that stood to the right of the Akalays', and to the four that lay between it and the corner. For nothing.

Could he have been stolen, like a bicycle?

Another group of shops clustered between the first tram stop and the next. She went into them all, and finally into a milk bar. It was owned by the man she always bought her father's cigarettes from. A man who was used to foreign worries.

'Of course I know your brother. Queer little fish; everytime he comes in he wants to shake my hand. Holds it out and doesn't say a word. You tried in your street, you tried the shops? Then go round to the police. They'll have him back for you in no time, it they haven't got him already. You know where they are, in Bell Street? It's not far. Like me to ring them for you?'

'I can find. Thank you.'

She had nearly run home — how many more times would she do this? — before she remembered that she should have asked him to ring, not the police but her mother.

She decided to wait for Osman. At 20 past three he had not arrived. This was not unusual, for he was a dawdler. She went out into the street, hoping to see him coming. Ten minutes passed. What was making him so late? She decided to meet him halfway.

As she walked she cried.

Levent was dead. A car had run over him. They had taken his body away, bleeding, with his eyes that were like polished chestnuts, wide open. He would never again stand in the milk bar, holding out his hand to be shaken.

Why, instead of walking straight on to Osman's school, did she turn into Bell Street? Fatma, torn between two despairs, could not have explained it.

Opposite the police station she stopped. She knew what their first question would be in there. And what would come of her answer. Her mother would have to give up working. The money for the car, the television and the lounge suite, the money they were putting by to bring out her grandparents, would melt away. What the Akalays had built up and suffered for, she, their daughter, would have smashed to pieces.

People were walking in and out beneath the purple lamp. A tall policeman emerged in a white crash-helmet, with fawn breeches and high, shiny boots. He turned into an alley. In a short time he came riding out on a motor cycle.

Fatma crossed over.

A woman came down the short flight of steps. She stopped and glanced round as if looking for a friend. She was dressed like the hostesses on the plane from Istanbul. She had the same perching cap, under which her dark hair was smartly set.

She had seen Fatma.

'What's the trouble, child, why are you howling?'

'My brother . . . '

'What about him?'

'I lost.'

'Lost your brother? Never mind; he'll turn up. You want us to help you get him back, is that it?' She pointed to the doorway.

Fatma shook her head.

'I think you do, really. What's your name?'

'Fatma Akalay.'

'You would be from Turkey. Come, I'll take you in. Here, you can use my hanky. No need to cry any more.'

Fatma guessed that in some way this woman was part of the police. To run away was impossible. They entered a large room divided by a counter. Policemen were leaning against it with the indifference of clerks, while in front, and seated on a long bench, were the people who had dealings with them. She was led through to a small room where two young women were drinking tea. A strip-heater glowed above their heads. There were filing cabinets and typewriters. Everything was bright and warm.

'Sit yourself down and just tell me what happened.'

Fatma was wearing slacks. She noticed, seating herself, that they were splattered. What she had to tell sounded like someone else's fate, unimportant and slightly funny. One moment a girl was holding a small boy's hand, the next he was not there. Could such a thing be? Before she had finished talking a cup of tea appeared on the table; she was drinking it and nibbling the biscuit which lay in the saucer.

'Good. Now write down for me on this paper where your dad

works, and your mum. The street, yes. And your own. Nice and big.'

Fatma had been taught it by her brother. The policewoman scanned what she had written. She told Fatma to be patient and not to think she was not coming back. Then she went out by a second door.

The girls settled themselves behind their typewriters. One pushed a magazine over to Fatma, who pretended she was looking at the pictures. An electric wall-clock moved with trembling, hypnotic jerks. It was five minutes to four. Osman would certainly be home now. Neighbours would tell him what had happened, and he would be wondering where she had got to. She felt so tired, she could have lain down on the floor and gone to sleep. But the biscuit was good: she could still taste the ground almonds.

The hour-hand had advanced only a little when the woman came back.

'Well, Miss, what do you say to this? We've already got your brother, safe, sound and undamaged. All we have to do now is collect him.'

The typists looked up from their machines. Both were smiling. One was an Australian, the other not, Fatma thought.

'The usual thing,' the woman told them. 'Hauling off into the next street. Some lady saw him, took him in and phoned us. We've had him on the book for nearly an hour.' She turned to Fatma.

'Do your parents speak much English ?

'Little.'

'Sadie.' She addressed the darker of the two girls. 'Find out who the Turkish interpreter is, will you? If these toddlers had identity discs we'd be spared all this nonsense.' To Fatma she said, 'I'll take you home in a car. Your brother we'll pick up on the way.'

'Thank you,' said Fatma. It was a black car and it was parked in the lane from which the motorcyclist had come riding out.

The house which sheltered Levent was not in the first but in the third street from the Akalays. It was a wide street, and the plane trees in it grew from the edge of the roadway.

'I kept asking and asking,' the plump woman who opened the door said, 'but you can't make out what he's saying. You hardly ever can when they're that age. First he played with my little girl, and now he's fast asleep. I gave him a biscuit and he gobbled it all up.'

'Thank you,' Fatma said.

'And some milk.'

'Thank you very much.'

'Pity you can't hobble them. I'll go and see if I can wake him.'

As she shepherded him through the gate Levent stopped and gravely shook her hand. When they drove off he blew the woman a kiss. He pulled out a piece of chocolate she had put in his pocket and, unwrapping it, let the paper fall to the floor. Fatma retrieved it for him. All the way back he grumbled and complained. The linesmen's tent was still at the corner, and so were their lamps.

Outside her house stood Mrs Akalay. She was paying off a taxi. Osman, by her side, was holding her bag and trying to read the cab's meter.

He's phoned the factory, Fatma thought. He can do what I cannot.

'Home again, home again,' the policewoman said.

Osman's school cap was on his head and he was still in his blazer. As the black car slowed to the kerb he touched his mother's arm and pointed.

Over his shoulder the policewoman said to Fatma:

'That big chap, is he your brother? By the way, dear, I should have asked you — why aren't you at school today? And which one do you go to; what form are you in?'

FRANCO PAISIO

The Enemy

The enemy is after us with flowers

• • •

He is not gaining ground

• • •

The enemy is singing bucolic songs

• • •

We will not listen

• • •

The enemy is trying the back door

• • •

The enemy is on his knees

• • •

The enemy is asking grace

• • •

We'll never forgive

• • •

The enemy is drinking wine with us
Reminiscing

Under The Sun

Under the sun
My hat
Under the hat
My skull
Under the skull
A flower
Looking for the sun

Autobiography

Franco
Paisio
Open parenthesis
One thousand
Nine hundred
Thirty six
Dash
Leave a space
To be filled in
Later
Close parenthesis
Full stop

LILIANA RYDZYNSKI

The Husband

Day vanishes and I feel the link
between you and me, who live in different worlds
that meet only at twilight. I know you will come
as always, as dawn or evening comes
with an amazing honesty — accordance with time.

Sometimes it is the only certainty
in my unreal, scattered world; that when you come
a holy time of everyday will reign
with the smell of food and a hearty talk.

You are the real one, who never can afford
to escape or to betray the commonplace.
In amazement I watch your human endurance:
day after day, year after year
your hands realize what your mind would postpone
— for you have only two hands to build our dreams.

Nobody wonders, nobody writes about you,
you keep nobody's mind in suspension
but in you, life will find its solid symbol
like a piece of perfect pottery hardening in the hearth.

The Polish Sculptor

Light in the window — swift movement —
      he is there
  alone   planted in the everyday
His head appears, white-haired, slender,
the eyes, the sentinels of his youth,
penetrating, rapacious, yet tender —
the eyes that (after Ezra Pound)
had never surrendered perception

Eternally eager, vivacious,
still like an astonished child;
his speech awkward, yet touching;
with shy fingertips he touches life,
surprised at its vastness.
Always ready for the first love
in everything.   Eyes cast down
he still dreams of her . . . his elusive dancer
who went away — forever — while he
toiled in the Australian forest.

Wartime misfortunes
his memory touches carefully;
when called back, they become like stones
weighing on his soul.
On the canvas, in the sculpture
she endures — the eternal woman.
It's he who reigns, a hundred times repeating
his favourite self-portrait
with a nasty, ironic expression.

Down the hill the sea roars
singing of the larger world;
the flowers lure him to the gate
where he has written in his own hand
his place on Terra Australis:

    Lucjan Michalski — Sculptor.

The Father

I saw my father after so many years —
he looked smaller, his hair was white
his will was bent to the ground.

I always wanted a very brave father,
a rebel, a dear friend, a mate.

As a girl, I used to fight with boys
eye to eye, determined to win;
the fringe on my forehead
was like a challenging shaft of light.
At school, I hated all kinds of discipline
and had bad marks for geography;
but all those with the best marks
somehow had never tried to move
outside their backyards and brackets.

I travel very far from those days
crossing mountains and seas
discovering their names with the wonder
of a very first love,
creating my own geography.

Wherever I go, I remain a rebel
whose external power is practically none:
my whole energy is used as a fuel
to burn in a stubborn, yet creative mind.

My father is a quiet citizen,
his will bent to the ground.

Greece in Winter

The roses you have just received have a firm beauty, a dense colour. The small cockroaches in your hotel room are rather friendly, slow and sleepy, very much in your favour; you deny them the right to exist, because of your Taurean aesthetics.

Dancing on a Greek arm, under a big umbrella although it isn't raining anymore, you've just seen a wedding in a quiet place with a church. Now you are lost in the narrow streets warmed with the innumerable copper pots and woollens, with a model-puppet at the corner — a healthy, velvety Arab with a big smile.

You go into the kitchen of the taverna at Panos St and choose *horiatiki* and *tsatsigi,* and *szustsukala;* although you have already tasted it somewhere in Sydney, those half-cold dishes become your very first Greek dishes. You drink beer and worship the special colours of the primitive paintings on the taverna's naked walls. '. . . they try to paint whatever they feel, they try to express, they *are* expressive.' The people from koala country are still learning how to be expressive; with their lips sealed by the years of silence, they still learn how to articulate their genuine emotions; though when it comes to colours, they went so much ahead . . .

Dimitris always talks about his islands. 'You will never know Greece without its islands.'

'But I already know it. I could feel the spirit of the land when coming from Patras in the bus. The others, the English-speaking, wandered about poverty and disorder . . . I inhaled the new, the unusual, the exotic . . . I drank it. I saw my first Greek sunset, I saw the hills and cypresses and the sea in silver, silent love with the moon. The moon looked Greek to me . . .'

You want to eat and drink everything Greek . . . the water elsewhere should be Greek. Greek coffee, baklava . . . the streets almost as in Paris, and yet different: no sadness, not the Piaf's dramatic, slow and ascending sadness.

You come back to the hotel, and suddenly feel happy again . . . wanting absolutely to change the dress, the colours, to make your eyes shiny . . . the small key of your suitcase suspended on a black ribbon on your neck becomes your only jewellery, like a key to your own heart.

The receptionist, Mr Jean, likes speaking in French and tells you a pleasant story: 'You remind me of your sister . . . the women in your family (I don't know, how many there are — I know only two) have something in common: they make us, men, surprised with this something. They can attract us without knowing it, far beyond wanting it: their eyes and lips speak without words, they make us intrigued and nourish us with hope . . . they never deprive us of a suggestion of a certain kind of hope. You just need to believe and endure a little longer . . . they fill you with a new admiration for woman as a symbol — like a rose, whose petals are always closed upon its own ripe life.'

'Monsieur Jean, you should have been a poet . . .'

'Woman is my inspiration, I am forever drawn to her tenderness and mystery. Woman knows what we do not, without realizing it; she will always want to tell us with her lips, with her eyes; she will touch us and tell us if we are truly needed on this earth, or if we must still learn . . . still learn the courage to live with love, with which she, the woman, has been blessed since her birthday.'

This is what Monsieur Jean tries to express, with his tired, ever-curious eyes, his smile of a shy boy, his soul drawn to excitement and subtlety at the same time.

The door of the lift closes, the Greek door opens . . . the street running like a lighthearted dancer takes possession of you. With your hand in a Greek hand, you climb up the streets like the stairs and cannot believe your eyes — the Acropolis is there! the Acropolis like la Lune, who married the enchanted hill. The image full of shadows and iridescent reflections in your bewildered mind.

Different . . . different from all you have seen and all you have known. With its grave, breathtaking beauty, Greece opens to you, then takes possession of you, slowly, silently sinks into your being.

La Lune, sun rising and sun setting . . . from now on never free of her sight, you become its Earth bathed in its light, enriched in ever-explained periods and moods, turning its nightly face covered in moony veil, enchanted, returning again . . . bathing again in its blueish light — the flying dove whose wings turn into moonlight.

Nicos's house in Plaka, near Acropolis, the house of his grandparents. Nicos invites: 'I pay tonight, you are all my guests; I cannot lose any more than I have lost today: the government takes my house, the whole suburb will be like museum. But I've just gained a friend, and I want to drink a toast . . .'

If it was not for your vigilance, he would lose his heart promised for his lady-in-waiting.

The boys — guests in the house — comb their hair, black and shiny, with a special gesture, a special look in the mirror. 'You would think they are vain — but they have good hearts, I assure you.'

Dimitris speaks again about his beloved islands. ' . . . Ionian Islands. In summer, we don't wear any clothes. People learnt to wear clothes because of cold, nothing else . . .'

The conversations. 'There might be a solution. I know communism. I know capitalism. There must be something in between, something new . . . no old garments.'

'No politics now' somebody says.

'And what the hell do you think I am talking about? . . . there are no politics in my words.'

You all leave Nicos's house and go to another place, another bar. Athens at night, winter night. There is something tender and warm in the winter air; people wait for taxis, embraced, animated. They are drunk with each other in a sure, quiet way . . . it is *different* than with the Italians: they *don't* need to show. Men clasp, join their arms in cordial embrace, there is no one gap between their arms, between their souls, at such moments. Such moments carry them into life and streets, and nourish the air . . . the city . . . the land. Their land breathes in tenderness and emanates tenderness.

Back at your hotel, overwhelmed with emotion, exhausted, begging 'enough!' — you are still bewildered, shaken with surprise and unknown feelings.

La Lune . . . its light . . its mystery; how does it marry with such sensuous human as the Greek is — who uses all his five senses in such a feverish and yet assured way?

And your own, reassured heart has a ready reply: AND HOW CAN THE MOON MARRY WITH THE EARTH?

BARBARA SCHENKEL

The Anniversary

It was a dull party and Maurice felt bored. The guests, all elderly people, had known each other for years. Their social contact had lately grown rather loose but they still met regularly, each year at somebody else's home, on the 25th day in the month of April.

They all had survived World War II in Germany, were liberated from a concentration camp together and since then always celebrated the day as their new joint-birthday.

Each year at 12 midnight they drank champagne, sang 'Happy Birthday' and parted soon after. Tonight all of them became '35 years old'.

The party started with excitement. Fryda and Jack, the hosts for 1980, had just moved into a brand new home built in the most coveted area of Caulfield. It not only had a swimming pool but next to it, a sauna as well: no one knew for what purpose as neither Jack nor Fryda could swim, their children were by now happily married, and had their own swimming pools and with Jack's heart condition taking a sauna would have been dangerous. Still, it was a sign of prosperity, it was fashionable and Fryda was always trying to outdo her friends. Last Christmas she and Jack had decided to close their dress shop for good, had a liquidation sale and spent the next three months harassing the builder to make sure that the house would be ready for tonight.

The guests were taken for a little tour of the place and were truly impressed. Then they all sat down to dinner. Now, the meal over, the party moved to the beautifully furnished lounge room where coffee, liqueurs and a great variety of the most delicious cakes were served. Fryda never disclosed the recipes for her cakes to anybody. It was a well-guarded secret and nothing could induce her to give them away. The conversation was sluggish. There were 14 people in the room. There were more than 50 of them back in 1945 . . .

* * * *

At dawn of that memorable day, 35 years ago, all the camp's prisoners were driven from their barracks in the middle of the night and lined up for roll-call. They were left shivering for six hours, but no roll was called. Roll-call usually meant standing endlessly under the blaring lights of the reflectors, but tonight all around them was darkness.

When the Allied air attacks became more frequent, blackouts for the roll-calls were introduced. Just at that very moment planes were circling low but nobody dared to look up. As the planes roared overhead, the SS-men with their dogs, and the warders, were running amok. Foaming with blind anger they yelled and screamed, shooting at random, kicking, punching. The dogs, excited by the smell of terror and blood, growled, or set on by their masters, tore big chunks of flesh from the shrieking victims.

As time passed, the pitiful formations grew smaller. All round them were dead bodies, stench, and misery. No one felt hunger any more, only a painful pressure inside the ribs. Each breath was a problem. To inhale or to exhale was such an effort that those not strong enough to close their mouths kept them gapingly open, taking little, fast, shallow breaths like fish out of water. All were silently praying for the bombing to start. Their only wish was to be killed by friends rather than by the wild animals running beserk amongst them. Their only thought was not to fall asleep. Falling asleep meant dropping to the ground and dropping to the ground meant instant death.

They were all destined to die, never to see the morning, and yet . . . by some incredible twist of fate more than 50 of them survived. They were bombed by Allies, shot at by the Germans and now it was morning and the madness in the eyes of the SS-men and warders rose to a pitch. They stopped shooting and started to crack the skulls of the prisoners with their rifle butts.

A sharp whistle of the camp leader summoned them to a meeting. Leaving the warders behind to guard the prisoners, the SS-men ran towards their superior who appeared on a small podium immaculately dressed, boots polished, a horsewhip in his gloved hand and observed the whole pandemonium with a contemptuous grin. The podium opposite the gallows was built for the camp's band which assembled there to play the happy tunes that usually accompanied public hangings.

After a short briefing the SS-men returned and ordered the warders to push the remaining prisoners back into the barracks. The last group was locked up in a small shed further away from the camp gates where *'Arbeit macht frei!'* was written in fat black letters. Work gives freedom! Indeed . . .

* * * *

'It is a beautiful chandelier' — said Maurice blowing rings of smoke from a cigarillo. Fryda was beaming at him. She looked well but was much too plump. Once, long ago, Maurice loved her. They had a brief affair, she was slim then. He didn't like fat women and had considered his wife Pola's good figure her greatest asset.

Maurice sighed and blew another smoke circlet into the air. The cigarillo tasted foul. He was trying to stop smoking and someone had suggested cigarillos for the transition period. Looking at the glittering chandelier Maurice sighed again. Pola was dead. Last year, when on their way home from a theatre show, she had suddenly died of a stroke. 'In duty bound' — a play written by a young Jewish doctor had good reviews, but the Jews didn't like it. It antagonized them as too provocative, too blunt . . . Why — mused Maurice — when their own son brought home a gentile girl he was in love with, Pola had made a similar fuss as the mother on stage had done. Unlike the story in the play Tommy did marry his girlfriend and Pola got over it all right, yet during the performance she became agitated and fainted as they were driving home. He took her straight to the Alfred Hospital but it was too late.

Maurice never believed that it was the play, though. Since that time in the camp hospital Pola always had high blood pressure. He remembered it well. One night their block's capo gave him a note from her. 'Am in the experimental ward — they are doing something to me. Don't know what yet.' He gave the capo his last three cigarettes. It became known later that doctors at the camp hospital manipulated her blood pressure putting it up and down. It had stayed high ever since.

And now Pola was dead and he was an eligible widower. There were three widows in the room and each of them had him in her sights. Maurice did not intend to marry again. Besides — he had slept with every one of them in the past and wasn't impressed in the least. He looked at the three women and at Fryda and blew one more shaky ring into the air, wrinkling his forehead in amazement that once he could look at her with desire. With the widows it was a different story. They were an easy lay and with his reputation as a local Don Juan it was effortless. But with Fryda it was love. When she broke it off he was bitter and thought her heartless. He understood now that she was busy looking after her children and helping Jack to develop their business. Money was coming in. They were moving to a new, better home. She had simply no time for secret love affairs. They were getting rich. Yes, Fryda and Jack had done extremely well for themselves. It wasn't like that with the others.

Maurice was never wealthy. Comfortable yes, but professional people who came to Australia after the war seldom did as well as those who had little or no education at all. Professional men like himself worked hard to learn the language, to find office work and not to slave 12 hours every day as the others did.

All migrants usually started their life in the 'Lucky Country' working in some large factory — men mostly at Holden's; women in the rag trade — all doing overtime whenever possible.

After the 'factory times' the ways of the migrants parted. The professionals learned their English and either had their qualifications verified or had completed studies started before the war. They were returning to their professions. The others stayed on at their machines and saved. When there was enough money a small business was bought, a milk bar or a green grocery, where they toiled long hours every day, seven days a week. Hard working people could get into money then. The less educated one was, the better one could endure the strain of uninspiring labour, lack of entertainment and social life.

There was another advantage: these little shops usually had a small dwelling at the back, so the children — they all by now had one or two children — could be taken care of properly and do their homework under the watchful eyes of their parents instead of running around unsupervised. The education of their progeny is always of paramount importance to Jewish parents — regardless of their backgrounds or social status.

And look at them now — thought Maurice — most of our kids are doctors, solicitors, dentists, architects . . . who could have imagined this on that day back in '45 . . .

* * * *

Their group was the last one to be herded into a small barrack. It stood on elevated ground, separated from the others by a wide ditch and was unoccupied for a long time.

Somebody once mentioned to Maurice that it was built to house the children. Now looking at the undersized bunks a thought flashed through his mind that it probably was true. No one from his 'generation' of prisoners remembered children ever living here. In Pola's and Maurice's time, children were treated like everybody else.

The doors bolted fast behind them, the prisoners dropped exhausted to the floor. An old man dragged himself towards the Eastern wall. Too weak to stand in reverence to his God, he sat on a tiny bunk lifted his emaciated face and rocking his thin body, prayed in a sorrowful voice. A few women cried, the rest remained quiet in a strange indifference to their fate as if what was going on did not concern them at all. As if hypnotized, they waited for the unmistakable smell of burning petrol and wood mingled with the pungent odour of frying human flesh and the permeating sweet scent of melting resin. They knew that soon one barrack after another would burst into flames, turning everything into ashes. It happened in other camps; it was happening here now. Their building was the last one in line, they were the last ones to die.

* * * *

'Why are you so quiet tonight, Maurice?' — asked Mary, one of the widows who still had some hopes about them both — 'Jack' — she called out to the host — 'put on some music, I'd like to dance!'

'O.K. We've installed a terrific hi-fi with speakers in all rooms. Just wait a sec.' Jack disappeared into the adjoining room surprising a couple cuddling on a settee. It was the other widow, Sonia, with Zyg — whose wife Erna was busily discussing with the third widow Rosa, the recent marriage of her daughter Vera to Rosa's son John, and didn't even notice her husband's short absence.

As Jack stared at them, Zyg and Sonia — embarrassed — disentangled themselves from each other and vanished into the lounge room. That was something new. Lately their meetings grew more insipid with each passing year; gone were the days of drinking, dancing, flirting, little affairs . . . Jack shook his head in wonder and chuckled . . . The party won't be so dull after all. He put on a sentimental tango and the whole house echoed to the hit of the 1930s 'The Blue Heaven.'

Zyg danced with Sonia, Mary dragged Maurice to the floor and Jack, using the brand new dimmer, dimmed the lights. At last something was developing. He decided to ask Fryda for a dance.

'I told you' — he said as he pressed his wife's plump body to his chest 'we need the dimmers, and you said we won't use them, look' — he whispered happily into her ear as more couples joined in 'what's happening!'

He felt a sudden desire and put his hand on Fryda's large breast.

'It's our new home' — Fryda pressed her thighs against her husband's in a willing response — 'it has an atmosphere' — and she pressed harder.

Now the sugary tune of 'The Isle of Capri' was coming from the speakers. Maurice felt Mary's hot breath on his face, her whole being melting into his with a quiver and all of a sudden he remembered how she had looked 35 years ago on the barrack floor, her enormous blue eyes wide open in mortal terror.

* * * *

The inferno had just started at the other end of the camp, inhuman screams of people burning alive became louder, crackling of the flames more audible and smoke was already penetrating through the cracks in the walls. Above the wails and moans they heard swearing, wild barking of dogs, thumping of heavy boots, single shots aimed at people trying to escape. The air inside became intolerably stuffy, the smells choking. The fire was moving closer. Each time a new barrack went up in flames the howls rose to a pitch, turned to moans and died out only to start anew when the next building was set alight. The silence inside was absolute. The old man stopped his prayer and they all listened to the noises coming from outside. It was as if an evil, cacophonic music was played there, a monstrous symphony of staccato rising wails, screeches, moans, intervals filled with the hissing sound of fire — like a damaged record — crackling fire, screams, pause, hiss . . . crackling fire, moans, hiss . . . on . . . and on . . . and on . . .

The last building over the ditch was burning. The prisoners in the children's barrack huddled closer together . . . The old man recited 'Shma Israel' — the prayer of the dying Jew . . . Unexpectedly a storm started . . .

At first it appeared to be a new barrage of shots but seconds later a true outburst came, a deluge. It was as if the skies opened up and poured torrents of tears over the wicked, mad world.

The inhuman groans from nearby were already dying out. It was their turn now . . . only . . . that nothing happened . . The rain was pounding on the tin roof but there were no flames.

The silence was so incredible that it hurt their ears. The rain changed to a trickle, there was a faint thunder and the storm ended as abruptly as it had started . . .

Terrified eyes looked at each other, bodies too scared to move — froze, no word came from the parched lips. They sat listening to the silence — not comprehending . . . without feelings . . . beyond hope . . . oblivious of the time passing by . . .

Suddenly — from all directions — the air resounded with youthful voices. The happy calls and laughter gradually changed to whispers of disbelief, then to outright silence. Only steps were audible but even the steps became fainter as if the men outside were scared to walk and started to tiptoe. The smoking ruins, the charred bodies, the desolation were so terrible that their feet in the heavy soldiers' boots didn't want to add any weight to the tormented soil . . .

* * * *

'You dance so well, Maurice' — said Mary smiling and put the tip of her tongue out like a little girl just about to eat an ice-cream. Then she licked her full lips and half opened her mouth waiting for a kiss that didn't come. Maurice disengaged himself instead: 'Sorry, Mary, I don't feel well, excuse me.' He went to the table littered with the remains of the supper and sat there with his head resting on the palm of his hand. Mary followed without a word — looked at him with resignation, noticed the leftovers and loaded a plate with a mountain of small cakes. With a deep sigh she sat down and started to eat with uncontrolled greed.

Not understanding that sweets became to Mary a substitute for her unfulfilled longings, Maurice looked at her with disgust. And again the enormous blue eyes and the emaciated face from 35 years before appeared in front of him. She still had beautiful eyes, the rest was submerged in fat.

* * * *

When the shrill command broke the silence it was Mary who first realized what was happening.

'Company retreaaaat!' — there was a shuffle outside as the soldiers were moving away. She tried to get up, was too weak, sat back on the floor and began hopelessly, piteously to sob. Maurice looked at her, understood and started to cry.

There was bottomless sorrow in his voice. He moaned, he howled, he groaned. All the misery of the last few years, all the pain and suffering, all the woe and grief, all the held back tears were surfacing in this lament.

The others joined in . . .

The retreating soldiers listened: from the lonely, little barrack wails were rising. Their officer came rushing back. The doleful weeping rose in a crescendo of dejection.

'Haaaalt!' The soldiers stopped.

'Turn baaaack!' The soldiers turned back.

'Doooors!' Four soldiers jumped over the culvert and tried to kick the doors in. The people inside were silent now. More kicks. The doors did not yield. This time stifled sobs were heard. The doors burst open. The soldiers stopped outside outlined against the now sunny sky. The day turned lovely after the morning storm. From the barrack a stench similar to the fetor of caged animals was coming out; a stench when excrement, urine and dust combined with dirt, sweat and fear. The officer joined his men at the threshold; hit by the odour they recoiled and squinting their eyes tried to look into the darkness,

where the wretched humans gripped by an unspeakable panic were withdrawing to the farthest corner.
The men holding their breath advanced towards the shivering prisoners who, sheilding their skeleton-like bodies with meatless arms, were looking with terror at the approaching legs.
They did not dare to lift their eyes higher, and Mary again was the first one to recover. She looked up from the muddy boots to the unknown uniforms and half crying, half laughing called to the others: 'We are saved! We are saved!'

* * * *

Maurice looking at her sitting alone with the now nearly empty plate of cakes, felt remorse and smiled at her. Mary didn't notice. Big tears were rolling down her puffy cheeks. The lights were dimmed and no one could see. To be smart and clever was evidently not enough — so she let herself go, alternately eating and crying. Maurice felf very, very sad . . .

* * * *

From then on things moved fast. The ambulances arrived, the stretchers were brought in and the survivors taken to a field hospital. They were nursed back to health. Slowly, patiently, step by step. The news spread, the press came. They gave interviews, were photographed, the numbers tattooed on their arms were examined, endless questions asked. The war ended. They were lodged in a displaced persons camp. Papers and documents were provided, the Red Cross searched for their families. A few decided to return to Poland, the rest tried to establish normal life elsewhere. A group of 30 reached Australia.

On 25 April 1946, they landed in Melbourne. It was Anzac Day and the first anniversary of their deliverance from the concentration camp.

Waiting to disembark they decided to celebrate. Singing and dancing on the deck they drank champagne crying and laughing at the same time. A reporter who boarded the ship became interested, began to ask questions. They didn't understand. No one spoke English, so they showed their tattoos, pointed to the shore and repeated: 'Australia, free country!' The journalist was impressed. This was a good story. He arranged them in a circle with the numbered left arm stretched towards the centre like spokes in a wheel, the other arm on the shoulder of the person in front. Then he climbed the railing and took a photograph.

Next day, it appeared on the front page of a leading Melbourne newspaper. 'Wheel of history' — ran the headline — and underneath: 'Victims of the Holocaust rejoicing on their arrival in Sunny Australia.'

From then on they decided to celebrate an Australian national holiday as their own personal double anniversary, but today after 34 years, Maurice felt so sick and tired of it all, bored to tears.

His life — he thought — went by unnoticed, he was a nobody, an insignificant speck of dust. To suffer so terribly during the war, to cling to life so desperately had not been worth the effort. At 65 now, he was a lonely unfulfilled man. An alien without ties or roots like the rest of them. They're only kidding themselves that it is otherwise. They all pretend that they are happy and carefree and successful, but deep down in their souls the wounds never healed, never could, never would . . .

It was not boredom he felt a moment ago; it was loneliness, abysmal, profound loneliness. In this room full of people he was alone. Great tiredness overcame Maurice. A moment later came the pain. Such a penetrating, piercing pain that he lost his breath and could not even cry out. His eyes turned up and the last thing he saw were the dimmed lights of the brand new crystal chandelier. Clutching his chest Maurice fell off the chair. Little gurgling sounds came out of his mouth and foam collected in its corners . . .

Mary again was the first one to notice. She sat still for a second, the last cake in one hand, the empty plate in the other. Then she screamed. Jack stopped dancing and turned the dimmers up. Now all looked at the body spread on the thick carpet. As they stood frozen to the floor the music came to an end. In the ensuing silence loud miaowing of a neighbour's cat imploring his mistress to be let indoors, came through clearly . . .

* * * *

Suddenly the doorbell rang. Loudly, impatiently. Startled, Jack went to open it. Outside stood a crowd of young men and women.

'Surprise! Surprise!' — they called, their arms full of flowers and bottles of champagne — 'Happy Anniversary!'

For the first time their children had decided to join in the celebration. They had plotted to liven things up a little because the old folk had complained that it wasn't any more what it used to be . . .

Judea

The hills of Judea
are soft and round
like women's breasts
with large, black nipples
of Bedouin tents
pointing up to the sky.

They look so inviting
spread around you
so sensual
and lusty

The hills of Judea
look golden brown
and soft from afar . . .

But deceived
is a wanderer
who enticed
submits to their call
and steps off the road
to seek abode
among their
tawny curves.

There is no milk and honey
to be gathered here;
no cool shade
to rest a tired body;
no water to quench
a burning thirst.

So yielding and alluring
from afar —
the hills of Judea
are harsh and cruel
when approached from nigh . . .

'Go away!' — they command
through the cracked lips
of their parched
with drought
soil.

On the Site of Jericho

Where is thy glory.
Oh, Jericho?
Oh, where is thy glory?

Hidden under the rubbish
amassed
over centuries?

Where is the horn that made
the walls
of thy temple shatter?

Oh, Jericho,
where are the stones
of thy temple?

* * * *

Deep in the pit
of history
lies the ancient city,
and nothing is left to us
but a few dusty ruins . . .

Olive Trees

The olive trees
are grey
and nothing much
to look at —
but they are
hardy and strong;
their roots dig deep
into the dry ground
to reach water.
Their fruit
bring the life-giving oil
for the hungry
and faith-balming
ointment
for the Holy.

PETER SKRZYNECKI

Migrant Centre Site
Orange Road, Parkes

Galahs and crested pigeons
scatter at my intrusion
into the paddock of autumn grasses
where horses continue grazing —
where agaves, pines and oleanders
have been planted like exotic memorials
among the native eucalypts.

Climbing over a barbed-wire fence
I discover the remains
of the migrant centre where we lived
on first coming to Australia —
where the lives of three thousand refugees
were started all over again
in row upon row of converted Air Force huts.

Broken slabs of concrete
lie baking in the sun —
pieces of brick, steel and fibro
that burrs and thistles have failed to overgrow
even after thirty-three years.
Several unbroken front-door steps
still stand upright and lead nowhere.

Except for what memory recalls
there is nothing to commemorate our arrival —
no plaques, no names carved on trees,
nothing officially recorded
of parents and children that lived beside
the dome-shaped, khaki-coloured hills
and the red-dust road that ran between Parkes and Sydney.

Walking back to the car
I notice galahs and pigeons returning,
settling back to feed in familiar territory —
unafraid of the stranger that searches
in waist-high grass
                      and breaks the silence
by talking to them as if they were human company:
even though the rows and slabs of cement
make him feel all the time
he has come to visit an old cemetery.

Hunting Rabbits

The men would often go hunting rabbits
in the countryside around the hostel —
with guns and traps and children following
in the sunlight of afternoon paddocks:
marvelling in their native tongues
at the scent of eucalypts all around.

We never asked where the guns came from
or what was done with them later:
as each rifle's echo cracked through the hills
and a rabbit would leap as if jerked
on a wire through the air —
or, watching hands release a trap
then listening to a neck being broken.

Later, I could never bring myself
to watch the animals being skinned
and cleaned —
                excitedly
talking about the ones that escaped
and how white tails bobbed among brown tussocks.
For days afterwards
our rooms smelt of blood and fur
as the meat was cooked in pots
over a kerosene primus.

But eat I did, and asked for more,
as I learnt about the meaning of rations
and the length of queues in dining halls —
as well as the names of trees
from the surrounding hills that always seemed
to be flowering with wattles:

growing less and less frightened by gunshots
and what the smell of gunpowder meant —
quickly learning to walk and keep up with men
that strode through strange hills
as if their migration had still not come to an end.

Going To The Pictures

Going to the pictures on a Saturday afternoon was the social highlight of my pre-adolescent years — when Superman, Batman, The Spider and The Durango Kid were heroes in a serial world where communication of moral values was manifested supremely by a knockout punch and the 'bad guy' image of Evil would shatter like breaking glass. Truth and Justice always triumphed, whether they flew through the sky or rode on a horse.

The 1950s in Australia were years of rawness and unsophistication — a decade in which the effects of World War II had only begun to seep into culture and society: where exiled European migrants were referred to as 'Bloody Balts' or 'Dagos' and their children began to learn about the English language from the distillation of phrases such as 'mad as a two-bob watch' and 'yer silly galah!' Our leisure time consisted of exploring the length of Duck Creek, making bows and arrows, listening to radio serials, inspecting each other's bodies as we grew into puberty, riding into the developing suburbs of houses and factories on our pushbikes, swapping comics and going to the pictures on a Saturday afternoon — and it was the last two, bound inextricably, that were the ultimate joy, eagerly awaited through the boredom of classroom hours and family commitments.

Although we had our own little group or 'gang' — six or seven children who lived within a mile radius of each other — we depended on interaction with others, outsiders, for a continuous and fresh supply of comics, even though there might be difficulty in obtaining them and, when we did, they might be in a dilapidated condition; but we devoured their contents nonetheless — The Phantom, The Panther, The Lone Ranger, Tarzan and all the fantasies that Walt

Disney could create; and it was because of these comics that the pictures played such a prominent role in our recreation. It was there, Saturday after Saturday, that we met with others, swapped comics and returned home with a fresh supply of adventures to be absorbed, characters to be learnt by heart and emulated afterwards in our ramblings along the paperbark banks of Duck Creek.

With the exception of Jimmy Fussell, a newcomer to the district, our gang consisted of migrant boys and girls that were of mixed ancestry: Russian, German, Polish and Ukrainian; but that fact never seemed important in those days and the word 'ethnic' was never heard of. We simply accepted ourselves as we were referred to — 'new Australians', though class consciousness meant nothing and language only became important when it was used as a term of derision against us; then we would retaliate with slang words we had picked up or by stones delivered barbarically from our shanghais.

Included in the session of comic swapping at the Saturday matinee was the purchase to be made at interval. The first half of the programme would barely conclude when there would be a stampede towards the back door and its heavy velvet curtains. As lights came on and the two side exits were opened, the theatre would already be a quarter empty as dozens of children spilled across the road to the milk bar and its fairyland display on counters behind a mirrored wall: where Minties, Jaffas, Fantales, potato chips and peanuts shone in cellophane-wrapped packets like Christmas presents that handfuls of threepences, sixpences, shillings, pennies and halfpennies would buy. Elbows nudged against ribs, foot trod upon foot, bodies crammed and shoved against each other in order to get closer to that red laminex counter. Ice creams, too, and soft drinks were passed into sweaty little hands that returned laden with more then they could possibly carry — but they managed somehow; and the second half of the programme would be filled with the sound of crunching and munching that filled the stalls like a strange insect sound. My own favourite snack would consist of a large bottle of GI lime, a bag of Smiths chips and a packet of Jaffas — sometimes an ice cream and a few packets of PK or Juicy Fruit.

Friends would take it in turns to mind the comics while the interval shopping was done. When it was completed, in the darkness that followed, lollies — like the comics earlier — would be exchanged. Jaffas rolled on the wooden floor, cellophane paper crackled like flames and bottles clinked without ever seeming to break: as the minds of innocent and gullible children sat and paid homage to a fantastic hero who was more credible than God or parents.

The first session usually consisted of the National Anthem, the

Movietone News, a Tom and Jerry, Mickey Mouse or Donald Duck cartoon, but the second half of the programme, with its main feature (often a Hopalong Cassidy, Roy Rogers, Gene Autry or Randolph Scott title), included the 'shorts' of a forthcoming movie and the current serial. At the end of the programme we would charge out of the theatre clutching our bundles of comics and head through the shopping centre and then up the high climb of steps and down to Platform 4. In that brief moment of glory each of us was a Superman, Tarzan, Jungle Jim or whatever character was the hero of that day — as we raced through the shadows of late afternoon and the imaginary catastrophes that erupted along the way.

It was either spring or summer. Weeds proliferated in the paddock that adjoined the land on which the theatre was built. Peewits sang. Only a few of our group arrived that afternoon shortly after midday for the session that would begin at two o'clock. There would be time to buy our tickets and then sit on the steps and exchange comics with others we had come to recognize by sight. We were dressed casually, the boys in shorts, shirts and sandals; the one girl, Irene Pirogski, wore a plain cotton dress and sandals, with a red bow in her hair. As we talked, a stranger walked up to us.

He was not of the usual groups that frequented the steps of the Odeon Theatre. He was taller and older than all of us, maybe 15 or 16 and dressed in a white T-shirt and blue jeans — projecting the sullen, James Dean and Marlon Brando image, except it was on a younger frame. There was an unquestionable mockery and contempt in the way he walked among us, flexing his muscles and brushing his hair with a round yellow plastic brush he carried in his back pocket. Several times he walked among the group, backwards and forwards as if to make sure everyone had seen him — bumping against their legs without apology, without any attempt to avoid trouble. He pushed in and out of the queue as he made his way towards the front, bought a ticket and disappeared around the side of the building.

Admittedly, there was a certain degree of awe and apprehension among us when he eyed our group, sneered and half-laughed, hooking his thumbs into the loop on either side of his jeans; but we had bought our tickets already and became involved in the task of getting as many comics swapped as we could before the doors were opened and the scrambling rush for the seats in the back stalls began. No one sat in the front if possible, and if they did, it was because they arrived after starting time and there was nowhere else to sit.

'Hey, everyone, look what Dougie's got! Over here!'

It was a trumpet blast, a call to arms; in its shrillness and urgency it could have been a Mayday signal. Groups broke up and ran around the corner of the building, stragglers followed, while others remained behind, totally disinterested in what it was that Dougie had done.

Planting my comics under my arm I ran off, caught up in the delerium of discovery that was generated by the day's warmth, the pitch of the caller's voice, the joy in having made some good swaps and the hullaballoo created by this unexpected uproar into the day's lazy afternoon. My sandalled feet joined the haste of others and we bound along the footpath, bumping and laughing, screeching like motor cars, up to the throng that milled around Dougie.

Pretending I was a rocket, I nosed my way to the front line, followed closely by Jimmy Fussell, Irene and Bogdan Tomasciewicz. Children pushed like demons from behind, sensing, perhaps, we were saviours — or, more probably, hoping these interlopers would continue rushing forward and do something stupid in the process.

Dougie sat on a small pile of bricks, part of an old foundation, a king upon a crumbled throne — gleeful and triumphant, devilry blazing in his dark eyes. In front of him, in a bare patch of dirt among weeds, a forked branch held a frilled-neck lizard prisoner, pinned to the ground, its tail and hind legs twisting in pain. Its captor would ease the pressure on the branch for a moment and the lizard would cease fighting, flatten itself and prepare to escape. Then Dougie would press down slowly and convulsions would start again — and all the time the pink mouth with its yellow lining, its small, porcelain-like teeth spat out resistance at the circle of humans that surrounded it: some laughing, some feigning terror, others jeering and goading its tormentor to 'Kill it! Kill it!' Every time the reptile opened its mouth the spikey frill would rise — a defence mechanism intended to frighten off its attacker; but that action, like the struggling body, was useless. Deeper and deeper its claws scratched the earth, failing to grip; and still the fork of wood refused to relent. It was almost as though Dougie had done this deed before, precisely, and was expert in drawing out the torture for as long as he chose — claiming attention to himself as the main actor in a petty drama that was obviously going to end in the death of the lizard.

'Let it go!' I screamed, sweat and sunshine blinding my eyes.

Voices behind me, around me — sensing a direct attack on Dougie — urged me on and I rushed forward, overpowered by an impulsive sense of heroism. My comics dropped as I beat out with my hand, not knowing what it was I hoped to accomplish; but it was the lizard I saw, still trapped, even as Dougie's fist made contact with my left cheek and a warm blackness came down from the sky and I fell on my knee in the dust, the end of a weed stalk catching against my mouth.

What followed was a commotion of voices, bodies, arms and legs crowding around me, filling my head with a noise that just wouldn't obliterate the pain that burned across my face. I touched the spot under my left eye and felt nothing . . . And still I wanted to lash out as I visualized the tortured lizard and the grinning face above it.

'I'm all right, leave me alone,' I lied, as Irene and Bogdan comforted me and pride could not bear the prospect of opening its eyes to encounter their faces or that of Jimmy Fussell who, I noticed, was absent.

When I did stand up the crowd of thrillseekers was dispersing except for those two that sat nearby and never took their eyes off me. Beyond them, a few girls and boys looked back, still curious to see what happened to this fool who rushed in and dared to question Dougie's superiority. My comics were scattered around me, and in all the excitement they too, like siblings, seemed to have suffered the shame of defeat.

As I watched Irene and Bogdan walk towards me, I cried out again and waved my arms threatingly, 'Go away, leave me alone.' Perhaps the bluff worked or perhaps they just felt sorry for me, in any case, they did walk away, glancing back over their shoulders until they'd turned the corner.

I slumped back in the dust, scooping handfuls of it and letting it run through my fingers. The day smelt of earth and grass, of sweat and heat; there was an insinuation of wrongdoing and its consequences in the air that I supposed to be nausea. My cheeks felt wet, smudged with dust that I could taste. My throat produced a dry, scraping sound as I tried to cough. Gobs of phlegm fell at my feet and I kicked at the ground in anger. Where were my super heroes — Superman, Batman and the others . . . ? Why hadn't someone come to my rescue . . . ?

Time was the innocent bystander, but I carried no watch to measure how long I remained under its gaze as I alternatively stood up and sat down, collected my comics, dusted them and moped around in that wasteland. I had no intention of now going to the pictures and neither did I want to return home too early. Whatever I chose to do, there would be the awkwardness of confrontation, of embarrassment. If I elected the former, there would be the possibility of another fight with Dougie.

Bundling my comics under my arm and dusting myself off as best I could, I began to walk away from the Odeon and towards the railway line and its steep embankments where peppercorns grew.

Four, five, six steps — and I saw the cause of my ignominy: the reason I had rushed forward into a crashing fist and now sported a swollen and throbbing cheek. The lizard. As if impaled by an invisible arrow, it clung flatly to the earth, blood running from its eyes and its sickly pink-and-yellow mouth open wide, threatening me with its frill.

The day seemed to have become hotter, I was angry and confused, yet a chill shot up through my body and I recoiled momentarily, afraid to move. The reptile had run itself into a corner of grass; its tail flicked sideways and it made pathetic attempts to rush forward, to intimidate the shadow it must have sensed across its path.

Horror and fascination seized my attention and I knelt down in front of it. What was it I hoped to discover, to learn as a secret or discard as unnecessary knowledge from that day? What was it I feared and thought to be an attack on my self-esteem? The two pits that had once been its eyes were caked with bloodied skin and tissue — a mockery to the serrated features that could have been the delicate artwork of a master sculptor. The more I stared, the stronger grew the bond that I felt was drawing us towards a physical encounter. Impulsively, without an iota of thought, I dropped the comics, lifted a brick that lay nearby and brought it crashing down on the lizard's head. Its body shot into the air, its hind legs and tail twitched erratically, madly.

Scooping up my comics I ran off, my hands and legs trembling — this time across the main road and towards the line of shops that lead around the station. My eyes were blinded by tears, my lungs gasped for air. I looked neither left nor right, whether or not I might bump into people or even if I ran past the station. My act of destruction seemed to spur me on, my notion of guilt refusing to accept any reasonable explanation that might lessen the severity of what I felt had been done.

No, I did not want to return home too early, but neither did I want to confront the rushing crowd that would bolt from the theatre at interval or at the end of the matinee session. After running through the shopping centre, I slowed down and hung around the hotel and masonry works opposite the railway station where headstones and crosses in granite and marble were cut by Italian workmen. I went into a milk bar and bought a large bottle of Coca-Cola, sat myself on the steps of a side entrance of the Royal Oak and perused my afternoon swaps. My comics seemed fairly intact, and despite some torn covers, none were missing. For the next hour or more, Uncle Scrooge bathed in tubfuls of money, the Phantom stalked ivory hunters through the jungle, Batman and Robin outwitted the Riddler, and the Superman saved Metropolis from a tidal wave and earthquake . . . but my hands still trembled and I could not forget the sight of the maimed lizard rearing its head beseechingly in front of me like a ruined Oedipus.

My parents chided me upon my return, warned me of the dangers of brawling and told me to keep away from that boy if I saw him again at the pictures. As it turned out, I returned earlier than usual and made no pretence of what had happened. I was in the security of my home and had the company of my new comics to read for the remainder of the afternoon, once I had taken a bath and eaten. But it was not the fight that bothered me any longer, the cheek that was swollen nor the fact that I had missed the afternoon's movies — it was the secret I never divulged to anyone and which burned in my head: the act of cruelty I believed I had committed without thinking and which plagued me for months and months afterwards — even when Irene revealed at one of our meetings in the bush that I had not rushed forward and attacked Dougie: that it was Jimmy Fussell who had pushed me from behind and that was why he had stopped coming around to our places. I believed and I didn't, even though I had not seen him for a long time and felt no pangs of absence when he no longer came with our group to the pictures. We never saw Dougie again and, without more incidents, life on the Saturday afternoons continued on its carefree path: the serials, the drinks and lollies, the comic swapping and the mad race to the station to catch the 'All Stations to Bankstown' from Platform 4.

The lizard, itself, remains a mystery to me: its marking, the frilled neck, the yellow-and-pink mouth and bluffing approach; and I believe that the respect I hold for all forms of wildlife stems from that incident in the vacant lot. What happened, however, I understand perhaps a little more and can speak about it now without fear or ridicule. As I stared at its blind face that afternoon I heard a summons — a voice — that was the sum total of all the noises around me: a plea, a cry for me to kill it and destroy its pain. No Superman nor Durango Kid had raced in to my rescue, yet I understood the lizard somehow knew who was confronting it in that clump of grass: knew and chose its own executioner, as well as the nature of its death.

If the 1950s left a remainder of their rawness and brutality in my nerves, of my inadequacies in coping with the Australian language and the customs of its people, they did not destroy the continued belief of childhood fantasies created during those matinee sessions on a Saturday afternoon, even though change occurs to create a new world of adult experience, irrespective of language or customs, and we are powerless to alter the nature of that catalyst — whether it is in the form of a bundle of comics that has been lost over the decades or the brick that I unconsciously lifted in the heat and dust of that Saturday afternoon.

TAD SOBOLEWSKI

Free As A Bird

I stood at the ship's rail trying to overcome the still lingering effects of the sea-sickness.

We were sailing valiantly across the turbulent Great Australian Bight and I peered eagerly towards the thin, hazy line becoming more and more discernible on the horizon — the shores of the Promised Land, Australia.

I simply could not believe it. A few months earlier, in Paris, we had been still awaiting the outcome of our endeavours. We always dreamed about sailing to some distant and peaceful country from the war-devastated Europe. Our activities in that direction had become quite feverish when the Korean war started.

Another global conflict?

That was what we could read between the lines in the French daily press.

Oh, no. Our children, born in Paris, had to be taken away and saved from the horrors we remembered so vividly. After surviving several years of the Nazi atrocities in Warsaw, we were frantic about taking our kids away, away, away! As far as possible.

I mused about all this while gazing at the thin, hazy line on the horizon. I was in a good mood in spite of the prolonged sea-sickness that had plagued us first when we were wallowing across the Bay of Biscay in the middle of the European winter and later again in the Great Australian Bight, in that hot mid-January weather.

But just at that very moment I felt like yelling against the roaring waves, the screeching seagulls and the muffled noise of the ship's motors: 'Australia! 'Australia in sight!'

I was awakened from my sweet dreams by the appearance of a bulky shadow on my right side. Glancing against the glare of the rising sun — the Australian sun! — I saw one of my travelling companions, Pan* Adam, leaning heavily against the rails and vomiting and swearing horribly.

When he finished and stood, bleary-eyed, clinging desperately to the rail and panting heavily, I thought he might need some consolation to lift up his sagging spirits.

'Look here, Mr Adam' I ventured, 'did you notice the size of the seagulls here? Compared with our European birds they seem to be

* Pan in Polish: Sir or Mister.

much larger and fatter, don't they? No wonder. It appears that this part of the world is much better to live in.'

Seeing that Pan Adam was not really interested in the size of the seagulls, or, for that matter, in anything even remotely related to the sea, I came closer and added:

'You know what? I am sure that finally we may be close to another stage in our lives — the stage when we may become as free as these birds.'

Pan Adam gave me a prolonged glare, spat far away on the turbulent waves, wiped his mouth with a colourful handkerchief and retorted in beautiful Warsaw slang defying any attempt of translation:

'Free as a bird! Are you crazy, or something? How free are they, eh? Look how they chase every bit of that, . . . ahem, offal there. You went to schools, or something, as I can see from the funny way you speak, and what have you been taught there? Some useless rubbish. Poetry, perhaps. Or other garbage invented to brainwash the working man. They have obviously never told you that there is no such thing as freedom in this bloody world of ours. You are scurrying to a remote place on the other end of the globe to find freedom and prosperity, and what will you find there? You'll be only chasing offal already digested by someone else. Just like those silly birds there. Free as a bird! Aren't you crazy?'

I elected to regard his last exclamation as a rhetorical question that need not be answered.

Pan Adam was an interesting personality. An able shoemaker from Warsaw, powerfully built, he betrayed the well known tradition reigning among the Warsaw bootmakers: he drank only milk and fruit juices.

He travelled with his de facto wife.

We had shared a room with them in a West German transit camp on our trip from France to Australia.

We occupied with our two children one half of the room while Pan Adam and his lady lived in the other half. The room was large enough and furnished with many two-tier beds, so there was a degree of privacy.

Usually I went to the kitchen, situated in another building, and brought meals for my family. It was rather cold outside.

One night I went to get coffee and whatever the kitchen had to offer for our tea and left my wife and kids in the room. Our neighbours were absent when I returned and my wife told me what had happened in the meantime.

Soon after I left, Pan Adam's lady shyly suggested that he, too, could save her from walking outside and could bring her coffee. He rose, speechless at first, then grabbed her by the scruff of the neck and administered a few blows.

'Coffee?' he bellowed, 'and, perhaps, some cake, eh? How about some cream, eh? Want some more of it, eh?'

My family, scared stiff, huddled in the corner not knowing what might come next. But Pan Adam, still heavily panting after his physical effort, turned to my wife, bowed politely and said:

'You, lady, have no fear please. Forgive me if I made you and your charming children scared a bit. I am not a criminal, my dear lady. I am not going to touch you. You will understand, however, that I have certain duties bestowed on me, too.'

He stopped for a while, leaned against the table as if preparing for a longer speech, and continued:

'There are certain principles that have to be upheld if this world is not to go to the dogs entirely. If these principles are not upheld, we all may finish in a ditch.'

Then, turning towards the sobbing woman, he raised his finger like an ancient god admonishing the sinful crowd, and bellowed:

'So! You wanted me to bring you coffee because you saw the husband of the lady doing so, eh? Do you realize what you have done? Something blasphemous. Yes! Blasphemous. Can't you see the obvious difference?'

He paused and took a deep breath.

'The lady is married in a church. In a church! And what are you?'

He seemed to be reaching a climax of his oratorial effort.

'What are you, may I ask? A whore. A woman living with a man in sin. In cardinal sin! Yes. And you want to be treated like a legitimate wife? Never. Never as long as I live. That would be truly the end of this imperfect world. Never!'

I met Pan Adam some time later in the Bonegilla camp. He toiled heavily, digging ditches in Albury in the February heat, to gain some money to buy bananas and other things for the woman who lived with him in sin. He need not work at that stage, we were living in the camp free while awaiting employment. But he wanted to supply the sinful woman with some luxuries not obtainable in the camp kitchen.

There were more people landing here with rather complicated sets of thinking on a variety of topics. The Pan Adam types, naturally enough, went through a series of clashes with the new surroundings. This was a stumbling block — one of many stumbling blocks for many an immigrant. Not all of them managed to fly over such hurdles.

But at that moment, there we were sailing towards Port Melbourne, and more and more people were coming out of the dormitories and gazing towards the bluish line on the horizon. To many that sight was as incredible as it was to me.

The Land of Promise!

Many had left behind many years of suffering and frustration, often hunger and dire poverty. To some, however, that hazy, bluish line on the horizon meant an escape from well deserved punishment for common or war crimes. That was one of the most unfortunate aspects of the otherwise great Australian immigration scheme.

We could already discern some blurry contours and shapes appearing and vanishing above that line. Were they tall trees? Church spires? But the most interesting question was: what are they like, those lucky people living there? They should be wearing cork helmets and bright flannel suits. Just like in an English novel describing the life in the colonies.

But the first glimpse of the land was not up to our dreams and expectations. We looked down at the maze of railway lines, at the workers wearing heavy felt hats and, often, pullovers — on a hot January day.

'Those English are always the same,' murmured a man standing next to me at the ships's rail, 'they would not change their way of life no matter where they are.'

I was amazed. That was not quite in line with what I thought of the Australians. The whole literature we had been given in the Australian consulates depicted them as manly, carefree types, hefty pioneers, good outdoor people. The sight of the port we were in was not much different from that of any European port. The people, too, seemed to have nothing distinctly different from their counterparts in Europe.

Finally we were allowed to leave the ship and were ushered into a funny train with a funny whistle. Then we were slowly careering across the railway yards, greeted by many workers who, apparently, were the immigrants who had arrived earlier.

'They seem to be happy with their lot.' I said to my wife, who sat quietly contemplating the new situation and what awaited us in that new, very new country, on the other end of the globe.

The train left the port and soon we were travelling across what to any European looked like a moon landscape: vast, empty spaces on both sides, reaching the blazing horizons. The grass was mostly burnt — ugly, black splotches — or yellow, at its best. The trees — naked, or with tatters of bark hanging off like rags on an emaciated beggar — jutted their partly blackened boughs towards the pitiless skies as if begging for mercy — in vain.

No animals, wild or domestic were in sight. It was a depressing landscape, sparsely dotted with vestiges of miserable life: some wooden huts, sometimes surrounded by clusters of visibly dying trees, also without a sight of a living creature around them:

'They must be shelters used by itinerant shepherds.' I said to my wife, remembering those shelters in Polish mountains.

A man sitting in the same compartment gave me a curious look and smiled and told me I was in error.

'These are the homesteads and not shelters. They are the residential homes of the owners of those vast latifundia you are admiring. From a distance, they look small; but some of them are quite comfortable. The trees . . . It is a dry continent, and it takes some effort to keep it the way it is done in Europe.'

He informed me that his sister had arrived in Australia earlier and he gained his knowledge from her.

When told that I was planning to settle on the land, he smiled, rather ironically, and unveiled more knowledge of the country:

'You are, permit me to tell you, a victim of old legends about those migrant pioneers who went to America and started from clearing the forests and managed to own large estates and prosperous businesses. Yes, of course, there are such people. They toiled heavily for some time, then, with a bit of luck, they really achieved personal successes. They were coming to Poland as wealthy visitors, and we looked at them with awe. But you must also bear in mind those unsung pioneers who perhaps toiled even harder — and who perished. Or, at best, they led miserable lives on small plots, owned small and not prosperous shops or businesses. Some of them perished bodily at an initial stage of the pioneering period: social services were unknown then! No legends nor songs have been created about them. The world you are entering is cruel to the weak, to the less prosperous. Forming one's opinions on the legends is rather risky.'

We discussed this further, till the train stopped in Seymour, where we were offered refreshments in the station's waiting room. The refreshments lifted our spirits: an excellent lunch, consisting of choice ham, bread, butter, some salad, milk for the children, tea and other good, wholesome things. We forgot the pessimistic remarks of our fellow traveller; Australia treated us at the threshold with its delicacies.

The railway officials who ushered us into the station were courteous and patient with those who spoke little or no English, but some of them observed us with very obvious apprehension.

True, we were coming from the moon. From the places known as turbulent and almost continuously in turmoil. So the people who lived in such places had to be more or less monsters causing trouble about any trifle. Our behaviour, certainly, was unusual, we showed nervousness, a lot of curiosity, and gaped at anything and anybody like village children watching a car that accidentally got bogged in the middle of the road. The way we spoke: loud noises, in unknown languages, with very different, sometimes raucous accents.

That was the initial, peaceful clash between the different people from distant, various countries, each one with a different background, history, and a set of moral, political, social principles. I watched the scene before me and had some misgivings about the possibility of adapting our people to those quiet, soft spoken Australians, who, with all the similar misgivings in their minds, smiled to us and helped those with small kids.

I thought about the scenes I could see during our journey on board *Fairsea*. There were many nationalities, some of them hostile to others. There were numerous arguments, even brawls. Women sometimes fought in the bathrooms. A German woman, married to a Pole, swore badly at a former Polish officer of the anti-Nazi resistance and called him, in front of a large crowd, a Nazi bastard. He took it calmly. To my mind, as I recall it now, he had already been 'assimilated' into the Australian way of life — most certainly many other Poles would be yelling back and telling the cheeky German what was what.

After the refreshments in Seymour we started the last leg of our trip by train and arrived at dusk at the small, deserted and hardly discernible, in the falling darkness, wooden shack. It represented, as much as it could, the Bonegilla railway station.

We left the train and looked around — the whole crowd of tired, worn out people, with children either already sleeping in the arms of their parents, or crying, and frightened. We shuddered — the images of similar crowds rushed to unknown destinations were still lingering in our minds.

But it was only a bad, recurring nightmare and we sighed with relief, realizing that we were far away from all those past tragedies.

* * * *

It was at midnight that we were ushered to our barracks, after going through a routine check made by customs officials in a huge shed. One of the officers found a simple soft drink bottle in our luggage. It was fitted with a rubber-clad cap which, thanks to an attached spring, could be used to close the bottle again after drinking part of the contents. The man examined it closely, opened and closed it twice, was obviously impressed by this simple device and put it aside. We understood that he confiscated it and asked him why it was so, but he dismissed our shy inquiries with a wave of his hand.

The cap that intrigued the customs officer had been in use in Poland long before the 1939 war, and we were at a loss to understand what could cause the confiscation.

'I'll tell you what' ventured one of my travelling companions, 'obviously the rubber patch on the cap could contain some bacteria, and this is why . . . '

A woman who nursed her sleepy child and was obviously fed up with the whole belated procedure, snapped:

'They have never seen that sort of a bottle here, so the idiot was fascinated and will use it as an exquisite present for his wife.'

Bewildered, we could not believe in such an interpretation of the case, but we did find later on that the angry lady could have been right. There were many items used a long time ago in Europe which still were unknown here. For a while, we thought it prudent not to start any row about a silly bottle on the threshold of the Promised Land.

* * * *

The hot, northerly wind and the monotous murmur of the loudspeakers producing a radio programme greeted us when we opened our weary eyes the next morning.

The barracks were made of fibro sheets, covered with iron roofs. The heat, towards noon, was becoming unbearable. We tried to find some shelter under the huge gum trees growing nearby, but they offered little or no shade.

While loitering around we met some earlier arrivals. One of these was Count Komorowski (not to be confused with the Count Tadeusz Bor-Komorowski, the former C-in-C of the Polish resistance forces in the Nazi-occupied Poland). The Count was married to a Russian woman doctor. He presented a classic example of a man totally uprooted, unable to adapt himself to the new realities. Once rich and in an elevated social position, the Count — who was then perhaps in his 40s — was certainly unfit to start a new life in a factory or on a farm.

However, he watched the new world around him with a benign smile of an aristocrat who, just for fun, found himself among the crowd he usually watched from the windows of his mansion. In spite of his downfall, he usually smiled and took whatever came his way with a good humoured joke. This, more than anything else, showed in him that true aristocratic streak that cannot be imitated.

I do not know what has happened to him. I hope that some time I may still hear from him, or about him. I greatly appreciated the conversations I had with him. I admired his sense of humour, good education and humane philosophy.

Other acquaintances were Mr and Mrs Tomasz Karski, and their son Andrew, who was our son's age. Mrs Maria Karski was a sister of my colleague from the Polish cadet school, Stanislaw Woloszowski, later known as an excellent horse rider serving in the cavalry. Unfortunately, he died a hero's death in an assault on Monte Cassino. We spent a lot of time remembering that brave and brilliant soldier. Mr Karski, too, was an aristocrat, although he laughed when called 'Count'. He had owned large latifundia in Poland.

They, too, could be regarded as totally uprooted, having difficulties with adapting themselves to their new position. The life in primitive barracks, the daily feasting on mutton fat and the prospects of a job in a factory became their world.

It was rather strange that they had left France: they were more in the picture there, having both an excellent command of French and good connections among other members of their elevated clan. After a few years in Australia they left for London where, I was told, Mrs Karski, formerly an inmate of the dreaded Ravensbrueck camp, died.

The life in the Bonegilla camp was by no means dull. The clash with the new realities and environment was more than evident. I decided never to accept any job that would require me to leave my family in the camp, as was the case with many other newcomers. My attitude was formed after certain experiences gained there, and also enhanced by a story narrated to me by Count Komorowski.

There was a Polish lady there, living alone in a barrack and working in the kitchen where she rubbed shoulders with a variety of people. One of her workmates, a burly type, one night paid her a visit and generously offered to sleep with her. Her prompt refusal made him mad and he bashed and kicked her.

When the terrified woman went the next morning to the police station situated in the camp, she went through an extraordinary experience of the local adminstration of justice.

The policeman listened patiently to her complaints and assured her that he would deal with the attacker if she, in case of another assault, brought the culprit to the police station, but without causing bodily harm to him!

The terrified woman, who feared another attempt of rape, found that she had no protection in law. To us, the newcomers to this fair land, this peculiar way of dealing with criminals was a revelation. It was also a revelation to many mean types who had found, to their extreme joy, the liberty to do as they pleased.

The things that went bump in the dead of night! Many husbands used to work far away and visited their wives only during the weekends. Some husbands, however, arrived when they were not expected. That was obviously the case with that Ukrainian who could not make his wife open the door when he arrived at 1 a.m. one morning. He also noticed that someone was leaving his wife's bedroom through the floor — after dislodging some boards. He struck a match and looked under the barrack — but the Casanova was already out and escaping, his trousers in his teeth. I saw two shadows darting with incredible velocity along the barracks, but the enraged Ukrainian roaring 'I'll kill you you bastard' repeatedly. The hot pursuit, however, was fruitless as obviously the Casanova was much younger. The enraged husband took it out on his beloved wife and we had little sleep on that particular night.

The hot, sultry nights induced anything but sleep. Once I heard some sounds which made me suspicious. I peered out of my window and spotted a crouching shape of a man at the door of Milda, a nice quiet Latvian girl, married to a Pole who worked in Melbourne. The door to her room was ajar, owing to the hot and stuffy weather. The man tried to peep inside and struck a match. I did not wait longer but leapt out of our hut and rushed at him. The culprit ran away and I suddenly realised that I could not chase him — all I wore was a singlet. I retired hastily to my hut, hoping that Milda did not see me. The next day I advised her to bolt the door every night, no matter what weather.

The girls from the Baltic states appeared to be real sirens. One of them particularly knew how to dress to look undressed. When she paraded along the barracks clad in the most alluring playsuit I had ever squinted at, she was admired by all men and hated by all women. Her husband worked in Melbourne; once he came home on a Saturday after an accident in which he had injured his feet. He asked his wife to change his dressings and take care of their kids, who, as a rule, were loitering and scavenging for food in the dustbins.

She retorted haughtily that she would not do anything that could spoil her make-up — she was going to a dance where she had a date with the entire local soccer team. At that very moment her husband rose from his bed and began strangling her. We heard some shrieking but took little notice as it was nothing extraordinary in the camp. The neighbours restrained the man and she went to the dance after heavily powdering her neck to cover the red and blue marks.

The next day I discussed what had happened with one of her ardent admirers. He laughed.

'It would be a pity to waste such a gorgeous bitch for one bloke' he said.

But the real siren was Linda, a fisherman's daughter from Dagoe Islands. It must be an interesting place.

She was a buxom beauty, a bubbling personality, and her night life would make many Parisians blush. She was delighted when she managed to have her two little daughters hospitalized with cold. Alone in her love nest, she sang Russian songs and entertained her lovers whom she changed more often than her underwear.

She was endowed with a particularly strong voice and used it freely all night, with intervals when her singing changed into guttural chuckles and powerful sighing.

Several of our neighbours decided to complain about all that to the man in charge of our barracks, a Pole, Mr G. He patiently listened to our complaints and promised to talk to the bubbling personality.

The next day he told us that she had lodged a very grave counter-claim: our children were a nuisance. She was greatly annoyed by them. We should rather look after our kids and try to improve their behaviour.

Puzzled and astonished, we asked for more details. Well, he said, gravely, she liked to have a good sleep during the day and our kids used to play in the street. We should take them to some other places, otherwise the lady could not have her rest.

How about our nightly rest? Mr G. refused to discuss the matter any further.

That was one more mystery we met at the outset of our great Australian adventure.

Mr G. represented, to us, the camp authorities.

The camp authorities represented the administration of the country.

Thus our first impressions had been formed on the strength of our own experience. The only way to learn about Australia at that stage was through the people in charge of our barracks — and our interests.

That first impression was rather bad. Such a dignitary in charge of a half a dozen barracks would, for instance, yell the name of a woman through the public address system, and when she appeared in his office, he would sit leisurely spread in a chair while she would stand. He would not condescend to invite her to take a seat. He deliberately wanted to show his temporary, brittle authority by rude manners.

His only qualifications for the job were that he had arrived a little earlier and had a smattering of English.

This first experience with my fellow migrants came to my mind at later stages, when — after passing through the stage of the 'initial clash' with some Australians — I have found that most of the troubles I have experienced in this country have been caused or aggravated by my fellow immigrants.

* * * *

While awaiting my interview in the employment office, I spotted the name of my former mate from the army school on the notice board. He had murdered his fiancee and had been sentenced to life imprisonment (in Poland murderers were not put on bail!) Obviously he managed to get free when the German bombs were falling all over the place. I decided not to contact him.

I rather turned my attention to a burly Russian who was being interviewed by an annoyed employment officer. When told that he was to be sent to work in Tasmania, the Russian objected by saying that he had come to Australia and not to Tasmania. Urged by the officer to accept the assignment, the man pointed his finger at the officer's nose, uncomfortably close, and stated firmly:

'YOU go to Tasmania. I be in Australia.'

The officer developed a nervous tic in his left eye. I did not see the final outcome of that exciting conversation as I was called to another table.

I was asked questions about my previous working experience and decided not to reveal my educational standards; I was well aware of the circumstances in which any studies in philosophy or philology were completely irrelevant and insignificant. I found that the people who interviewed me were of the same opinion — they were interested only in my abilities to perform manual jobs.

I did not mind. The legends about the successful immigrants who sailed to America and became rich by hard work were very strong in every refugee. We were glad to reach the shores of the Promised Land and dreamed about mighty jobs and efforts finally crowned by well deserved material independence. I was prepared to settle on the land. I was fed up with big capitals going up in smoke, overcrowded, bombed like Warsaw and impoverished like the post-war Paris. I looked at the vast expanse of empty lands surrounding the camp and thought that all of us there could be settled on those empty spaces and offered some help to start producing food and other goods then in short supply. I remembered similar schemes in Poland and thought that it could be even easier implemented in Australia.

One day we decided to see a piece of that real Australia and went to Albury by bus. It was a very eventful trip.

We found that the cakes we bought in a shop were not bad, that bananas were of lesser quality than those we could get in Paris, and that sugar was unobtainable. We got a small quantity in a shop where we met an educated Pole working as a salesman. Another shopkeeper told us that sugar was short simply because the hardly civilised newcomers who had never tasted sugar before rushed at the shops and bought all of it. He also told us that here at least we could buy some butter while in Europe one had to get police permission to buy a pound of butter.

The day was warm so we left our two children on a bench in a small green enclosure with a bag of bananas and made for the pub next door. Our arrival was greeted with murmurs and chuckles, and a waiter informed me, in a whisper, that women were not allowed inside.

Confused and embarrassed, we decided to go to a bank in order to open a savings account. But first we loitered at the entrance trying to make sure that women were allowed in banks!

It was in that bank in Albury that our experience with what is termed as the language barrier made its first appearance. I approached a teller and inquired if I could open a savings account, and wanted to make sure that I could withdraw the money on call, without any waiting period. I did not know how to formulate my question, so I asked if I could have the money on request on the same day. I pronounced these words the way I had been taught in Europe.

The teller smiled and replied:

'Yes, you can have the money the *syme die*.'

I was taken aback by his pronunciation, but he repeated, as if teaching me to speak Australian: the *syme die*.

Obviously my face betrayed utter bewilderment and a prosperous looking gentleman spoke to me in German and offered to help with interpreting, but I politely thanked him and said that I was keen on learning English as soon as possible even if this seemed to be rather difficult.

* * * *

On the strength of a contract we had signed before landing in this country I was obliged to accept any job assigned to me during the first two years of my stay here. We had only some $60 in our possession and it would not last long as we had to buy a lot of food owing to the rather indigestible mutton fat offered to us in the camp kitchen. I eagerly awaited the first job.

It came. We were told to go to Mildura for fruitpicking. This caused problems as I would have to go on my own and leave my family in the camp. When called to the employment office I stated firmly that I would accept only such a job where I could go with my family. To leave my family at the mercy of rapists who have to be caught by the victim and delivered to the police station? Sorry!

I flatly refused to go, was called to the office, solidly grilled for about one hour by an officer, told that I would be deprived of social welfare payments, ten shillings weekly, not to be sniffed at, and would have great difficulties in finding any job long afterwards. I insisted that I would go anywhere — but with my family. Fed up with threats and oppressive talk I demanded to be deported back to France. This ended the stormy conversation.

Walking back to my hut I felt guilty. Here I was coming to work in an hospitable country and the very first thing I did was to refuse to work. That, I thought, was a very bad omen.

Depressed and in despair, the next day I went to see the people in authority to try to justify my attitude. While facing some of these big nobs I had an impression that I was facing a wall — an invisible but formidable wall. They were at least interested in my arguments and in the whole story as well. I thought that they were giving not a damn to everything that was going on. Their expressionless faces told me that they had no human feelings, they were the puppets, doing their job in a most primitive way, not prepared even to argue with me.

Finally I went to the highest authority, the camp director, an amiable, elderly gentleman in an old army tunic. He listened to my halting narration very politely, with an expression of some profound suffering on his face; from time to time he gave a deep sigh and rose a few inches from his seat. He grunted twice and finally told me that he could not do anything about my plight.

Frustrated, I left the office and was stopped on my way by the gentleman's secretary, a beautiful and refined young lady, a Hungarian, I was told later. She spoke to me in German, listened to my narration, and very kindly tried to cheer me up. She told me that her boss suffered from haemorrhoids, especially on a hot day. And I thought that he was showing his compassion when he grunted and showed profound suffering on his face!

Finally, I understood that my actions were silly, that really nobody was interested if I went fruitpicking or not, they were all small cogs in a bureaucratic machinery and desired nothing more. My silly actions were dictated by that confounded way in which I had been brought up — at home as well as in school, including the army school. I had always been told to be honest and never to do or say anything untrue.

I am ashamed to say that I was one of those idiots who took it seriously. Hence my misfortunes.

I watched my mates who were issued with railway tickets to Mildura, and were going to earn good money as fruitpickers. On the day of departure their names were called over a loudspeaker and the trucks were waiting to take them to the railway station.

There was one name called repeatedly, and impatiently, but the man, a Mr F., did not appear. I knew that he had agreed to go, and had been issued with a railway ticket after passing through all the formalities I refused to pass. I met him the next week in the canteen.

'So you are still here' I exclaimed, 'not in Mildura? But I heard your name trumpeted all over the camp through the loudspeakers . . .'

'Yees' he smiled. 'I did not feel like getting out of bed. To be frank, I had little sleep on that night, so . . .'

'But later you informed them about all this, did you not?'

He gave me an unhealthy grin.

'What for? Those muttonheads . . . They were calling me for half an hour and never came to think of finding me in my hut! They are incredibly stupid, their minds are clogged with mutton fat. Do you want me to apologize to them, eh?'

'But they did cancel your welfare payments, did they not?' I insisted, with a faint hope in my voice.

'Not at all. I have just collected it and intend to spend it here.'

I watched him with awe.

'But . . . the ticket. The railway ticket. Did you return it? It costs money, you know.'

He fumbled in his pockets, produced some scraps of paper, a handful of crushed peanuts and finally the ticket.

'Good, you reminded me' he said, 'I hate carrying too much junk in my pockets.'

He extracted the ticket and deftly tossed it to a distant dust bin.

I gazed at him with envy and sheer amazement.

Later I trudged to my hot barrack and, in my hoarse voice, warned my wife of the calamities awaiting us in this Land of Promise. I'll never succeed here, I wailed, my face buried in my hands. Oh, to be as smart and happy-go-lucky as Mr F.! He and his ilk will go very far here, in a country where you are punished for being honest and rewarded if you are as clever as Mr F. In vain my wife tried to convince me that the same laws govern all other countries: I retorted that I did expect so much more from Australia than from other countries and this should make me even more unhappy here.

Tutama followed the woman he loved everywhere

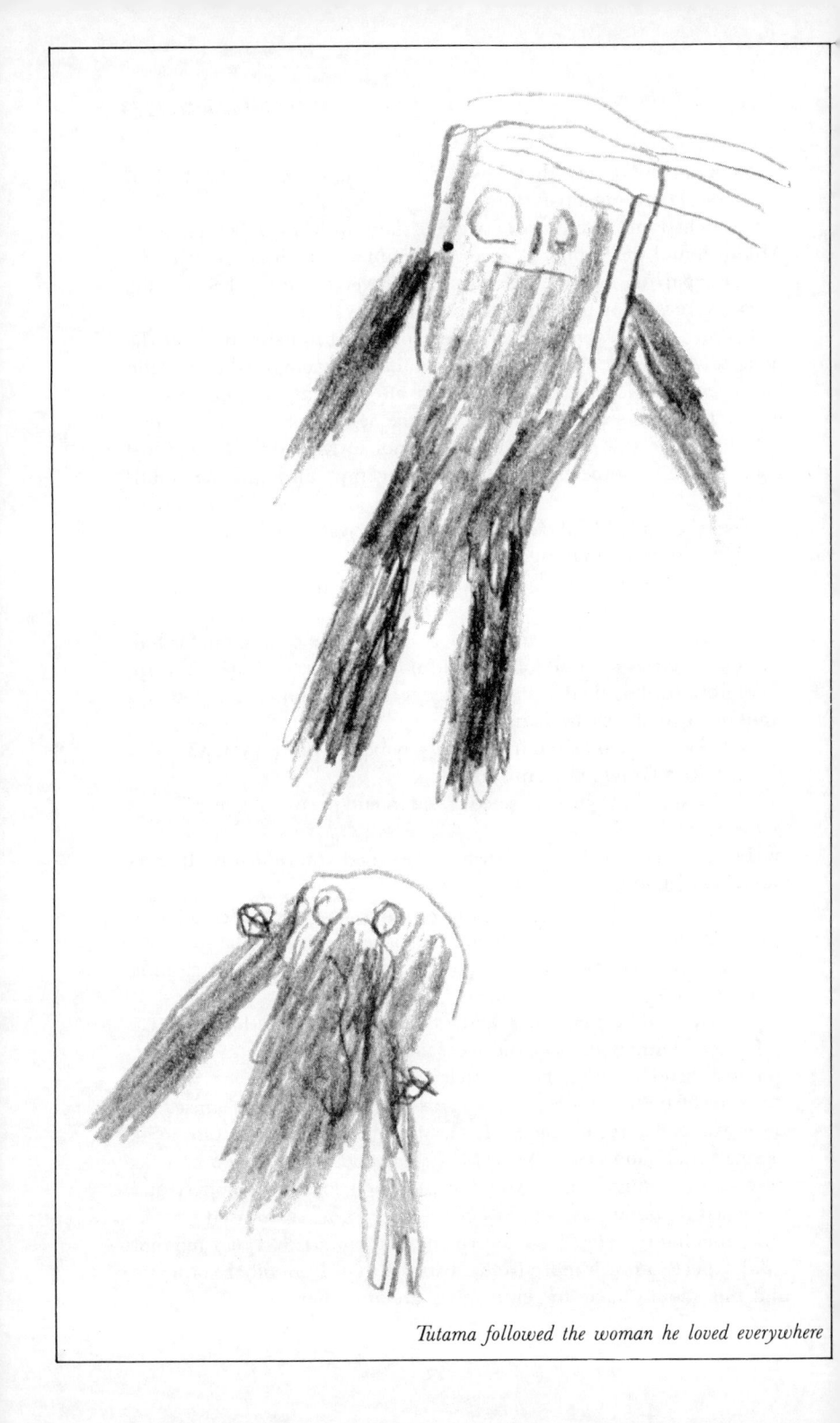

TUTAMA TJAPANAGARTI

Getting a Wife

(translated by Paul Bruno Tjampitjinpa and Billy Marshall-Stoneking)

I slept. I told the woman, you come; but she didn't listen to me. Make a camp, I said, sleep. Together. No. Only I talked; she didn't talk to me. So I slept. I slept, and in the morning I got up and went hunting for meat, out in the bush — different bush meat. Then, again, I said to that woman, come, to sleep. But no. And all the time I'm going out tracking meat.

One day I'm tracking for kuka[1] and I see the tracks of two women — and that woman who I wanted to come, her tracks are there! So I follow those cracks until I can hear those women; they're making some noise. They can't see me, but I see them hitting on some hollow wood. The other woman is down, bending over, looking in the hollow log, maybe looking for *something*. I say to myself: Ohhh, maybe I might *poke* you! But that woman's poking in the hollow tree trying to make something come out, some animal. When it comes out she hits it, and then they're both busy hitting that animal, and when they turn around it's the first time they see me and that other woman says to her sister: 'Oh! it's Tutama! Maybe coming for wangii!'[2] But that woman I'm after, she's gone; and that other one starts fighting with me. Fighting and fighting and fighting, ohhh, too much fight!

I shout: 'Don't go, don't go!' I'm calling after that woman. Then I say to that one who's fighting me: 'Wiya, stop, no more fighting!' And I grab her and say:'All right, you're going back to the camp with me now!' And we stamp off toward the camp.

When we get to camp I see that woman who ran away and I say: 'Come here.' Then she starts crying so I say: 'Come on; I'm not going to kill you! We're gonna cook this wintaru[3] you got out of that hollow log.'

They cook their wintaru at one fire, and me, I have a wayiyuta,[4] I'm cooking at another fire. After cooking, I sit down; then I look around. Oh no! I can see a lot of men coming to fight with me, and even my friend is with them, *my friend!* The sun is just going down; only a little bit is showing. I get up and walk toward them. Then I stop and put my spear and boomerang down by my feet. Standing up straight I can see those men coming toward me; they're ready to fight. Then one man throws a spear, but it misses me, so I grab my spear and say: 'That's enough! You threw a spear at me, but we shouldn't fight. I didn't do anything silly with that woman. I just grabbed her and brought her back to camp, that's all.'

I tell them I only got those two sisters to come back to camp, nothing wrong with that. Then I have a long talk with that man who threw the spear, and everyone finishes up satisfied. After that those men leave for another waterhole.

Next day a whole group of us also go to a different waterhole, and those two women come along too. We keep going and going a long way. All the time we are looking for food. Finally, I get some kuka and I make a fire to cook it. I tell the others to keep looking around for more kuka. I don't go; I'm still watching that kungka,[5] and wondering why she's not going with the others looking for kuka. I get up and, walking toward her, I say: 'Okay! I'm going for more kuka now.' But she doesn't say anything.

Later. I'm back and she's gone! She's run away again: nothing there! Can't find her anywhere. Then someone tells me: 'She's gone.'

I get up and drink some water. I'm not going to worry about getting anymore kuka now. I just go, and go and go and go. Lonnnngg way!

First thing next morning I wake up. I start tracking that woman. I can tell from her tracks that she is going slow now. Then, when I come around some bushes, I can see her. She's facing me and she sees me coming. I see her face, shaded by a tree, and her face is saying: Oh no! Same bloke still following me. I hold up my spear and say: 'Why did you run away?' Then I run towards her, ready to throw my spear. There are men there too, but they aren't sitting; they're running. I'm standing with a spear, like this, but I don't throw it, wiya. I'm just trying to scare them, pointing it to scare.

I stop there and make a fire to cook some kuka. The others keep to themselves. I eat; we all eat. We are all sitting down.

This bush tucker I have, ohhh, it's a really sweet one: skin em and eat em, scoop it all out with a stick. Oh, too sweet! Tucker from Tingarri.[6] Like that, I'm eating and everyone is sitting around, eating.

Then one old man wants to fight me; he growls at me. I tell him: 'You mob never give me that woman, always take her away. She's supposed to be my wife!'

Everybody's getting angry and then everybody stands up. Big fight now. Spears coming and coming: miss, miss, miss, miss, miss, miss, miss, miss. Every spear misses! After that, they tell that woman she's got to come with me.

She comes. Sleeps. Next morning, we two go for kuka, and that night we make song — singing Tingarri, happy. We sleep again, and then we sing again, different song.

Next morning I went to Wikilirri.[7]

Glossary
1 kuka: meat.
2 wangii: taking a girl with the intention of copulating with her.
3 wintaru: bandicoot.
4 wayiyuta: a possum-like animal.
5 kungka: young woman.
6 Tingarri: pertaining to the Dreamtime. Also refers to song cycles that teach Aboriginal law.
7 Wikilirri: place name, ceremonial site in Western Australia.

The Payback

(translated by Paul Bruno Tjampitjinpa and Billy Marshall-Stoneking)

A long time ago a lot of bush cats and possums changed into devils. This is a true story. A man from the south sang[1] them because someone had killed his son. He was going to pay back these other people for killing his son.

Those bush cats and possums killed a lot of Pitjapitja[2] people — women, men, blind men, blind women, kids, whole lot. This is in olden times.

Kaawakaawanya was killed; he was just a young fella. Pilpiltjanu, another young fella, was killed too. My father, Karlytal, he was middle-aged at this time. We all heard about theses cats and possums that had changed into mamu.[3] The news spread everywhere.

At one camp, some people had been sitting around and these cats and possums came out of the bushes, making a lot of noise. The people that couldn't run climbed trees. They climbed really fast, but the cats and possums followed them. Those animals followed the people into the trees. People and mamu were squeezed in together. Then the cats and possums killed those people, chucking them out, throwing them down, and any that were still alive when they hit the ground, they killed those too.

Some people got away and made another camp, but the mamu followed them. They killed another person. So the people went to another place and made another camp, but they couldn't get away. The cats and possums were still after them, and this time they took a woman and killed her.

After the cats and possums killed people they would eat them. Then they'd climb up into the trees. They rested in the trees and waited for more people to come along and camp.

No people came. They were all running away. They didn't look back. They were running and crying for help. Those mamu had too much power.

Later, some of those people that were left made another camp. Just before the sun came up those animals caught up and killed another person. The people started running again. Only sons and daughters were left from that mob; all the parents had been killed.

Then the mamu started after another mob. There was one old man in that mob who tried to stop them. Everyone was really frightened, but Kurupaawinytja was really strong, a really strong nangkari.[4] He was powerful, but even he couldn't stop them.

When the sun was almost down Kurupaawinytja called all the people over to him. Everyone stood close around Kurupaawinytja. He whispered to the people: 'Look. Look in the trees.' And he pointed and all the people looked and they could see that all the trees, all around them, were full of bush cats and possums, sitting in the trees, quietly, watching, waiting.

When the sun was down that devil mob killed almost everyone. Only those that had a lot of power escaped. Everyone else was finished — poor buggers.

Glossary
1. sang . . .: a magical chant. 'Yingkangu' literally, 'to curse by singing.'
2. Pitjapitja: Pitjantjatjarra people, south and east of the Petermann Ranges, Northern Territory.
3. mamu: an evil spirit, a devil, often in the guise of a living form.
4. nangkari: Aboriginal doctor; medicine man.

DIMITRIS TSALOUMAS

Prodigal

Fanatical mosquitoes and persistent fetid stench
   hold absolute dominion
over the twilight bogs. Evening comes early
   full of mutterings. Our days
were never rich — but now!
   The ox is skin and bone and the goat
barely yields enough for the baby. Therefore
   make no rash decision.
The other day Eros was seen in the market-place
   unrecognized in cast-off clothes,
grown old. Come of course since you insist, but
   whatever you remember, now forget.

The Return

The war's been over now for forty years
and you've still to take the enemy off the wire.
Who opened up his back so that his lungs hung out
from behind? Haven't you tired of his shallow moans
in a whole lifetime? I sent you word to empty out
the bucket with the arm and other bits,
to stop up all the cracks. The house
stinks like a shambles. You haven't even sealed
the holes in the cellar and who knows what
might suddenly creep out on us? I don't like
this weather at all. Already my sleep is taking
water, and there are tentacles stretching out,
feeling in the dark. I'm sorry to tell you,
brother, but I'm not spending summer here.
At our age some caution is called for.

The Pale Knight

The Pale Knight dismounted at the inn
and made his rounds of the neighbourhood
with his saddlebag of old pamphlets. What luck
that the people should all be out, and Spring
should sit alone among the garden's gossamers
and the traceries of birds. The passing rain
had barely left us. One hello at the window
and it became a chandelier, a necklace
round a Gypsy throat, a lizard's coat of mail.
Never stopping at the gate at all, but passing by
bent and raving like a beggar, the bone
clothed in flesh, he had, I swear,
for a carnation at his ear, the irony of my heart.

Televised Message of Comfort

Thunder from the abyss and hurricane wind
bending the forests like barley-fields —
horizon demented in pomegranate reflections
as there arises, symmetrical and beautiful,
the great cloud. Without effort,
silently, the Babel towers collapse
and on the world fall salt-dust shrouds.
A living soul — nowhere. Only he,
handsome in the glitter of decorations
telling of freedom's triumph and of hope's
extension to our children's children,
in the desolate heart of this Sunday evening.

VICKI VIIDIKAS

Darjeeling

Imagine a road
binding a mountain's shoulders,
the earth running like a ribbon
with cool wind humming,
the sky a mauve carpet
so deep
it buries where you look

The mountains rumble and purr
as wind tickles their bushes,
a hawk is floating in air
while cypresses
tongue each other's fur;
the winds carry solitude
and snow

A tin roof gleams
under a veiled red sun,
Tibetans vanish indoors,
the mountains smile and ruffle
icedrops from their sides;
imagine a road is a gateway
there is a hawk
circling, searching

To My Father, Viidikas*

Your favourite violin plays, Paganini,
dark forests bloom in the night

Through Russia the horsemen gather,
even the foothills are alive, sub-zero,
the breath freezes

* named after Estonian fish

And at Tallin the phantom ships
sail out in search of summer, carrying timber
and escapees . . .

Your one silly fish
is flashing and fast, mercury through bone,
the skin peels, but never the spirit

Your violin is an ancient one
fashioned from wood, the horses' hair, you
return to earth

Lover of music
your colours delight the memory, wick
of energy, bastard husband, Estonian tower

The rain tells me now
of your streaming . . .

The Relationship

One

She was adrift in her repression, afloat in her sealed fear, and she said, he might chop off my head; he needs psychiatric help.
 I couldn't be bothered talking.
 Nineteen letters he sent to her, all insults; 19 times she's decided, to retaliate might be dangerous.
 What's this? Fear sprouting like cauliflowers from her eyes, her knuckles, her mouth — 19 times of evasion.
 There is this fear of men, she feels, they might chop off her head — men are dangerous, she said. Nineteen letters of attack, and she's taken them all lying down; 19 times to break through, yet she's refused.

Two

She is mad, he said, you know that don't you? Ever since we met she's done nothing but snipe at my personality, he sniped. I am giving her up; she needs psychiatric help, he said. Nineteen times I've tried to help her, broaden her mind but it's useless; all women are mad.
 At the age of 19 I couldn't be bothered talking to them.

I've had women, he said. I've travelled this green planet and discovered the world is stupid. And women are the same. They all want to change me — and she, she's done nothing but snipe at my personality.

And his tongue became a wasp and glowed orange with the sting, and the black stripes on the wasp's wings banded his mind and locked him in.

Three

A thick mist glides down and clings to his gloom.

At the masonite factory he pushes boards into a machine, levels them till their surfaces become smooth.

He levels and stacks, he levels and stacks. All women are mad — he hates as he stacks — they all want to change me. He smoothes his reason back until it's that of a child's — I've travelled the world and discovered it's useless: there's too much sun in Afghanistan, not enough quiet in Tibet, too much fog in England; and women are mad and everyone is stupid.

He pushes the boards into the machine. I am alone — and in this he takes consolation. I am superior — he wallows. I've suffered for years, yet I'm still here. His pride swells with the . . .

He smooths and stacks, he smooths and stacks. The factory bristles with accusation, in every corner among the shavings he finds a new loop hole — I am superior — alone — I have suffered — I have to live with people's ignorance. SUPERIOR. I AM SUPERIOR. I'VE READ THE GREEK CLASSICS. The factory echoes now with reassurance.

He is mad, his fellow workers whisper.

Four

Hold on, hold on. I must keep to the rails, she tells herself. I've never met a decent man, they all want to dominate me. I'm sick of their egos.

She turns this ancient habit over in her mind.

I've tried my best with him. Cooked him nice meals, washed his underwear. I sewed his buttons and tried to humour him when he came to me full of despair. I've been good to him. But he'd never see anything my way; always treating me as if I were inferior. And now he sends me 19 letters saying, like all women I'm irrational, and if only I'd done what he said, and changed, we would have . . .

Now I realise he's dangerous, and my instinct was right — all men are mad.

Five

There is a train, something phantom and loose in her mind, but strong enough to hold, the wheels are greased.

My marriages have failed — always the same. And with him it's no different; the talking down so I'm afraid to speak; his taking for granted my cooking meals, just because we're lovers. And he's convinced he's superior. I could tell him one day, I could really tell him, just once I'd . . . but he's mad and could be dangerous. Why shoud I suffer at the hands of madmen?

I have enough problems. I am alone.

Six

You know she's stupid, you know she's mad, he said. I've done my best for her — tried to show her the right path, to broaden her mind, make her more aware. But it's useless, she's like everyone else. She refuses to think.

And she's done nothing but try to undermine my character. All women are the same — they want to change me.

At 19 I couldn't be bothered.

I have tried, she said. I have endured, he said. You'll understand when you're older, they said.

Seven

Cauliflower fears and misted despair.

I've never insulted anyone, she says. I've tried to enlighten many people, he says. They will go on a journey together, on their separate rails.

Somewhere a train rattles along narrow lines, lamps sway as it lurches, old ghosts fill the walls. The multi-faced driver is fixed like a wooden puppet to the wheel; the sliding landscape on either side bursts into colour, plants like lush sentinels beckon in the vibrant air, birds throw notes like pebbles at the shadowed windows — the train does not stop, but rattles on, in fixed motion.

CORNELIS VLEESKENS

Street Talk
Two sonnets on a theme

1
Her brother never took to him.
Felt she'd married low though who's to say
for no one really knows where he was from.

The name had not been heard around before
(when was it? — November 1667, I remember
I was doing the Christmas shop the year
young Paulus had his first — yes . . .) 1667
when Gundy Copermans and he announced
they were engaged.

And a short one that was, too!

Three days later she paraded
as Mrs Vleeskens, married mind you,
right here in the St Sulpitiuskerk
with special dispensation from the priest.

2
Three days! There must've been
good reason for the rush.

I've heard some say
but I don't know the truth
he was a soldier
conscripted, wanting out
and saw this as his opportunity.

Others: Ah!
Joos Vleeskens
he was just a drifter
don't know what Gundy saw in him
but she made sure he stayed around . . .

Dragged him to the altar
before he drifted off again.

At Every Step

They've let him keep the motorcar. Had it been his mother's ancestors rather than his father's that carried the German blood, he would not have the advantage of a good Germanic name, nor its attendant privileges. Of course, it also carried a stigma in the community. While the occupying forces will take a German name as proof that he will never act against the Reich and thus betray his own Aryan blood, in the city of Amsterdam the mere bestowal of simple privileges, such as the continued use of a motorcar when so many others have had theirs taken forcibly off the road, places the traitorous stamp of collaborator on him.

Gerrit Hoffnung takes the icy corner with the necessary care to avoid a nasty skid. There are so few cars on the road now that the ice takes longer to melt into slush, turning winter driving into a constant trial. He steers the big black Ford into its customary parking place outside the *Amsterdamse Universiteit,* where life does not quite proceed as normal, but does in some way proceed. Gerrit is the Associate Professor of German Studies, one of the few departments which has suffered little curtailing in the current strife, a department seen by the occupying forces as being no threat, rather a voluntary propaganda machine. Gerrit stares a minute at the walls of his office, the windows hung with the thick drapes necessitated by this damn war.

His knowledge of German studies, the politics, the manner of thought, is extensive, and although his area of primary interest now lies in the vast body of literature produced by that race over the centuries, his initial contact with the department had been for more personal reasons. As a first year student he had displayed a keen interest in a subject he felt might shed some new light on his own peculiar character, on his origins and the divisive loyalties he felt whenever the Great War was discussed.

Over the years, first as a student and later as a member of the department, he has formed a solid basis for his beliefs. Aften ten years of delving into the depths of the German mind, through their literary achievements and their philosophical debates, he can well understand the logical processes that turn out a Hitler. Whether he agrees with these processes is something not even his wife is sure of anymore. All she knows is that in the past year, this terrible year of cold stares from their neighbours in the food queues, Gerrit seems to have been on an inordinate number of trips in the car to centres around the country, but most often to The Hague.

* * *

Sheets of rain fall across the windscreen on another grey day. The black Ford moves steadily along the country lane not far from the city. Gerrit avoids the main road, tries to relax with the serene scenery of windmill and canal.

Relaxation does not come easily, however, and beneath the reasonable, assured features of the academic a troubled mind struggles. The black Ford is conspicuous. Villagers and farmworkers, those who remain, stare at its passing shape, more used to the sight of horse and cart plodding slowly along.

* * * *

Johan de Groot pulls tight the heavy blackout curtains, turns up the wick on the lantern. He looks across the kitchen table at the drawn face of Theo Hoogevaar, spits out:

'And how's that Hun brother-in-law of yours keeping? Trudy says she saw him driving through the village today like a one-man victory parade . . .'

Theo mulls over the ersatz flavour of the would-be coffee and the attack on a member of his family by someone who *should* know better: should know better because of his position as co-ordinator of the local resistance cells, but can't. Can't be let known what must remain a secret between Theo and his sister's husband, Gerrit Hoffnung. It is enough that the resistance knows Theo has a contact for moving Jewish refugees safely to the North Sea pick-up points. Gerrit is already vulnerable because his black car is so conspicuous. Not only the Hun, but every unsuspecting villager around the Dutch countryside is aware of each move he makes, each road he takes.

'Hit a sore spot, have I? Well, I guess it must be trying to hold rank in the resistance when it is common knowledge you have dinner with a *German* at least once a week. But no, there are more serious things to talk about.'

'How many this time? And when?'

'They'll put a boat ashore at Katwijk on Friday night. We have two men and a woman ready to go. And they're important. Some pretty high connections.'

'That only gives us five days to set it up. You know we need at least a week . . .'

'They're important, that's all I can say. *Can* you do it?'

Despite below-freezing temperatures Theo finds a sweat breaking out on his forehead as he leaves the rendezvous. He could never understand Gerrit's constant pre-occupation with roots and heritage, knows little of his own ancestors beyond the grandparents he visited for the first six years of his life. And little cares to know more. It is enough that he knows the land he works, the small farm with its herd of Friesian milkers. He is a simple farmer with simple tastes and little education. Yet war has thrown him a bit off balance. He feels impressed with the higher education his brother-in-law has always advocated, longs at times to understand the workings of the mind that can drive a whole nation to follow one man's dictum, but finds it enough just to keep his own life together now, when so many once simple things depend on the smooth working of the underground.

It isn't the first time he's asked himself what he's doing here. It isn't the first time he's failed to come up with a convincing answer.

* * * *

Gerrit has stopped asking himself about his involvement with the underground. He knows from his studies of history that in times of national strife a strange bondage born of fear and pride works its way into the people. He's tried to think it through as an academic problem, as though it were some strange phenomenon that the mind can comprehend. He's laid aside the rational approach. War has no time for rationality.

He seldom thinks about the risks involved, but somehow tonight it nags him. Detection, although he doesn't care to admit it, would leave a deeper, more lasting scar on his wife and children than on him. For himself, it is only death. For them . . .

* * * *

It is short notice to get the necessary clearances for yet another trip to The Hague. Only a fortnight since the last seminar with his counterparts in the coastal city's *Instituut van Leerkunde*. Of course, the advancement of German doctrine is important, but how many intervarsity meetings can be called without calling even his position as the National Co-ordinator of German studies in to suspicion. Although the cover is a good one, its use, perhaps its life, is limited.

Last time he'd obtained clearances for himself and two colleagues, and it had taken all the efforts of the underground to supply fresh identities and well-used papers for his passengers. Passing through the roadblocks and checkpoints was a minor headache, nothing compared to the task of explaining the disappearance of his colleagues at the other end, should he ever be called on to do so.

Usually they travelled on papers which needed little explanation,

those of academics purportedly returning from another part of the country who'd stopped off briefly at the *Universiteit*. But there is a strict limit even on *their* movements.
   No. They'll need to use a different ploy this time. The thought of travelling without permission comes up, but is dismissed. There'll be at least three roadblocks to negotiate and without the necessary papers it would be impossible. You might fool them once, but no more . . .
   Backroads are also ruled out. Gerrit knows from his drives in the country just how obvious the big motorcar is. It would stand out like a hearse in a funeral procession, and would surely turn into one.

* * * *

Theo's chin sits heavily on his hands. The dried potato-peel in his pipe leaves a vile aftertaste, but the act of smoking relaxes him a little.
   'I still don't see how it could work. A funeral . . .'
   Gerrit, however, is quite worked up about the idea:
   'It would explain the urgency, though. There are enough rotten smells around the place already, and surely a Professor of German should be allowed a decent burial in the place of his birth.'
   'But still, no . . . What if they want to open the coffin? No . . . It's all too unbelievable.'
   'And that's exactly why it'll work.'
   And then he explains the whole idea was handed to him on a plate through the unfortunate, but timely death of the head of his own department at the *Universiteit*. All that remains to be done, aside from contacting the family in The Hague for the funeral arrangements, is for an extra three mourners to be provided with the papers.
   Theo's breath comes more easily.

* * * *

Gerrit's feelings of unease stay with him as he drives behind the hearse. Only two cars have been allowed for the mourners, and to occupy three precious seats with people who, to the rest, are total strangers, causes some minor friction. But their papers lay claim to family ties which must prove stronger than even a lifetime's association in the department.
   After the funeral three refugees are left to mingle with the people on the streets and make their own way through danger to Katwijk, some kilometres north along the coast.

* * * *

Theo brings word from de Groot that the pick-up went smoothly. Gerrit's passengers are safe in London where the Allies are pleased with the information they've brought through. Gerrit is not so pleased, feels somehow that this time he has been used.

His association with the resistance movement has at all times been for purely humanitarian reasons. Extensive research into the German race has not blinded him to the atrocities that race feels compelled to inflict on others, both in the countries she ruthlessly invaded and on those people of Jewish origin within her own borders. His position, he feels, is less like that of a chess player intent on using strategies designed to save his own pawns while inflicting the greatest possible damage on his opponent than that of the human observer to whom the pawns on both sides appear as sacrifices too great to make lightly.

And now he feels this last escape, when he was called on to do the near impossible and succeeded only through the peculiar twist of fate which must always look to have been in rather poor taste, all smacked too much of politics, of espionage. His passengers had not had the frightened look and stilted speech of refugees which he had seen and heard too often. They had the cold assurance of agents who had placed themselves in danger for their own, or their country's strategic purposes and then relied too heavily on the movement to get them out again.

He does not want to be involved in this. Not this which is designed to bring about more bloodshed, even if it is in the interest of eventual peace. He wants only to see an end to this war and suffering and a return to normal life, to remove as many people as is humanly possible from this cruel theatre. Not to collaborate in the scripting of the play . . .

Snow had been falling from leaden skies these past few days but this morning the sun begins its struggle through the thick layers of cloud. Gerrit pulls the oppressive drapes and lets the feeble sunlight find its way into the dampened office.

* * * *

He looks down on the big black Ford parked in the lot below. There are smudges on the rear window where a youth has scrawled obscenities in the dust. There are the equally obscene remains of snowballs still clinging desperately to the runningboard. For Gerrit to continue in his work he must remain forever an outcast . . .

* * * *

The rhythmic plodding of de Groot's workboots is broken by a heavy footfall and a halfturn to face Hoogevaar. He's never really taken to this weedy Boer, but has relied heavily on his contact for the most difficult, most dangerous cases passing through his sector. This farmer who has held out on the identity of his contact for all this time, who has maintained a greater silence and secrecy than anyone else in this sector and, perhaps because of it, perhaps in spite, has managed to develop the safest and most reliable escape route. And now he comes here, the offensive beast, to say that it's finished, over, no more . . .

'But Theo the movement . . .'

'No Johan, no more. You broke trust trying to pass off those British agents as refugees. I can't ask my men to take that kind of risk without knowing what he's in for . . .'

'But it was urgent. We had to get them out quick . . .'

'You didn't think my man a fool . . . To even try . . .'

'But Theo, all my other channels are clogged. The movement needs your man more than ever. Just when we're making some headway . . .'

'Damn your headway Johan. And damn you and your trickery. No!'

'But just once. We'll look to establish something else for next time, but this is right on us now. Can't you at least talk to your man? See what *he* says? One last time . . .'

* * * *

One last time. The black Ford draws in to the kerb outside Gerrit Hoffnung's house. His wife has heard the car coming, opens the front door, steps out . . . to see Gerrit's blood-caked body thrown viciously onto the lawn. To see the muddied clothes torn off, re-opening the wounds. To see the blood run again from a lifeless body while these animals mutilate it.

She draws the children to her side, buries their faces, rushes them inside. She draws the heavy drapes, their weight almost defeating her. Defeating her. Why her? Why Gerrit? Shut out this sight. Don't let the children watch . . .

The soldiers push their way into the house. Tear down the curtains. Make the children watch. Make the wife watch. The darling wife, yes make her watch. Make them all watch. And leave the body there a week. There, where they fall over it at every step.

KATH WALKER

Namatjira

Aboriginal man, you walked with pride,
And painted with joy the countryside.
Original man, your fame grew fast,
Men pointed you out as you went past.

But vain the honour and tributes paid,
For you strangled in rules the white men made;
You broke no law of your own wild clan
Which says, 'Share all with your fellow-man.'

What did their loud acclaim avail
Who gave you honour, then gave you jail?
Namatjira, they boomed your art,
They called you genius, then broke your heart.

Acacia Ridge

White men, turn quickly the earth of Acacia Ridge,
Hide the evidence lying there
Of the black race evicted as of old their fathers were:
Cover up the crime committed this day,
Call it progress, the white man's way.

Take no heed of the pregnant black woman in despair
As with her children she has to go;
Ignore her bitter tears that unheeded flow;
While her children cling to her terrified
Bulldozers huddle the crime aside.

White men, turn quickly the earth of Acacia Ridge,
Plough the guilt in, cover and hide the shame;
These are black and so without right to blame
As bulldozers brutally drive, ruthless and sure
Through and over the poor homes of the evicted poor.

Homeless now they stand and watch as the rain pours down;
This is the justice brought to the black man there,
Injustice which to whites you would never dare,
You whites with all the power and privilege
Who committed the crime of Acacia Ridge.

Bwalla the Hunter

In the hard famine time, in the long drought
Bwalla the hunter on walkabout,
Lubra and children following slow,
All proper hungry long time now.

No more kangaroo out on the plain,
Gone to other country where there was rain.
Couldn't find emu, couldn't find seed,
And the children all time cry for feed.

They saw great eagle come through the sky
To his big stick gunya in a gum near by,
Fine young wallaby carried in his feet:
He bring tucker for his kids to eat.

Big fella eagle circled slow,
Little fella eagles fed below.
'Gwa!' said Bwalla the hunter, 'he
Best fella hunter, better than me.'

He dropped his boomerang. 'Now I climb,
All share tucker in the hungry time.
We got younks too, we got need —
You make fire and we all have feed.'

Then up went Bwalla like a native cat,
All the blackfellows climb like that.
And when he look over big nest rim
Those young ones all sing out at him.

They flapped and spat, they snapped and clawed,
They plenty wild with him, my word.
They shrilled at tucker-thief big and brown,
But Bwalla took wallaby and then climbed down.

The Curlew Cried

Three nights they heard the curlew cry.
It is the warning known of old
That tells them one tonight shall die.

Brother and friend, he comes and goes
Out of the Shadow Land to them,
The loneliest voice that earth knows.

He guards the welfare of his own,
He comes to lead each soul away —
To what dim world, what strange unknown?

Who is it that tonight must go:
The old blind one? The cripple child?
Tomorrow all the camp will know.

The poor dead will be less afraid,
Their tribe brother will be with him
When the dread journey must be made.

'Have courage, death is not an end,'
He seems to say. 'Though you must weep,
Death is kindly and is your friend.'

Three nights the curlew cried. Once more
He comes to take the timorous dead —
To what grim change, what ghostly shore?

Note: The curlew was brother of the Aborigines. He came to warn them of a coming death by crying near a camp three nights in succession. They believed that the curlew came to lead the shade of the dead one away to the unknown world.

ANIA WALWICZ

europe

i'm europe deluxe nougat bar i'm better than most i'm really special rich and tasty black forest cake this picture makes me think of germany make me made me europe made me i keep my europe i europe this town is just like my polish town where born where is where am here is europe all the time for me in me is europe i keep it i got it i get it in me inside me is europe italy warm palms lovely palace chrome chair street busy alive me my end pier with a little lamp what i remember i don't forget keep this keep lighter and brighter now this is it this europe in me in me my only what i have what i have i keep europe hold on to that i thought i lost what i didn't had carl's mother said don't get out of bed there are goblins goblins they eat his white long leg i was so so so jealous jealous of what he had fresh new young just came two weeks from frankfurt and i'm too long gone left too quick didn't stay what what what i could have been exactly like him exactly like him they took my europe away they took my europe away they took my europe away they took me they stole me they boat me they float me take me took me away took but but but but but but but i bounce back i get back i add ten years to my life i look younger all the time i get it again the it how look my europe now i look fine i ride in my forest at night with goblins i look pictures i win i don't lose i always get another chance and i'm europe again and again and again europe better than it really is better soir de paris perfume my wrist my picture paris from photos is perfect i never saw paris i distill i don't have to travel i'm in europe i'm europe i get europe it comes to me what she said venice after the railway through door to lagoon i can just see it i can feel it you can go to europe but you can't be europe like i am i suck my finger and i taste europe i touch europe i travel on my map with my fingers in my newspaper floods rhine carl saw little mermaid carl eiffel tower climb famous people every thing very important just tell me europe come to me now my city crowd friday could be rome now my europe my my my better than really better than is could be magic feel and taste carl smells of europe his coat is europe two weeks just came just came ran away from the german navy bought this trenchcoat in germany i'm young man i'm young man got this vest in stockholm beret in berlin i'm young fair strong long tall long tall my europe is best only best only nicest loveliest sweetest creamiest i only want best most kind most marvellous i'm homesick for where i haven't been i miss france and i miss norway i only want what i should have had what i should have been where i now am i come home to that in my europe is europe all green all fresh all green i shot geese with my gun white feathers fell in my eiderdown dear carl i hope everything is well with you i'm young and now new i'm looking forward exciting to i'm twenty two i'm studying physics i'm young man young man everything is going to be

stories my mother told me

be careful on the street close all the doors tight don't open the window at night i was smuggling arms on my bicycle german soldiers flirt she said hurry up caught us going to shoot i get away he hides me in the attic my hair turned black overnight don't go out by yourself i hide under the stairs everybody looks a soldier to me now put away gold fake fur i won't need it now who knocking on the door too loud what is that now who is it i have to watch out they come boots i climb over the wall they switch the electricity hid me haystack i was so hungry never throw out food now i am so hungry all the time and scared who comes now don't go out the door there's danger after easter pogroms* don't tell anybody who you are no don't tell them it is five o'clock now it is too late they'll come again i knew false passport i change my name to singer the siren's siren put me up night i leave the next day don't trust them stole her ring and cut off her finger they inform me car lights in dark winter he reports me i run through snow i was in another town i didn't look like it have to be quiet now don't breathe i get away they come now up the stairs can't you hear best seats for the germans stacks of shoes everybody gone now i could not find them if someone leaves the house they might not come back take your clothes hide the silver it's the same again now take this it will be useful don't cough don't make too much noise they hear now walking walking up knock shadow walls get dusk close curtain don't put on the light i was on my bicycle don't tell them who don't trust them don't trust anybody now black cars maria have sirens they come at night don't tell them never tell them keep secret don't leave the house they steal our suitcases hide the whole family till the money run away now quick mud make soup out of potato peelings save everything i can't sleep i listen for footsteps and knocking keep awake now look out shut the door properly test if shut and again close the windows tight don't trust them the man who worked for my father gives me away i run i get drunk keep me warm now don't trust anybody ever the germans

* (pogroms: organized massacre of jews in russia)

come back thirty years later take jewellery hide it close the doors all the doors they come now i wait for boots footsteps on the stairs knock knocking don't let anybody in now don't go out on the street danger black car night siren maria don't tell them anything i run through mud in my dream hide me will you hide me now look look are they here they can come again don't tell anybody i'm here i'm on my bicycle smuggling arms i change my name he hid me in the attic don't tell him who you are don't tell them anything be careful on the street danger don't go out the house at easter pogroms stay inside close doors windows don't put on the light be careful save all the food come useful i run through snow i was in another town underground i didn't see the sun don't go out at night stay here i was all alone he hid me attic under the stairs don't tell anybody be careful on the street they steal our suitcases they come now

JUDAH WATEN

A Writer's Youth

The first writer in my life was Sholem Aleichem, the great Yiddish comic writer. I heard him read aloud in Yiddish by the elderly Chaim Frankel from a Yiddish paperback with the picture of the writer on the cover. I was about five and it was during World War I when we lived in a country town near Perth. We had arrived in Australia early in 1914 when I was two and a half.

Sholem Aleichem was not the only Yiddish writer read aloud in our house but he was the funniest and the saddest, always managing to strike some humour out the of the plight of the Jews in Czarist Russia and New York's East Side. Most of the stories came out of New York Yiddish dailies which published short stories and *feuilletons*. My father, always being short of money, could not subscribe to them but several better-off friends did, and they brought them to our house where they were read to us and other indigent migrant hawkers who gathered for the occasion. Chaim Frankel was an impressive reader, acting out the stories, using different voices for the characters.

All of us waited for the newspapers with a mixture of anxiety and excitement, like farmers in a drought waiting for rain. In those days New York and Perth seemed to be planets apart and with a war going on, travel from one to the other took longer than crossing Australia on foot.

When the newspapers finally turned up, the news was stale but the stories and *feuilletons* were still fresh and alive, only some were better and funnier than others. They were read and re-read. 'What is a man without reading — a nothing,' the same Chaim Frankel declared and my mother often repeated this aphorism.

My mother loved Sholem Aleichem whom she had once heard read his stories in Odessa. My father also recalled that in 1907 or 8 he had bought a paperback collection of Sholem Aleichem's stories on the Kiev railway station when he was on his way to Warsaw.

As the writer died in New York in 1916, in the year when I first heard his name and stories, there was a period of mourning after the news reached us in our little enclosed world. Chaim Frankel said our lives would be much sadder without him but we would still have his work which would console us. The writer consoled mankind; he was the only one that did.

Even now I remember the day when the newspaper arrived with the account of Sholem Aleichem's funeral attended by hundreds of thousands of New York Jews, the biggest procession of men and women ever to follow the hearse of a Jewish public figure, it was said. The Jews, like the French, are good at giving their writers a grand send-off. Even attending such a send-off bestows a kind of distinction on you. Years later when we lived in Carlton, one of our neighbours, a Mrs Fanny Segal, was always spoken of as the cultured Mrs Segal, as she had been in the vast crowd outside the cemetery in Warsaw when that other great Yiddish writer, Isaac Leib Peretz, was being buried. I don't know whether having attended Jean Paul Sartre's funeral would add something to you in France, but perhaps it would.

My mother actually liked Chekhov even more than Sholem Aleichem, saying that he was the deeper writer, only second to Count Leo Tolstoy who was the deepest of them all. She thought the *Kreutzer Sonata* was Tolstoy's masterpiece and should be compulsory reading in schools everywhere. The hero of that novel was a voluptuary and it worked his destruction, she said. Tolstoy showed that the sowing of wild oats in youth produced an immoral man only interested in a woman's physical attributes, and when that man married he inevitably produced misery. 'Got behitten (God forbid) that any woman in our family should fall into the hands of a voluptuary,' she once said, referring to a cousin who had spoken well of a certain unmarried draper who had a reputation. Reputation for what? I really didn't know what mother was talking about and I didn't get around to reading Tolstoy or Chekhov for a long time.

In the meantime I went to a state school where I learnt to read and write English. I had arrived in the class speaking English quite fluently, having acquired the language from the neighbours and the children in the street.

I took to reading like a bird to flight and before I was seven, I had joined the Carnegie Library in our town and went there regularly on my own. My passion then, and for the next few years, was for books about cowboys and schoolboy heroes and Lamb's *Tales from Shakespeare* and Defoe's *Robinson Crusoe*. Sitting in the dour Carnegie Library in the country town, a type of library no longer in existence in Australia, I put myself in the skin of Robinson Crusoe, living his life with him, refusing to accept the story as merely a kind of fairy story, as the librarian called it. But then all good fairy stories, even now I imagine, convince children by their combination of an exact literalness about the visible with an unquestioning acceptance of the impossible.

I also liked poetry and committed to memory those famous Australian poems 'My Country' by Dorothea Mackellar, 'Faces in the Street' by Henry Lawson, 'The Man from Snowy River' by Banjo Paterson and 'The Sick Stockrider' by Adam Lindsay Gordon.

At the weekends I recited those poems to admiring friends although most of the old ones didn't understand a word. I was encouraged to think I was a good reciter after a Jewish concert in Perth where I had recited in Hebrew a poem by the famous Hebrew poet Bialik, another one of mother's favourite writers.

Being able to remember poems once came in handy for my father. When the school holidays came I sometimes spent whole days on my father's bottle and junk cart. At one guest house in Kalamunda I impressed the guest-house keeper, old Annie Mason, by reciting 'The Sick Stockrider'. The last lines brought tears to her eyes:

> Let me slumber in the hollow where the wattle blossoms wave,
> With never stone or rail to fence my bed;
> Should the sturdy station children pull the bush flowers on my grave.
> I may chance to hear them romping overhead.

It was Annie's favourite poem and as I was word perfect, she immediately gave father permission to collect the bottles, iron, everything stacked in a heap in the yard. Father could have the lot for nothing; he was really proud of me that day. Annie must have thought that a bottle-o couldn't be all bad if he had a son who could recite Adam Lindsay Gordon. Bottle-os weren't highly thought of, not by guest-house keepers, who knew what they were capable of doing when nobody was looking.

Annie's sister, Dot, watched father put the goods in the cart. She ran the outside, assisted by their brother Percy, another ancient. He drew the water for the washing up and turned the mangle. He had once been a gold miner and had turned a windlass for God knows how long. He milked the cow and drove the horse and phaeton to meet guests at the railway station.

It was at this guest house that I first fell in love and also suffered my first humiliation.

Dot had another assistant, Beryl, who was always hanging washing on the line whenever we appeared. She also collected the eggs. She was about 14 or 15 with pale eyes, pale lashes and fine blonde curls. Those blonde curls were irresistible to me and I had fallen in love with her the first time I had seen her. The heroines in the cowboy novels I read and in the films I saw, all had blonde curls, unlike the women in our community who were mostly black or brown-haired and looked sternly at the young.

I must have been staring at Beryl when she called me to the line where she was hanging up washing as usual. When I came up to her she tickled me under the chin and my vocal chords instantly ceased to function. I must have looked alarmed.

'I'm not going to swallow you.' She said.

Just then a Muscovy duck was escorting her brood past us. Under the blue sky the duck looked snow white and the ducklings, little balls of golden wool. Our presence seemed to make the Muscovy very angry and she stamped her feet and hissed:

'Muscovies don't quack.' Beryl said. 'You're like that duck, you don't quack either. But can you hiss?'

When we returned home I wanted to write a sad poem about myself but I didn't know how, although I had learnt acres of poetry, good and bad. I never managed to write poetry but soon I was beginning to write prose sketches and even novels which never got beyond chapter one, and were suspiciously like the cowboy novels I'd read, the heroes looking like Tom Mix and William S. Hart the silent one, and the heroines with blonde curls.

When I was 11 I met writers in the flesh, real writers as my father said. The first was Katherine Susannah Prichard. My earliest memory of her was coming out to our cart standing in front of her house in Greenmount. She was very different from most of the women on our rounds who were suspicious of bottle-os and not always pleasant especially to the foreign ones. Katherine Susannah Prichard was gracious and understanding and I imagined that being a writer somehow made you all those things.

Every fortnight or so my father, wearing a leather arm-band with a metal disc on it engraved with the words 'marine dealer', drove round the hills stopping at private houses, boarding and guest places. But he was almost at the end of this bottle-oing as business was going bad. It wasn't that the inhabitants of the hills had given up drink, but there were now many Russian-Jewish marine dealers on the road and they cornered a good deal of his former business in Kalamunda, Mundaring and the smaller timber settlements.

So he decided that rather than drive to every house that had previously been on his list he would only stop at those houses where he could have a yarn or a good cup of tea or both, even if there was nothing to buy or collect. Katherine Susannah Prichard's home in Greenmount was one of those.

Another stopping place was Molly Skinner's guest house in Darlington, a few miles from Greenmount. Molly Skinner had written a book on nursing: she was not as famous as Katherine Susannah Prichard who in 1915 had won the Hodder and Stoughton £1000 All-Empire novel prize, one of the biggest literary awards of the day.

My father knew a lot about his clients, customers or whatever you call them, and Molly Skinner and her brother and her friends were no exceptions. Big talker though he was, he also listened. He had an insatiable curiosity about his fellow beings and women liked to confide in him.

It was at Molly Skinner's that D. H. Lawrence and his wife, Frieda, stayed a week or so in 1922 when they were on their way to Sydney. I don't think father saw them but it wasn't too long after the Lawrences left Western Australia that he told stories about them. Apparently Katherine Susannah Prichard who had lived in England just before the war and was probably the first Australian to have read Lawrence, was the only person in Western Australia who knew that Lawrence was a really great writer. And Molly Skinner who was later to enjoy the collaboration of Lawrence in her novel *The Boy in the Bush* thought him to be a marvellous person as well as a great author. My father accepted everything she said without hesitation. He had a great regard for Molly Skinner who had once been a midwife in the slums of London. So had my mother been a midwife, and once father took her to the guest house so that they could talk, about midwifery presumably. I wasn't there on that occasion.

Of course Lawrence didn't and couldn't mean anything to our circle. One of our friends however did hear that Lawrence wrote love stories 'with a bit of paprika' as erotic tales were delicately, and in hushed tones, described by the more knowing. This friend had learnt this from a Mr Cohen who had stayed at Molly Skinner's at the same time as Lawrence and had read one of his books.

Many years were to pass before I read Lawrence or Katherine Susannah Prichard for that matter. We shifted to Perth and I went to Christian Brothers where all the literary talk was about Cardinal Newman and Francis Thompson. I learnt 'The Hound of Heaven', not that I was encouraged to recite it in class. I felt that my teacher, an elderly Brother, didn't think it quite appropriate for a Jew boy to be spouting such a holy Christian poem. Be that as it may, I did shine as Shylock. We were forever doing *The Merchant of Venice,* writing about it or performing the play. The elderly Brother teacher always said: 'Waten, you'll be Shylock'. And so I was. Now and again I felt as Shylock did when Antonia insulted him, especially when the Brother led the laughter after I had pronounced some words with a Russian-Yiddish accent.

I liked Francis Thompson well enough, but I liked Shelley and Byron more and secretly I read Swinburne who was considered rather naughty by our Brother teacher and not suitable for growing boys. I was also reading Dickens who touched me like a poet. So did Hugo.

My reading was not all literature and highmindedness. I would furtively buy the *Gem* and *Magnet* and read them in my bedroom. I also read several bestsellers and I had a feast of Poe and Conan Doyle.

Virtue certainly had its reward then; it sold well. Two virtuous novels that I remember were A. S. M. Hutchinson's *If Winter Comes* and *Simon Called Peter*, by Robert Keable. The heroes in both books were searching for answers to their own problems and those of postwar mankind generally. In *If Winter Comes*, the hero declared that he had 'got the key to the puzzle that had been puzzling me all my life . . . Here it is: God — is love.'

Simon called Peter, after a lot of soul-searching and acute woman trouble, came up with approximately the same explanation of everything. He got his revelation on a Sunday morning at breakfast time in Westminster Cathedral where he had gone for a breather before returning to his mistress's bed in the Piccadilly Hotel. The lofty words at the end of the novel were used in the subsequent play that it evoked. My view of this and the other novel was best expressed by the drama critic of the play who went into verse:

> The dowagers wept in the stalls,
> And I really can't see
> Why the man next to me
> Repeatedly said it was balls.

When we left West Australia and settled in Melbourne at the end of 1925 a new world opened up to me. I discovered George Bernard Shaw and he beguiled me with his humour and although different from Sholem Aleichem, he brought back my childhood days when literature meant laughter. I also found at Coles Book Arcade and Fykes books, the Haldeman-Julius little paperbacked blue books which introduced me to the European classics, although in a condensed form — some of the blue books hardly being more than 70 pages. I became familiar with Molière, Voltaire, Schiller, Goethe, Ibsen, Strindberg, and Gorky, all edited by Mr E. Haldeman-Julius in Kansas City.

Somewhere about that time I began a Marxist diet, reading Marx, Engels and Lenin and socialist novelists and poets. Jack London became my favourite fiction writer. The Californian hobo, the participant in Coxey's march on Washington and the admirer of Marx's *Communist Manifesto* was a good example to follow.

He was in my mind when I took part in a free speech fight which resulted in my doing seven days in Pentridge, my first taste of prison. The day before I was arrested an old left-wing said to me, 'If you get nabbed put up your age and you won't get bunged in with the young fellows. They'll do you in all ways — belt you and root you. But in with the older ones there'll always be an oldie that'll sympathize with you and keep an eye on you.'

I did as he advised and I was placed in the section that housed the long-termers, as there was no empty cells anywhere else in the jail.

In the shower house several prisoners asked me what I was in for and I said I was in a free-speech fight. Well, what did you get out of it? I didn't understand what they meant. When I explained the defence of the principle of free speech they dismissed me as a simpleton, a nut in a word. The place was overrun with nuts: another harmless nut was neither here nor there.

One man did understand. He was an eminent smash and grab artist doing ten years for seizing jewellery from a posh shop in the heart of Melbourne, and he was a highly respected inmate of Pentridge — respected for all kinds of reasons, above all, his knowledge of the law, his ability to provide grounds for appeal, the complete bush lawyer he was. He said to me 'I was a rebel once but nothing'll ever happen in Australia. Forget it boy.'

Every day he spent hours writing his memoirs. He said to me 'When this book sees the light of day many politicians, policemen and pimps will flee the country.'

He left several chapters in my cell when I was out in one of the yards breaking stones which was a busy prison occupation in Pentridge. His memoirs weren't all that revealing but I thought they were good and I promised to talk to the editors of several radical publications about his work in progress.

But as soon as I left jail I promptly forgot about him, immediately caught up in my affairs, not understanding how cruel I was to him. I was still reading Jack London when I decided to go to Sydney and I stowed away on a passenger ship, sleeping and eating in the fo'c's'le with the stokers, greasers and trimmers. I changed bunks every four hours: when the watch came off I went into the unoccupied bunk of one of the men going on the next watch.

As well as Jack London's *The People of the Abyss* I also had with me Marx's *Communist Manifesto*, *The Autobiography of a Super-Tramp* by W. H. Davies, and Oscar Wilde's *The Soul of Man Under Socialism:* when one of the stokers caught sight of the booklet he laughed loudly and recited an obscene limerick about the poet-playwright. He called to other stokers that I was reading Oscar Wilde and there was more laughter and dirty jokes. One elderly trimmer lying in his bunk said I had pink girlie hands and they certainly looked like that in company where hands were larger, even those of small men. The old lad went on tormenting me. He said my dad must have thrown me out and in a croaking voice he sang an old IWW song:

> Where is my wandering boy tonight?
> The boy of his mother's pride?
> He's counting the ties with his bed on his back
> Or else he's bumming a ride . . .

That was in fact just what I had done — bummed a ride. It was a difficult situation but my ingenuousness rose to the occasion. I was not a homosexual but how did one go about proving that in the fo'c's'le. The innuendo in itself didn't upset me but somehow I understood that homosexuality could stir their feelings, that in a strange way it mattered to them, and that the good humour could take an ugly turn. So to their surprise I set about defending Oscar Wilde. The great writer had been framed because he believed in socialism and because he'd been one of the few English writers to plead for clemency for the Haymarket martyrs.

Did they know that? I asked. No, they didn't. Just as I thought, I said. Wilde was defamed just like all rebels were defamed, framed and jailed. I then read out bits from *The Soul of Man Under Socialism* which must have impressed them as the dirty jokes and the innuendo stopped. When I finished I gave the booklet to the ship's delegate or shop steward, and asked him to read the lot and tell his fellow-workers whether there was anything objectionable in it.

After that there was no more talk about my girlie pink hands. If there was one human being they respected in that fo'c's'le it was a rebel.

But just as we were about to enter Sydney Harbour the old persecutor, pretending not to look at me, sang another IWW song, this time about the girl who gives way to the temptation of a procuress and sells herself:

> Girls in this way, fall every day . . .
> Who is to blame? You know his name,
> It's the boss that pays starvation wages.
> A homeless girl can always hear
> Temptations calling everywhere.

In the Mitchell Library I met an old poet named Pat Michaels who had known Henry Lawson and had been at his funeral, the biggest Australia has given a writer. Old Pat was a bit of a derelict who lived in a doss-house behind the Town Hall. He took me to a wine saloon where supposedly I would meet other poets and writers. The great Christopher Brennan came often, he said.

There were no poets or writers in the saloon, only drunken men and women. If there were any literary people around he didn't introduce me to them. Pat Michaels bought two three-pennorth darks and ran out of money.

'Have you got the price on you?' he asked me and I said yes. I had a pound which was more than plenty as he only drank the three-pennorth dark. He persuaded me to have some too. The only time I'd ever taken liquor was on a Passover night and then only a couple of thimblesful.

I didn't like the bilious sweet taste of the wine but I swallowed the liquid manfully, watching Pat Michaels all the time and listening to his words which became more and more portentous. For every glass I drank, he drank four or five.

'So you want to be a writer, young fellow? he suddenly said.

Then he fell into a kind of silent reverie. Then he muttered into my face, 'Don't.'

'I've always wanted to.'

'It's an awful business, writing. Don't for Christ's sake. Nothing comes of it.'

He looked down to the floor, his lower lip drawn up as if the wine in front of him had become sour, and he began to cry, tears running down his nose.

'I did nothing. Nothing. Just a mediocrity. And that's what most writers are — mediocrities.'

'I'll give it a go.' I said.

He had stopped crying and stared at me, as though studying me or maybe it was just alcoholic vacuity.

'Well give it a go, young fellow. You'll find out you're only a mediocrity. You just think of this: for all the hundreds of writers there are, how many write books that live a day after they come off the press?'

With gloomy words in my head I returned to Melbourne and I began my first novel which I called *Hunger*. Not an original title, considering that Knut Hamsun's novel *Hunger* was very much around then. Everything went into it — the unemployed, stowing away and jumping trains, gaol, burglars, religion and Communism. Not everything of course. Thee was nothing about my migrant background nor was there anything about sex. Perhaps the *Kreutzer Sonata* had got into me.

I was then eighteen.

B. WONGAR

Bralgu

Nganug the paddle-maker
ferries the dead
far across sea
to land of *yuln*

The canoe will be around
on time to fetch the last man
of the last tribe.

When Nganug dies
who will ferry him?

The Drought

When dry, all trees, spinifex
waterholes and flying foxes
sleep anonymously
as do *tamus,* the tribal spirits.

The day the drought strangled the country
pungals, the whites, noosed a cloud
to drag poor fellow away.

When hibernating
trees, spinifex, flying foxes and *tamus*
do not chant for *kapi,* the rain
— the fear of *pungals*
outgrows thirst.

The Legend

On bright side of the Moon
Man shapes a boomerang
With piece of flint.

On the side of the Moon
Old woman bakes *nyuma*
Damper from grass seeds

On the Moon, a swarm of ants
Charmed by scent of honey
Gather nectar in their humps

On dark side of the Moon
Shielded by huge boulder
Sits thorny lizard Niari
Our totem ancestor
Who made the world.

$U_3 O_8$

No man held kind words closer to his heart than Bungawa of Gunwin tribe, or so it was said. When the whites reached his country and began grabbing at the rocks no angry words were heard nor curses chanted. The spiritual ancestors who created the country for tribal man in the Dreaming, but now long gone to Bralgu, land of the dead, must have felt the same way. None of them came to trouble the minds of the tribal elders and it looked as though, wherever the whites were keen to dig and grind the rocks, no harm would come to the black man and his spirits.

Bungawa found it hard to grasp why anyone would bother with the rocks — boulders had no taste and only patches of lichen grew on them. A paper brought to him to sign hardly told him anything; it referred to rocks and $U_3 O_8$, a formula he had never heard of before and which undoubtedly had no tribal importance — the 'U' was too bent to symbolize a boomerang, and the 'O', though it was the shape of the egg of the totemic serpent, appeared to be too small to have any spiritual significance. As for the numbers — he could find nothing like them in the tribal world. Bungawa placed his thumb on the place marked 'signature' at the bottom of the paper. 'The whites have strange rituals', he told the people later, and however strange the arrangement sounded, he appealed to every tribal soul to respect it.

Much later, Bungawa learnt that $U_3 O_8$ is commonly called yellow cake. If it had not been for his standing as a wise old man the news would have set him laughing, but instead he wondered how the rocks would taste when ground into dust and baked to make a yellow cake.

Though personal tastes differ as much as the colour of the human skin, he was wise enough to know than a man eats only what his stomach can manage.

Tasteless and tough as the rocks were, they were not given away for nothing — when the whites came to take them they brought bags of tea and boxes of biscuits, and each tribal elder received a packet of tobacco and a steel axe. Bungawa, presented with a stainless steel pipe and a bottle of rum, felt that however odd the tastes of the whites might seem, trading with them could be pleasant. The mountains at Gunwin were large enough to last for years, but should the country run out of boulders, Bungawa would gather the elders, clap two wooden sticks together, blow the *didjeridu* and chant for the ancestors to come and make new hills again. At the end when the whites no longer needed the yellow cake, the chanting would be needed again to bring back the trees and the scrub to the bared earth — the scars on the land would heal quickly.

Bungawa went on a trip around the world carrying a dilly bag full of rocks, hoping to whet the white man's appetite. The tribal country he left behind lay under a cloud of dust too leaden for even the monsoon wind to carry it away. Little was heard and less seen of Gunwin for years, but it was always thought that, however thick the hanging dust cloud might be, it would eventually fall back onto the tribal ground and the ancestors would be there to see that the bush grew up again.

Even though hopes remained sky high, the tribal country never greened again. From the settling dust rose hills of mining waste, bare and dry. Bungawa wandered among them blowing his *didjeridu* now and then to gather the tribal elders to join him with their clapping sticks and chanting; but no one came. With the going of the bush, man had departed too. The new shape of the country was no place even for a fly.

Instead of the spirit world of Bralgu, the blowing of the *didjeridu* reached the white man's world — Bungawa received a flood of telegrams wishing his country a speedy recovery; the bells of Canterbury Cathedral rang for a whole week; Ayatollas sent their prayers too, and Stravinsky was commissioned to dedicate a concerto to the tribal cause. The effort achieved nothing — little patches of lichen grew here and there on the crushed boulders, but the leaves never came again. The country remained dry and dead and Bungawa knew, that if even an ant happened to appear there, it would be drowned in a sea of dust.

The Defectors

A rumour spread that Emu and Kangaroo had defected from the Australian emblem on the dollar note; with it came the fear that whole continent, after two centuries of progress, was about to be plunged back into the Stone Age.

The writing was on the wall, in fact — trading in uranium shares was suddenly suspended, the Seventh Fleet was put on red alert and Mohammed Ali cancelled all engagements. The defectors were spotted by the beady eye of a satellite as they headed across the desert country towards the deep north. Both were dressed ceremonially, the bodies smeared with *malnar*, red ochre, and sacred totemic designs covered every inch of their brown skin. The fugitives were thought to be travelling under their tribal names: Takipir, Emu-Man and Malu, Kangaroo-Man, from the Arta and Pitjantra tribes.

A warrant for their arrest was issued, and a number of RSPCA officers, vocal in the animal liberation movement were put under security surveillance. Files were opened on all marsupials and aliens in the country. The CIA and Interpol were called in to assist. The crisis snowballed into an international event — politicians instigated a move for banning animal gatherings, festivals and puppet shows.

There was a sudden upsurge in trading in wild game, fur and feathers, although nuclear reactors all over the world were on strike, due to the lack of high quality uranium *australis*.

Clouds of leaflets were dropped over the outback country of scrub and spinifex. The message appealed to the two defectors to give themselves up and save the world. The authorities recognized their strange spiritual associations with local tribes and noted that both the Arta and the Pitjantra, whose totem they were, had departed, leaving the white man as custodian of their land.

When captured, Emu and Kangaroo were suffering from a strange kind of gastroenteritis, which they had most likely caught by drinking from contaminated water-holes and eating dry spinifex. A trial was speedily set in action to deal with their case, but it seemed, for a time at least, that the defectors would return to their old post, despite their discontented, sick appearance. Their lawyers argued that Takipir and Malu had been in chains for nearly a century, kept in captivity in contravention of the *Abolition of Slavery Act* of 1833. The court found that had they been informed of that piece of humanitarian legislation, Emu and Kangaroo would have gone long ago. Their tribal relatives, whether human, animal or spirit-shaped, had long vanished; the spinifex country where they once lived had been contaminated for years and was not even safe for a fly.

As the affair drew to a close, the defectors returned to the dollar note; the only safe place the country could provide. On the national emblem below them, 1833 was inserted in invisible ink; but, even had the appropriate year been made visible it would still have been no help — the Arta and the Pitjantra never knew how to read, and could not have understood the sign should they happen to see it from the land of the dead. As for the white man, he reads only what pleases him.

SPIRO ZAVOS

Elvis is Dead

'Elvis is dead.'

Frank Gordon looked up from his newspaper uncomprehendingly. He'd been trying to work out what the latest series of proposals on Rhodesia meant. 'Elvis who?' he asked.

'Elvis,' said Sharon Archer emphatically. For once she was not buffing her nails, and then holding them up in the light in a way that infuriated Frank.

'Oh, Elvis'.

It was ten o'clock in the morning. The newsroom was almost empty. No gaggle of journalists sat behind their green-top desks fingering away at their typewriters. The *Clarion* was a morning newspaper and the journalists working on it tended to drift into work sometime after midday in much the same haphazard manner as sheets of newspaper being blown along an empty street. Only literary people were on the job. Frank, an editorial writer; Sharon; George Roberts, a feature writer; and Jack Mason, a columnist. The fluorescent lights, set into the ceiling, blazed down on a room as quiet as a mortuary.

'Yes, dear old Elvis,' Sharon repeated quietly, as if to herself.

'He'd been overweight for years,' Jack said. 'You know how preachers and parsons have called his stuff the devil's music for years, well,' he continued, smiling in anticipation of his punchline, 'if they're right, it'll be a case of the fat's in the fire.'

Frank did not want to hear the further development of a column. He turned away from Sharon and George and stared out the city building. The long, wide street it was on ran down to the wharves. Behind the cranes and the tops of sheds rose the sharp-edged lines of Mount Victoria.

In the street immediately below him, Frank saw a man step out onto the pavement and then jump back quickly as a car came unexpectedly around the corner. The driver shook his fist and roared on towards the Town Hall. The pedestrian looked around in a startled manner and then ran across the road and down the street.

If the car had knocked the man down, Frank knew he would not have been bothered for even a second. The man meant as much to him as a fly on the window pane. He didn't know him, so he didn't care about him. The day Kennedy was killed a bus overturned somewhere in South America, he remembered, and he and all the millions mourning for one man did not give this larger tragedy a second thought.

Suddenly he felt sick. His stomach dry-retched. His head was dizzy. He was gasping for air the way he used to years ago when he was an altar boy. It was as if a solid block of hot air were being pressed on every part of his body. His hair felt lank and sweaty. Beads of perspiration ran down his brow.

Elvis was dead.

'He never had a sense of timing or of time.' George was saying. He had a cigarette dangling from his bottom lip, a roll-your-own, and he was peering at the white copy paper in his typewriter carriage. He pecked several words and looked up. 'He's proved it, hasn't he?'

'What do you mean,' said Frank unsuccessfully keeping truculence out of his reply.

'Keeled over in the Tele's time. It'll be a front-page story for them. We'll get what crumbs are left, if we're lucky. They'll make a feast of it. The pickings will be meagre by the time we get to have a crack at the story. Elvis assailed our ears all his life, the least he could have done was to die after midday and let us have a big story for a change. Damn bad timing, I'd say.'

Annoyed at this light-heartedness, Frank passed up making a reply and continuing the conversation. He walked across to the telex basket. There on the top of the overseas cables was a short message:

'Memphis, Tennessee, August 16, Elvis Presley, the Mississipi boy whose country rock music guitar and gyrating hips launched a new style in popular music, died today at Baptist Hospital. He was 42, and a multi-millionaire. More to follow.'

Frank threw the message into the basket. His mind went back to his last year at school. He had been dragooned into organizing the school ball. One night, just before chapel, he had taken the list of the dances he had worked out to the Rector for his approval.

The study smelled of apples and tobacco. Black-cassocked, stern-faced, the Rector let his glasses slide down his ample nose as he read through the list. His fingers were darkly stained on the inside with nicotine. His hand shook slightly. Shouldn't you have the gay gordons before the valetta and the fox-trot?' he asked. 'You want people to relax and enjoy themselves. The gay gordons are just right for that sort of thing.'

Frank nodded in agreement. He waited for the Rector to read the dances on the other side of the paper. The Rector turned the page. A dark scowl came across his face. The scowl persisted for some time. Frank heard the shuffle of boys' feet as they marched up to chapel. The clock in the study struck seven loudly. The Rector looked at

Frank. Even though he was only 17, Frank knew that with the Rector he was the closest he would come to meeting a great man. The Rector had been a champion cricketer bowling legbreaks and googlies with all the flair of a Benaud. He was a gifted linguist: French, German, Greek, Latin: the language did not seem to matter. Currently he was coaching cricket, taking all the senior boys for languages, and working into the night trying to raise the thousands of dollars needed to build a new chapel for the school, as well as carrrying out all the functions of a headmaster. Within six months, he would be dead from cancer. Now he stared at Frank. He had a concentrated look that had the power to freeze a person, the way a snake mesmerizes its victims. 'Rock and roll', the Rector said.

'I thought perhaps . . .'

'Rock and roll.'

Frank mustered as much resolution as he could. 'It's the in thing, Father.'

'It's low grade, debasing, immoral and unmanly. People dancing like dervishes. The rhythms of the jungle at the school ball. With nuns and parents present? You must be out of your mind.'

'I thought it would make a bit of a change.' Frank said timidly. Why did the Rector terrify him so much?

'A bit of a change.' The Rector raised his eyebrows in mock amazement. He lit a cigarette, pulled on it hard, snorted out smoke and coughed viciously for some moments. 'Two years ago' he went on, when the coughing spasms had subsided, we had that business of people not rubbing the polish off their shoes and smudging the girls' dresses. The nuns are still furious about that. Last year some of you people wanted to invite non-Catholic girls. Girls from Marsden, I believe. Now you want to dance rock and roll. A bit of a change, you say. The next request will be for the lights to be turned down, that sort of thing. The rot's got to stop somewhere, and it stops at rock and roll.'

The Rector handed the list to Frank. 'Cross off the rock and roll. I won't have it. Put the gay gordons first. And now go up to chapel, you'll probably need all the prayers you can get.'

By the time Frank reached the study door, the Rector was already correcting an exercise book.

Something came over Frank at the ball. In the fox-trot before supper, he walked up to Miss O'Sullivan, the dancing teacher, and asked if he could dance with her. Miss O'Sullivan made an extravagant bow of thanks. They stood hand-in-hand waiting for the music to start. When it did, Frank pushed her away from him, twirled her around the way he'd seen in the Elvis Presley movies. 'Frank, said Miss O'Sullivan, flustered, 'I don't understand.'

Grim-faced, Frank took her hand and pushed her away again. He did a turn himself. 'Rock and roll, Miss O'Sullivan. Pretend the music is 'Heartbreak Hotel.' He pushed her away again. This time she twirled herself, her skirt swirling out like a suddenly-opened umbrella, and she came back to Frank. Frank took her hand, passed it round his back and the both of them spun away from each other.

Up on the stage, in a red-backed chair, sitting with the Archbishop on one side, Mother Superior on the other, and the committee ladies and their husbands further down the line, the Rector watched with mounting horror. When the amazing spectacle began, he tried to pretend it wasn't happening. He leant across to the Archbishop and asked him how his golf was coming along. 'Single figure handicap yet, your Grace?' he murmured nervously. The spectacle continued. The Rector leant past Mother Superior and asked one of the committe ladies if supper was ready. 'Perhaps we should think about putting it on as soon as possible, Mrs Fitzgerald.' Out of the corner of his eye, the Rector could see the boy continuing with his crazy antics, obviously embarrassing poor Miss O'Sullivan, something that was unforgivable. What would the mothers and young girls being pushed around the floor by stiff-legged boys think about what was going on? going on?

The Rector made a decision. He marched from the podium and seized Frank by the ear. Twisting it sharply, he pushed the cringing boy towards the door. 'Report to me tomorrow.' he said and the door slammed on Frank. Outside, Frank roared into the night, 'Long live Elvis, the king' and marched off to the dormitory.

Frank was caned the next day. The next year, every dance was a rock and roll one.

By then Frank was at university. He remembered now a party in an old house not far from the campus. In the front room all you could see were bobbing heads of people of people rock and rolling. A stack of Elvis records stood beside the record player. The host, a fat young man doing law, was smitten with the latest hit single. 'One Night With You,' and played it time after time.

Frank went across to a slightly built young woman sitting in an armchair. 'Dance?' he asked.

'You needn't be so nervous,' she replied. She gripped his hand and gave it a squeeze.

They danced all night. It was perfect. How unlikely this had been: only some hours before as he cautiously shaved trying not to cut off the pimples that blossomed on his cheeks. They threw back their heads and shouted out the words to the song, affecting Presley's southern drawl: 'Won nite with yu-hu . . .' She was so light in his arms. At the end of the song, while the sweating host flicked the record player arm back again, they hugged each other, hearts beating. Later that evening, at her flat, they had gone to bed. It was Frank's first time. When it was over, he remembered something: 'What's your name?' he asked, stroking the flat white belly of the girl lying beside him.

'Louise. Louise Barton.' She took his hand and moved it to her breasts.

The next week he missed his weekly confession for the first time.

He dialled the familiar numbers. 'Elvis is dead,' Elvis is dead,' he told the woman who answered the phone. There was a silence. 'I reckon,' Frank went on, 'we should have an early dinner and watch the TV specials. How about that?'

'I'm going out Frank.'

'You never told me, Louise.'

'Since when do I have to tell you I'm going out Frank? I don't belong to you.'

'But you are married. And to me. Where are you going?'

'Out, Frank, out.'

'With some stud, I suppose?'

'Frank, don't shout at me. I don't have to put up with that sort of shit. I'm going out, where and with whom is my concern only. Now I'm hanging up because I'm running late.'

'Louise, don't you remember that night we rock and rolled to those Elvis records? And then we went back to your flat?' But she had hung up before he had finished the last question.

A tall, leggy fair-haired young woman came into the newsroom. She was straight-backed, flat-stomached and gleaming eyed. 'Elvis is dead.' Frank said as she strode acros to the coffee machine. 'They reckon that people are going to the record shops and crying their eyes out.'

'Who'd want to cry about that fat slob? He was over the hill,' the lovely young woman said.

NIHAT ZIYALAN

Pigeon Flight

(translated from Turkish by Gün Gencer)

when the pigeon leaves the nest
when it pitches to fly
who can have anything but a heart throb,
its rising is white
flapping the sky
hope, hope for tomorrow

crows want to crow this flight
want to smear it in crow
this white
this tomorrow

I let the crow be the guide, it packed and went away
I kept the sky.
I gave a glimmer to the pigeons with their flight of poets
I gave a glimmer from my heart
for those tired to perch on

smoke expects the fire
It doesn't choke
anyway, it's unheard of for the fire to be late.
smoke, on the wing of a pigeon
reaches the sun
the sun that blooms in our open arms.

Poem of Missing Home

(translated from Turkish by Gün Gencer)

I stood on one side of the Bosphorous
and said to the other side:
'I'm in a hurry'
it stepped close to look into my eyes
never asked 'who are you' or 'where to'
but said:
'The fire within you
burns me too'
and joined in.

I did not run
I became a sword
stuck at the doors of the ones I love
opening their doors
they looked into my eyes
I don't know what they saw
they stood back
from my fire
my fire, head up and feet bare

you, the reader of this poem
when you look up the sky
I'm in that cloud you see
I got flying
I haven't rained anywhere else
I'm over my country now
not in tears
but a flying face
feeling the smell
of my mother, my father and my son
feeling the smell of my land
and to feel that smell
I will rain, will rain, and rain.

Acknowledgments

WALTER ADAMSON 'Five Minutes' first published in *Luna* and reprinted with permission of the author. 'Pietro' and 'Laughter and Tears' published with permission of the author.
ALMA ALDRETTE 'The Black Skirt' published with permission of the author.
GARY CATALANO Four poems from *Remembering the Rural Life* reprinted with permission of the author and University of Queensland Press, St Lucia.
MARIANO CORENO Three poems from *Yellow Sun* reprinted with permission of the author and Saturday Centre Books.
JACK DAVIS Three poems from *Jagardoo*, reprinted with permission of the author and Methuen Australia Pty Ltd.
MARGARET DIESENDORF 'Reading Akhmatova' and 'Woman Alone' published with permission of the author. 'From Exile' first published in *Quadrant*. 'The Escape' first published in *SCOPP*.
JOHN J. ENCARNAÇAO 'Coming of Age in Australia' and 'Football Like She is Played' published with permission of the author.
SILVANA GARDNER Three poems from *When Sunday Comes* reprinted with permission of the author and University of Queensland Press, St Lucia.
GÜN GENCER 'Mekong' and 'Killer Prayers' published with permission of the author.
KEVIN GILBERT Two poems from *People Are Legends* reprinted with permission of the author and University of Queensland Press, St Lucia.
LOLÓ HOUBEIN 'Fighting For Peace' from *Everything Is Real* reprinted with permission of the author and Phoenix Publications, Brisbane.
JURGIS JANAVICIUS Three poems from *Journey To the Moon* reprinted with permission of the author and Poetry & Prose Publications, Canberra.
MANFRED JURGENSEN 'object lesson', 'bonegilla 1961' and 'ethnic food' published with permission of the author.
VASSO KALAMARAS 'Mademoiselle' from *Other Earth* reprinted with permission of the author and Fremantle Arts Centre Press. 'A Christmas Gift' published with permission of the author.
ANTIGONE KEFALA 'Parish Church', 'The Old Palace' and 'Family' published with permission of the author.
STEPHEN KELEN 'The Intruders' published with permission of the author.
RUDI KRAUSMANN 'The Art Critic' and 'The Poem' reprinted from *Aspect* and published with permission of the author.
YOTA KRILI-KEVANS 'On the Other Side' reprinted from *Education*. 'Migratory

Birds' and 'To the Adopted Mother' reprinted from *To Yofiri* and published with permission of the author.
MARIA LEWITT 'Refugee 1944' first published in *Fin Magazine*, 1975 and reprinted with permission of the author.
SERGE LIBERMAN 'Envy's Fire' reprinted from *A Universe of Clowns* and published with permission of the author and Phoenix Publications, Brisbane.
UYEN LOEWALD 'Nightmare' first published in *Outrider* and reprinted with permission of the author.
ANGELO LOUKAKIS 'Being Here Now', first published in the *Bulletin*, 1983 and reprinted with permission of the author.
DAVID MARTIN 'The Turkish Girl' reprinted from *Foreigners* and published with permission of the author and Rigby. 'Letter to a Friend in Israel' and 'Gordon Childe' reprinted from *The Gift* and published with permission of the author and Jacaranda Press.
FRANCO PAISIO 'Autobiography', 'Under the Sun' and 'The Enemy' first published in *Aspect* and reprinted with permission of the author.
LILIANA RYDZYNSKI 'Greece in Winter' published with permission of the author. 'The Husband', 'The Polish Sculptor' and 'The Father' from *Celebration* reprinted with permission of the author and Saturday Centre Books.
BARBARA SCHENKEL 'The Anniversary' reprinted from *Ethnic Australia* with permission of the author. 'The Site of Jericho', 'Judea' and 'Olive Trees' from *Israel — Impressions of a Journey*, first published by the Australian Friends of Tel-Aviv University (Melbourne, 1981), reprinted with permission of the author.
PETER SKRZYNECKI 'Going to the Pictures' and 'Migrant Centre Site' published with permission of the author. 'Hunting Rabbits' first published in *Quadrant* and 'Going to the Pictures' in *Southerly*.
TAD SOBOLEWSKI 'Free As a Bird' from *The Perfume of Patou*, published privately and reprinted with permission of the author.
TUTAMA TJAPANGARTI Translated by Paul Bruno Tjampitjinpa and Billy Marshall-Stoneking. Reprinted with permission of the author and Billy Marshall-Stoneking.
DIMITRIS TSALOUMAS Four poems from *The Observatory* reprinted with permission of the author and University of Queensland Press, St Lucia.
VICKI VIIDIKAS 'The Relationship' from *Wrappings* reprinted with permission of the author and Wild & Woolley, 1974. 'Darjeeling' and 'To My Father, Viidikas' from *Knäbel*, reprinted with permission of the author and Wild & Woolley.
CORNELIS VLEESKENS 'At Every Step' and 'Street Talk' published with permission of the author.
KATH WALKER Four poems from *We Are Going* and *The Dawn Is at Hand* reprinted with permission of the author and the Jacaranda Press.
ANIA WALWICZ 'europe' published with permission of the author. 'stories my mother told me' first published in *Migrant 7* and reprinted with permission of the author.
JUDAH WATEN 'A Writer's Youth' first published in the *Bulletin* and reprinted with permission of the author.
B. WONGAR Poems and short stories published with permission of the author.
SPIRO ZAVOS 'Elvis Is Dead' from *Faith of Our Fathers* reprinted with permission of University of Queensland Press, St Lucia, and the author.
NIHAT ZIYALAN 'Pigeon Flight' and 'Poem of Missing Home' translated by Gün Gencer and reprinted with permission of the author.

Biographical Notes

WALTER ADAMSON Born and educated in Germany. Arrived in Australia in 1938. Has written novels, short stories, poems, articles. Past president of Victorian Branch of the Australian Goethe Society. Held a Fellowship from the Literature Board in 1978-79. Co-ordinator of German Travelling Book Exhibition 'Books on the Move' in Australia in 1981.

ALMA ALDRETTE Born in USA, of Mexican origin. Has lived in Adelaide since 1977. Writer of poetry, short stories and articles. Student of anthropology, history of Japan/China and Japanese literature of Adelaide University. Holds an Associate Diploma in Aboriginal Studies. At present in Nepal.

GARY CATALANO Of Italian and Australian parents. Born in Brisbane in 1947. Educated at Trinity Grammar School, Sydney. Left school in 1963 and has worked at a variety of jobs. In recent years he has become known as an art critic. Published books include *Remembering the Rural Life* (UQP), 1978), *Heaven of Rags* (Hale & Iremonger, 1982) and *An Intimate Australia* (Hale & Iremonger, 1985).

MARIANO CORENO Lived in Italy until 1956. Poet who occasionally writes for Italian newspapers. Has published two volumes of poetry in Italian, *Sotto La Luna* (Giuseppe Lucente Editore, Cosenza, 1965) and *Vento Al Sole* (Gastaldi Editore, Milano, 1968). Also one collection in English, *Yellow Sun* (Saturday Centre, Sydney, 1980).

JACK DAVIS Aborigine of the Bibbulmun tribe. His first collection of poems, *The Firstborn,* was published in 1970 and won acclaim in Australia and England. Has travelled widely, representing the Australian Aborigine and giving poetry readings. In 1976 he was awarded the British Empire medal. He lives in Perth, Western Australia. A second collection of poems, *Jagardoo,* was published in 1978 (Methuen).

MARGARET DIESENDORF Born and educated in Vienna. Sydney poet, translator and freelance writer, working in English, French and German. Was Associate Editor of *Poetry Australia* and of *Creative Movement* (Sumter, SC, USA) until 1981. Widely published in Australia and overseas. Has taught in various writing schools and published her collection in English, *Light,* in 1981 (Edwards & Shaw).

JOHN J. ENCARNAÇÃO Born in 1940 in East Timor. Of Portuguese origin. Arrived in Australia in 1942. Works in NSW Public Service. Poet and short story writer whose work has appeared in newspapers and magazines. Published collection, *East Timor Poems,* privately in 1979.

SILVANA GARDNER Born in Zara, Dalmatia. Arrived in Australia in 1952. Poet and

artist who graduated in Fine Arts and English Literature from the University of Queensland. Her art-work is represented in many galleries in Australia, Canada and USA. Has published three collections of poems: *Hacedor* (Planet Press, 1980), *When Sunday Comes* (UQP, 1982) and *With Open Eyes* (Queensland Community Press, 1983).
GÜN GENCER Born in 1944 in Antioch, Turkey. Graduated as an architect in 1965 from the Middle East Technical University in Ankara. Playwright and poet whose work has been produced in theatre festivals in France and Turkey. Graduated from NIDA in 1976. Works as a public servant with the NSW State government; also on subtitling for Channel O/28.
KEVIN GILBERT Born at Condobolin, NSW, in 1933. In 1957 he was sentenced to life imprisonment for murder. While in prison he began writing and, with *The Cherry Pickers*, became the first Aboriginal playwright. His poems were also published in a limited edition. After fourteen and a half years he was released and wrote *Because a White Man'll Never Do It*. He followed this with *Living Black* and *People Are Legends* (UQP, 1978).
LOLÓ HOUBEIN Born in Holland in 1934. She regards her childhood during the Depression and war years as a binding influence on her further life. Arrived in Australia in 1958. Lives in the Adelaide Hills. Poet and short story writer whose work appears in magazines and anthologies. In 1983 she compiled a bibliography, *Ethnic Writings in English in Australia* (Uni. of Adelaide, Dept of English). Her collection of short stories entitled *Everything Is Real* was published by Phoenix Publications in 1984.
JURGIS JANAVICIUS Born in 1926 in Lithuania. Arrived in Australia, in 1948. Editor and co-publisher of the 'Poetry and Prose Broadsheet', 1969-73. Contributing poetry and prose writing to magazines and anthologies in Australia since 1968. Published a volume of verse, *Journey to the Moon* (Poetry and Prose Publications, 1971).
MANFRED JURGENSEN Born in 1940, of German-Danish descent. Arrived in Australia in 1961. Holds an MA from Melbourne University and a PhD from Zurich University. Professor of German, University of Queensland. Poet, novelist and literary critic. Has published several books in Australia and overseas. Most recent book of poetry, *The Skin Trade* (Phoenix Publications, 1983). Edited *Ethnic Australia* (Phoenix Publications, 1981).
VASSO KALAMARAS Born and educated in Athens. Came to Australia in 1951. Poet and short story writer. Returned with her family to Greece in 1960. Studied drama at the School of National Theatre. Returned to Western Australia and now lives there. Holds an Associateship in Fine Arts from the Western Australian Institute of Technology. Received Literature Board grants in 1976 and 1977. Has published a bilingual poetry collection and a bilingual collection of short stories, *Other Earth* (Fremantle Arts Centre Press, 1977).
ANTIGONE KEFALA Of Greek/Roumanian origin. Poet and writer of novellas. Holds a BA and MA from the Victoria University of Wellington, New Zealand. Publications include *The Alien* (Makar Press, 1973); *The First Journey* (Wild & Woolley, 1975), *Thirsty Weather* (Outback Press, 1978) and *The Island* (Hale & Iremonger, 1984). She lives in Sydney and works for the Australia Council.
STEPHEN KELEN Born in Budapest, Hungary, in 1912. Educated in Budapest and Prague Universities. Served in the Australian Army and as a member of the British Commonwealth Occupation Forces in Japan. Novelist playwright and short story writer. Author of several books, including *I Remember Hiroshima* (Hale & Iremonger, 1983). Since 1975 he has been President of International PEN, Sydney Centre.
RUDI KRAUSMANN Born in 1933 in Austria. Poet, playwright and prose writer. Editor of *Aspect* (art and literature) and several books, including *Flowers of Emptiness* (Hale & Iremonger, 1982). His play *Everyman* has been produced by the Nimrod Theatre and another *The Leader* was broadcast by the ABC (Radio Helicon, 1980). He now lives in Sydney.
YOTA KRILI-KEVANS Born in Greece. Arrived in Australia in 1959 as a migrant worker. Poet whose work has appeared in various publications. Has a BA from Sydney University and a Diploma of Education from Sydney Teachers' College. Is a teacher with the NSW Department of Education. Writes both in Greek and English.
MARIA LEWITT Born in 1924 in Lodz, Poland. Arrived in Australia in 1949. Worked

at various jobs while attending evening courses with the Council of Adult Education. Novelist, short story writer and translator whose work has been published by Macmillan & Co., Reader's Digest, Scribe Publications and the St Martins Press, New York (1982). Won the Alan Marshall Award in 1978 for her story, 'Come Spring'. Has read on Ethnic Radio and addressed various literary groups, including the National Book Council in 1980.

SERGE LIBERMAN Born in Russia in 1942 and came to Australia in 1951. Short story writer whose work has appeared extensively in Australia and overseas. Is editor of the English section of the *Melbourne Chronicle*. Received Alan Marshall Award in 1980 and 1981 for his collections of stories, *On Firmer Shores* and *A Universe of Clowns* (Phoenix Publications, 1983.) Works full-time as a medical practitioner.

UYEN LOEWALD Born in North Vietnam, moved to South Vietnam in 1951. Married an American in 1964. Left USA in 1970 and settled in Australia. Has written three novels and a collection of short stories.

ANGELO LOUKAKIS Born in Australia in 1951. Of Greek descent. Has published stories in magazines and works full-time as a writer of fiction and screenplays for film and television. Received a Young Writers' Fellowship in 1979. Published *For the Patriarch* (UQP, 1981) for which he received a NSW Premier's Literary Award.

DAVID MARTIN Born in 1915 in Hungary. Grew up in Germany. Has lived in Holland, Palestine, Britain and India. Worked mainly as a journalist and settled in Australia in 1949. He is a prolific writer — as a novelist, poet, short story writer, playwright and critic. His works include *Spiegel the Cat, Tiger Bay, The Young Wife, Hughie, The Man in the Red Turban* and *The Gift*. A collection of stories, *Foreigners*, was published in 1981 (Rigby).

FRANCO PAISIO Born Milan, Italy, in 1936. Arrived in Australia in 1958. Poet and artist. Studied in Milan at Piero Vannucci Academy, Perugia, and in Australia at Bissietta Art School and East Sydney Technical College Art School. Has published two books of poems in Italy and was awarded First Prize by the Italian Society of Authors in 1961. Has contributed to literary publications in Australia and abroad. Has held several one-man exhibitions in Sydney, Melbourne and Canberra.

LILIANA RYDZYNSKI Born in Poland. Arrived in Australia in 1970. Lived in Paris during 1960s. Educated at University of Warsaw and Sydney University where she obtained her BA. Published *Castle* and *Earthquake* privately. *Celebration* published by the Saturday Centre (1982). Of her ethnic background she writes: 'Not to be proud of one's ethnic self, but essentially being it and consciously growing beyond it is most important.' Writes both in Polish and English.

BARBARA SCHENKEL Born in Warsaw, Poland, in 1919. Lives in Melbourne. Retired teacher of drama and health. Journalist and poet who has published work in English and Polish. Radio broadcaster for Special Broadcasting Service. Recipient of Silver Cross of Merit, 1977. Member of various Polish cultural and artistic organizations.

PETER SKRZYNECKI Born in 1945 in Germany. Of Polish/Ukrainian descent. Arrived in Australia in 1949. Graduate of University of New England and Sydney University. Poet and short story writer. Published five collections of poems, the most recent being his collected migrant poems, *The Polish Immigrant* (Phoenix Publications, 1982).

TAD SOBOLEWSKI Born in Poland in 1911. Came to Australia in 1951. Lived in Bonegilla. In 1955 moved to South Australia where he has lived since. Translator, writer of magazine articles and short stories. Published *The Perfume of Patou* in 1982. Working on a translation of Henry Lawson's short stories into Polish.

TUTAMA TJAPANGARTI Aborigine of the Pintubi tribe. He comes from the area south of Lake Hopkins and had no contact with Europeans until in his forties. He is now about 65 and his Dreaming is the Spiny Ant-eater. He has been featured in several documentary films and his work has appeared in the *Bulletin* and *Overland*.

DIMITRIS TSALOUMAS Born in 1921 on Leros in Dodecanese group of islands. Arrived in Australia in 1952. Studied at Melbourne University and joined the Victorian Education Department as a teacher of modern languages and English. Several collections of his work have been published in Greece and in 1983, UQP published a bilingual volume of poems, *The Observatory*, which won the National Book Council Award.

VICKI VIIDIKAS Born in Sydney in 1948. Of Estonian and Australian parents. She had published several collections of prose and poetry. *Condition Red* (UQP, 1973), *Wrappings* (Wild & Woolley, 1974), *Knäbel* (Wild & Woolley, 1978) and *India Ink* (Hale & Iremonger, 1984). She has also lived in England and India.

CORNELIS VLEESKENS Born in Holland in 1948. Came to Australia in 1958. Educated in Sydney's Western suburbs. Is a graduate of the University of Queensland. Travelled widely throughout Australia and South East Asia. Associated with *The Border Issue: Poetry in Queensland* and Makar. Started *Fling!*, which he still continues to publish from Victoria. Has published several books including *Hongkong Suicide* (Makar Press, 1976), and *Sketches* (Fling Poetry, 1982). *The Day The River* (UQP, 1984).

KATH WALKER Poet, essayist and public speaker. Well-known as a worker for Aboriginal rights and the preservation of Australia's environment. She spent her childhood on Stradbroke Island, where she now lives. Her first collection, *We Are Going*, was published in the early 1960s and became an international bestseller. In 1966 she published *The Dawn is at Hand* (Jacaranda); and in 1972, *Stradbroke Dreamtime* (Angus & Robertson). In 1970 she was awarded the MBE.

ANIA WALWICZ Born in Poland. Came to Australia in 1963. Graduate of the Victorian College of the Arts, School of Art. Published in literary magazines and represented in various anthologies. Has participated in numerous public and radio performances of poetry. Published *Writing* in 1982 (Rigmarole Books, Melbourne). Had a one woman show, Art Projects, Melbourne, October 1983. Of her work she writes: 'Visual work, like the writing, concerned with notation and enactment of inner states of feeling/being.'

JUDAH WATEN Born in Russia in 1911. Came to Australia as a small child and settled in Western Australia. Educated at Christian Brothers College, Perth and University High School, Melbourne. Has travelled widely in Australia and overseas. Novelist, short story writer and essayist, his works include *The Unbending, Distant Land, So Far No Further* and *Alien Son*. This first collection of stories, published in 1952, was one of the first books of migrant life, written from within a foreign community, to appear in Australia. Many of his works have been widely translated into foreign languages — including Dutch, Chinese, Japanese, German and Russian.

B. WONGAR Born in the late 1930s in a remote area of northern Australia; the birth was not recorded officially because at that time a register of births among tribal Aborigines was not kept; the State had power to separate Aboriginal children from their parents and take them to institutions to be indoctrinated in the white man's world; to avoid this B. Wongar was taken overseas; he grew up and was educated in Europe during and soon after World War II; he returned to Australia and was reunited with his tribal people.

His first published work appeared in 1970 and he has won many literary awards, including the Arvon Foundation Poetry Award 1980 (England). His last book, *Barbaru*, has been selected for Notable Books 1982 (The American Libraries Association Award). Other works include *The Track to Bralgu* (Jonathan Cape, 1978), *Bilma* (Ohio State University Press, 1983) and *The Trackers* (Outback Press, 1975).

SPIRO ZAVOS Of Greek descent. Born 1937. Educated at St Patrick's College, Silverstream, New Zealand and Victoria University. Received the 1978 Katherine Mansfield Fellowship and spent a year in Menton, France. He now works as a journalist on the *Sydney Morning Herald*. Published *Faith of Our Fathers* (UQP, 1982) for which he received a NSW Premier's Literary Award.

NIHAT ZIYALAN Born in 1938 in Turkey. Published in Turkish newspapers and literary magazines. His first collection was published in Turkey in 1962 and his second, in 1980. Worked as an actor in films in Istanbul. Has been living in Sydney for three years and received an Australia Council grant in 1981. His work has appeared in *Quadrant* and *Overland*.